I0817785

THE CALL OF THE SHADOW

THE POWER OF GOLD TRILOGY

The Power of Gold

J. J. LEACH

THE CALL OF THE SHADOW

• BOOK TWO •

Leach Books
Flat Rock

Originally published only in eBook format in 2017, and subsequently published in hardcover, paperback, and eBook in 2021.

Published by Leach Books, Flat Rock.

Printed in the United States of America

Map created with Inkarnate

First edition: 2021

ISBN: 978-1-7360144-3-1 (hardcover)

ISBN: 978-1-7360144-4-8 (paperback)

ISBN: 978-1-7360144-5-5 (eBook)

Library of Congress Control Number: 2021900590

The Library of Congress Cataloging-in-Publication Data is available upon request.

Young Adult Fiction/Fantasy/General

For Dolly,

your smile and encouragement are missed.

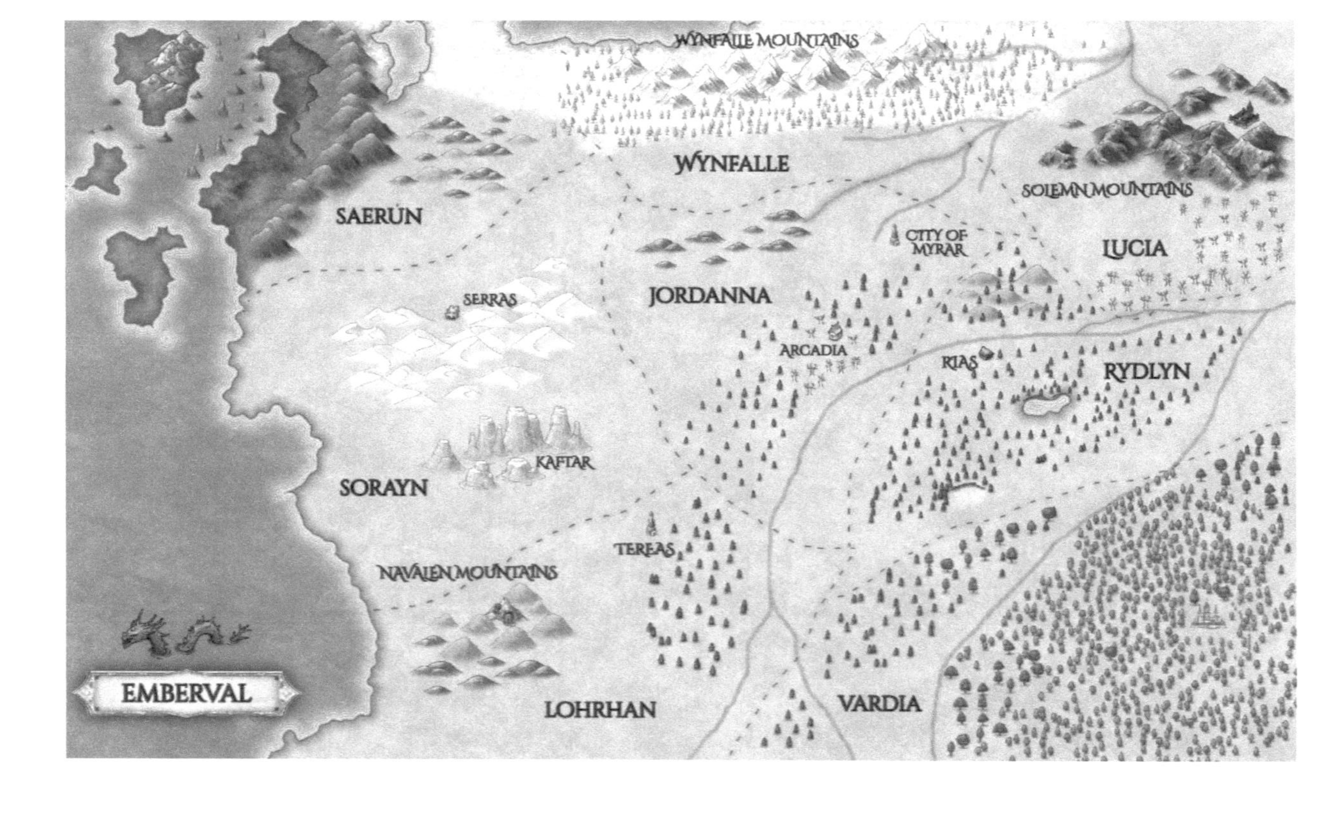
WYNFALLE MOUNTAINS
WYNFALLE
SOLEMN MOUNTAINS
SAERÚN
CITY OF
MYRAR
LUCIA
SERRAS
JORDANNA
ARCADIA
RIAS
RYDLYN
KAFTAR
SORAYN
TEREAS
NAVALEN MOUNTAINS
EMBERVAL
LOHRHAN
VARDIA

PROLOGUE

The passage smelled of mold and decay. Corvus picked his way through the rock debris littering the ground. He shook his head in disgust as he brushed against one of the Goblins tasked with clearing the tunnel. Red eyes narrowed. The mottled beast shrieked in terror at the contact. Corvus couldn't understand why his Master kept these repulsive creatures around—they were too slow and reeked of rotten meat. But the Goblins were eager to work for nothing as long as ale flowed freely.

Another creature crossed his path. "Get out of my way, filth," he snarled. The Goblin grumbled, baring his long, yellow teeth.

Moving into the new location was out of their control, all because of the elves. He couldn't understand how they found the girl. The concealment spell should have made her undetectable.

The brooch—the familiar design and its loaded meaning crowded the edges of his memory. His brow furrowed as he thought of the power emanating from it. Old magic. Magic with a life force—an energy he hadn't thought about in a long time.

Another memory surfaced—one that made the quick trip to their new home worth the trouble. The corner of his mouth twisted into a cruel smile.

The death of the Elder Healer, the great Hrafn.

Pleasure surged through his body. His only regret was missing the chance to witness the momentous event and capture his magic. But, alas, all in good time. He would have all the power he needed once he captured her again.

The overwhelming feeling hit him. His steps faltered as he leaned against the wall, savoring the memory of tasting her magic. Corvus's hand suddenly shot up, gripping his tunic and ripping it open. He then placed his hand on his markings—feeling them swirl and pulse with anticipation.

She was strong, unique, and she would be his.

Soon.

A loud thud echoed from the Throne Room. Corvus entered cautiously, aware that his Master's mood seemed especially irritable today.

"I need proper food. Proper meat. Get out and find me food worthy of your king, or I will have your head and feed it to the Kludde."

The servant quickly bowed and hurried off to find the elusive meal. Corvus sneered at the servant as he walked by, knowing his head would be separated by the end of twilight.

Kenrick barely glanced at Corvus as he settled onto his makeshift throne. Displeasure flickered in his eyes. Corvus knelt, waiting to be spoken to.

"Is the Lirrean ready?" Kenrick asked.

"Yes, Master. I believe the plan is ready to begin as soon as you approve."

"Excellent."

Kenrick pushed himself out of his chair and started pacing back and forth, a habit he's developed recently.

"Is the boy awake?" He stopped in front of Corvus. His eyes shimmered with a red glow.

Corvus couldn't help but notice the change happening in his Master more and more each day. A slow smile spread across his face.

"Not yet, Master. But he will be ready when it's time for action."

"Good, good. The Great One shall be pleased."

Kenrick turned away from Corvus, walked back to his throne, and sat down.

"Let the games begin."

Corvus bowed and headed back down to his workroom, smiling.

Yes, let the death commence.

ONE

I grasped the bow tightly, my knuckles turning white as I peeked around the tree. Elric gave me a quick nod. Halvard and Thyra were stationed in the branches above, ready at Elric's signal. Although I had accompanied the elf warriors on several reconnaissance missions, my heart felt like it was about to burst from my chest with anticipation.

Jack pushed to the front of my thoughts, and my feelings shifted to anger and revenge. I needed Jack back home.

Elric whistled, focusing my thoughts on the task ahead. We darted around the tree, bows drawn and arrows ready. Thyra and Halvard dropped right into the Lucian camp, catching the soldiers off guard. There were only five soldiers, a smaller group than usual. Still, we stayed cautious.

We quickly overtook the soldiers and bound their hands and feet. Now the so-called 'good elf/bad elf' interrogation would begin.

"Where are you heading, human scum?" Thyra yelled.

One thing I had learned since Jack's kidnapping was the fury of a mother. Although Jack was not Thyra's son by blood, or even from this world, she was clearly his mother through her emotions and actions. Rage fueled her, and she was determined to find Jack and bring him home. No matter what.

I had been observing her tactics throughout our journey and was very grateful that I wasn't the one being questioned. She was ruthless and deadly.

Nervously, I watched her move carefully around the soldier, her steps deliberate and exact.

"Where is Kenrick? What are your plans?" she whispered menacingly. She leaned into the Lucian soldier. "Where is the human boy?"

The man refused to answer, as expected. But Thyra was just getting started.

She reached for her dagger, pushing it slightly upward toward the man's throat and drawing a drop of blood. He sneered at her and spat in her face.

I shook my head at the man's obvious stupidity. I looked at Elric, who also had the same 'you must be an idiot' look on his face. Unknowingly to the soldier, he just signed his death warrant.

Now, I must issue a disclaimer because I truly do not condone violence, but after a few of these interrogations, I had to accept that you should not cross an angry elf. The thought that Jack might not be alive haunted us all—and that emotion was what we thrived on.

A shiver ran down my spine. I thought for the hundredth

time today about Jack's fate. I couldn't believe he was gone—I had to believe he was still alive.

I quickly turned my head when Thyra shoved the knife into the man's throat, killing him instantly.

The other soldiers started shouting and backing away from her. She swiftly grabbed the closest man and pressed the knife to his throat.

"So, answer me, or are you a dead man too? Where is Kenrick? Where's the coward hiding?" she sneered in his ear.

Now enter the 'good elf' scenario. Elric leaned down and peered into the soldier's wide-eyed, terror-filled stare.

"She will kill you, human, if you do not tell us what we need to know," Elric calmly said as he leaned forward slightly, his face inches from the soldiers. "I do not control her, young one. It will be hard to hold her back if you do not answer."

Elric leaned back again and fixated on the soldier, his pale blue eyes growing stormy and ominous. "Where is Kenrick?"

The man looked at us indifferently. I silently begged him to tell us, not wanting another bloody mess, but I knew where this was headed. Kenrick chose his men carefully; he must understand that their journey was essentially a one-way trip, with death almost certain.

Thyra moved her knife closer to the soldier's throat when he suddenly flinched upward. His mouth opened and closed, but no words came from his lips.

"Wait!" I exclaimed, quickly kneeling beside him. "Tell us, where is Kenrick?"

He gasped and clutched his throat.

"I can't understand you!" I screamed.

Words forced out with labored breath. The soldier clutched his throat once more.

I leaned closer to him and felt Elric's hand on my arm.

"Not so close," he murmured.

The man tried to speak, but no sound came out, not even a breath. His bloodshot eyes rolled back. Both Thyra and I jumped away from him.

All of the soldiers began to convulse and writhe on the ground. Blood oozed from their eyes, nose, mouth, and ears—as if some invisible force was pummeling their bodies to death. Immediately, their bodies stopped moving.

"What just happened?" I asked, stepping back even more.

Confusion and caution spread across our faces. A red cloud rose and hovered over the bodies—calling us to reach out and touch it. Elric and I stepped back even further. Our hands now stretched out in front of us, ready to fight the magic hanging over the men. But the mist vanished. Everyone exchanged glances, unsure if the magic had truly disappeared.

"They must have been bound by a spell," Elric said, shaking his head in disgust while lowering his arms, signaling that the danger was gone. He kicked the nearest tree. "Kenrick must know what we are doing. To gain complete control over his men's thoughts and actions, he binds them with magic, ensuring his whereabouts remain hidden."

"So, what does it mean?" I asked as Thyra turned away in anger, wiping her bloody knife on the ground.

"It means we need to change our tactics, young one," she

said with a frustrated sigh and stood up. The sharp snap of her dagger being shoved back into its sheath sent a jolt down my spine. "We will have to adapt to Kenrick's new plan."

I faced Elric, who was staring at the soldiers with a stone-cold expression; they were now completely unrecognizable—blood covered their faces.

"And how do we change our tactics? The Mage must have cast the spell on these men. Can we adapt and combat his magic with our own?" I asked with concern.

Elric shook his head once more. He looked at me and then at the others.

"We will have to, won't we, Anwen? We have been tracking Kenrick's men for months. It seems pointless to go on until we figure out how to break the spell." He looked at Halvard and Thyra. "Let's cover the bodies and set up camp for the night. We need to regroup with the others and then head back to the kingdom for now."

Thyra muttered in frustration, and I agreed with her. We were so close to getting something out of each group of soldiers, but never enough to move forward and find the new headquarters. Never enough to locate Jack. And now we have the magic to face and conquer. I placed my hand on Elric's arm.

"I will gather our bags. There was a small clearing about half an hour away that I think will work for our camp," I whispered. He placed his hand on mine and gave it a gentle squeeze.

"Yes, I know the place you're talking about. It's a good choice." He smiled and turned to help Thyra and Halvard with the bodies.

I gently wove through the underbrush, found all our bags, then kept walking ahead of them, knowing Elric was familiar with the place I mentioned. As I wandered among the trees, my body finally started to relax after the two-day stalking ordeal.

Whenever we came across Kenrick's men, we watched and observed them, trying to figure out where they were headed and hoping we weren't walking into a trap. My body stayed tense for days as I tried to adapt to the elf warrior way. I'm not complaining—over the past six months, my training, both magical and physical, had prepared me. And I have to admit—I was pretty good at both now.

With the help and guidance of my new teacher, Elric.

Imagine my surprise when Elric revealed his power to me. Most days, I still couldn't believe how well he kept it hidden from me and also from many of his friends. Both Halvard and Thyra were surprised by this new revelation. King Ansgar, Queen Eydis, my grandparents, and Vidar, my uncle, knew. And, of course, Hrafn.

My heart sank when I thought of the Elder Healer, my first teacher. Nearly a year ago, Jack and I were living in another world until we were suddenly taken to this strange land called Emberval—where mythical creatures roamed, and powerful magic thrived.

When we crossed over, Jack and I never thought of calling this extraordinary place our home. And I had never dreamed that I was originally from this world, an elf princess and a magical Healer. My life had changed so much that my memories of living in foster care were gradually fading away.

As I rounded one of the larger trees, I entered the small clearing.

I tossed the bags onto different spots on the ground. My stomach growled with hunger. Although food was hard to find in the area, Halvard always managed to find something for our dinner. I grimaced as another growl echoed—let's hope his hunt succeeds again tonight.

Picking up several large twigs for kindling from the ground, my thoughts drifted to the day I learned about Elric's magic. For some reason, after his parents' death, his people banished him from Wynfalle, the Mountain Elf Kingdom, and sent him back to his mother's people, the Wood Elves of Vardia. That much I already knew, as he told his story when we first met.

What he didn't mention was that his father was a Healer, or, as the Mountain Elves called them, a Volun, and, according to Elric, his people explored a more nontraditional energy, which they called Shadow Magic. Many people living outside the mountains described it as dark magic. Elric, on the other hand, argued that his people's way of life and his magic were highly misunderstood by outsiders.

When he moved in with the Wood Elves, the king, queen, and Hrafn forbade Elric from using his powers—keeping the secret from the people of Vardia. I was surprised by their demand, but Elric seemed okay with it—though he didn't have much choice.

After his general explanation, Elric refused to discuss anything further with me. I didn't pressure him. What was strange, though, was that, with the exception of Halvard and

Thyra, most of the kingdom seemed afraid of Elric.

Fear and anger grew among his friends and allies. My heart ached for him as his own soldiers—those he had commanded for years—recoiled from him. Their hesitation was clear. But Elric never questioned their actions. He appeared resigned to the punishment of his heritage.

Twigs snapped behind me, pulling me out of my thoughts. Elric, Halvard, and Thyra slowly made their way into the camp. They looked exhausted, so I finished gathering a few more pieces of wood and followed after them.

Halvard was already filleting several rabbits as I knelt beside the fire pit. Placing a few branches in the center of the pit with dry leaves stuffed between them, I raised my hands over the pyramid. Gold wisps of light flashed, igniting the wood. A smile crossed my face at the distant memory of Hrafn doing the same task.

We swiftly made our beds and then ate in silence; the thought of returning to Vardia without Jack weighed heavily on my mind. I glanced at Elric and saw him staring into the fire, his expression revealing his inner turmoil. Suddenly, he looked up and caught me staring at him, but I quickly looked away.

The secret glances here and there had become our ritual—our already strained relationship still stayed hidden. He was still holding something back from me, which frustrated me. But I knew he would talk to me when he felt the time was right—once again, the no-pressure approach seemed to be the norm.

I was patient. For now.

Thyra stood up and took our bowls, trying to hide her face

from us—her anguish in leaving Jack behind was clear. Fresh tears shimmered on her cheeks. Halvard briefly smiled at her but quickly looked away when he saw the emotion in her eyes. He suddenly glanced at Elric.

"So, what will be our plan on the morrow, Elric?" he asked, wanting to confirm what everyone else was thinking. "Are we truly going back to Vardia? Is the magic unstoppable?"

Without looking away from the fire, Elric sighed. He understood their frustration and anger.

"Yes, I believe that is our only option. Anwen and I will need to come up with another plan now that magic is involved, magic I am unfamiliar with. I assume Kenrick has bound all his men by now. But something else doesn't feel right. The magic smells of darkness and intent. A spell linked to another spell, magic that could harm the person trying to free the victim."

Thyra shook her head. "We are entering our second season, Elric. Jack needs to be rescued." Thyra looked away, her words catching in her throat. "He must be so frightened."

I turned away at the emotion dripping from her words—my heart lurched just thinking about him scared and alone. But Elric was right, we needed to prepare for this new obstacle.

"We are not giving up, Thyra, but I have to agree with Elric. We need a new plan. The magic is growing stronger in this area, almost overwhelming," I said. "Even standing next to the Lucian soldiers, the darkness inside them reached out to me."

Elric nodded in agreement.

"We will never give up searching for Jack. Something is wrong in the forest. Let us return to the kingdom for now. Even though we leave with no new information than when we started, I believe that will soon change."

Elric's gaze shifted cautiously toward the dark forest. Tremors ran down my spine. An ominous feeling overwhelmed my thoughts—something sinister was lurking.

Something powerful was hunting.

We needed to find a defense, or everything could be lost.

TWO

As the sun rose from its nightly sleep, we resumed our journey to Vardia. Our hearts were heavy with Jack's absence. Our bows were drawn and ready for any Lucian scouts we might encounter. Our rendezvous with the Vardian soldiers, Asmund and Einar, was still two days away. They stayed behind to watch the horses while we followed the fresh trail of Kenrick's men. Once we had our horses again, the journey home would be swift.

I looked around the Lucian forest with anger, my heart heavy with sadness. Kenrick destroyed Lucia. There were hardly any creatures scrambling around the dense forest—either destroyed or migrated to other areas for food. Kenrick ruined what was once a majestic kingdom.

My kingdom.

Most of the trees were blackened from fire or, worse, magic. A strange energy pulsed from the darkened trunks and leafless branches—surrounding us was a dying land, and there was nothing we could do about it. I shook my head in disgust, ready to leave this forsaken place. Elric must have sensed my anger and stopped me.

"Are you unwell, Anwen?" he asked with concern.

I looked up at him with a frown. "No, I am angry that Kenrick destroyed Lucia's land. *My* kingdom, Elric," I whispered. "I cannot help but feel saddened that my home, the place where I was born, is torn apart like this."

It was hard to even imagine that my ancestors had lived on this land for thousands of years in peace with the elves. My grandparents were the King and Queen of Lucia, along with their children—my father, Garrick, the heir to the throne, and his younger brother, Kenrick. Because of greed and the desire for power, Kenrick killed them all, including my mother, and he would have succeeded in killing me too if she hadn't sent me to another world. In that world, I was bounced from one foster home to another until I was eventually transported back to this world and found my true family.

Elric gently placed his hand on my cheek. His action caught me off guard—touching me so tenderly, especially in front of others, rarely happened anymore. But I didn't pull away, enjoying his boldness, as his thumb brushed my skin, sending warm, trembling sensations through my body.

"I am sorry, little one. We have been so busy hunting for Kenrick's men that I forgot this land is just as much your home." He looked around at the trees and the landscape. "Someday, when we have defeated Kenrick, we will come back and find a way to heal Lucia."

His eyes found mine again. My heart raced as our energies

connected. We were so close, gazing into each other's eyes, not caring that Thyra and Halvard were nearby. Until Halvard cleared his throat. We instantly pulled apart. Elric's hand fell away from me. Thyra offered us a warm smile.

"I believe we have a little more time to travel before sundown, so shall we start again?" she asked hesitantly, not necessarily wanting to interrupt our moment.

I stumbled a little, pulling away from Elric.

"Yes, of course," I said, trying to quiet the beating of my heart. Elric always had that effect on me.

I passed by both Halvard and Thyra, avoiding their eyes. Soon, I heard their footsteps behind me. We continued on our journey. They let me lead the group for a while, knowing I had proven I was capable.

I grimaced at the thought of the first real test of my abilities when I was kidnapped by Kenrick and his Mage. I endured torture and then faced a tormentor from my old world who originally belonged to Emberval. He was a spy for Kenrick and was the reason that Jack and I crossed into this world. I knew him as Travis, my foster sister's abusive boyfriend, but here, he was called Draugr, the leader of Kenrick's death squad, the Lokrum.

I kept looking around, my nerves on edge, and thought about that fateful day. The day my powers first showed their potential. But it was also the day I lost my beloved teacher, Hrafn.

Tears blurred my vision. His presence still lingered deep inside me. I kept wishing he was still here. He might have helped figure out why my powers were so different, since no one, not even Elric, knew why strange symbols appeared on my body when I used my energy. They didn't surface every time, so the reason for their appearance remained a mystery.

My eyes landed on Elric. He had mentioned a prophecy several times, but the link to my markings remained unclear. Sometimes I felt like he was holding something back—vital information that could reveal the true nature of my powers.

I didn't want to believe he would choose to hide important information from me, but I knew Elric had many secrets he was keeping.

Sighing, I turned back around and focused on the task at hand. Patience truly had become a virtue for me in this world.

***

There were many fears and uncertainties I had to face in Emberval. You might assume the biggest threats were dangerous creatures or vengeful kings. Surprisingly, though, it was a four-legged animal that was deeply rooted in both my old world and this one.

Horses.

It wasn't easy either, especially when everyone around you excelled at everything, including horse handling. It took me a while to get used to the power of the beast, and I had to eat my words, admittedly. My so-called beast was actually a gentle palomino named Glaesir. Over the last several months, we had become great, loyal companions, so when he saw me for the first time in almost a week, he broke free from Asmund's grip and ran toward me, legs dancing from side to side. I grabbed an apple from my pack, and his teeth nipped at the palm of my hand.

"Good boy, I missed you too," I crooned to him as I pressed my forehead against his neck, feeling the vibration of his chewing strength through my body.

Elric, Thyra, and Halvard passed us, laughing. They knew I was nervous at the start of my horse training, terrified, but now Glaesir was my best friend. I looked up and smiled at them.

"You are just jealous," I called out, laughing with them.

I watched as Einar approached Elric with an anxious look on his face. I grabbed Glaesir's bridle and walked toward the group. An uneasy feeling began to creep into my chest.

"Commander, Asmund and I have news," Einar said breathlessly as he crossed his arms over his chest in the traditional greeting. Elric stopped and waited for him to continue.

"Yes, what say you, Einar?" Elric asked.

"Sir, earlier this morning, Asmund and I were watering the horses down by the stream a short distance from here. The horses caught wind of something and became timid, so we hid them behind a line of trees. We then made our way back to camp to see what was wrong." Einar stopped and glanced at Asmund.

"Sir," Asmund continued, "it was Lucian soldiers. And there were many—too many to count. Regular soldiers as well as the masked fiends, the Lokrum. They were marching northwest toward the mountains."

Einar looked at Elric intently. "And sir, men weren't the only ones marching. The Rock Giants were among them, just a few, but more than what we usually see with the Lucians."

Elric shook his head and then looked up at the trees, his thoughts racing as he tried to make sense of their report. Suddenly, anger flashed across his face. He turned around and grabbed the reins of his black horse, Lyfir.

"Come, Halvard, let us ride. I want to see these demons," Elric said as he mounted Lyfir. Halvard quickly grabbed his horse.

"Elric, it's too dangerous. We should head back to Vardia and then plan our next steps," I pleaded. Glaesir started to dance around me, sensing my nervousness.

"She is right, Elric. We need to alert Vardia about their movement, especially if there are many soldiers," Thyra pointed out.

I looked at Asmund and Einar, hoping they would voice their concerns about Elric's actions, but Einar grabbed his horse and leapt aboard.

"I will show you the way, Commander," he urged, moving his horse forward.

"Elric, please. Don't do this now," I begged again. "Draugr might be among the group."

He looked down at me. "Anwen, there is a ridge not too far where we can hide. We will be back by nightfall," he softened his gaze, "do not worry, we will be careful."

Elric nodded to Asmund and Thyra.

"Take the horses and set up camp farther into the trees. We'll let you know when we're close tonight, so you won't be alarmed. Stay hidden and stay safe."

Elric was the first to turn his horse around. Halvard and Einar followed him into the woods. Frustrated, I placed my hands on my hips and turned to Thyra and Asmund.

"Well, that accomplished nothing," I fumed.

Elric was reckless. They should have stayed back and come up with a plan. I shook my head in frustration, leading Glaesir away.

Thyra and Asmund grabbed the supplies and followed me to the new campsite. The nervous twitching in my stomach came back.

My patience completely wore out, replaced by uneasiness and dread.

We waited for Elric's return.

THREE

The sun vanished, bringing the unsettling silence of night. The unusual absence of wildlife made my nerves flare. I couldn't stop pacing back and forth in front of the fire. They should have been back by now. I looked at Thyra's worried expression as she stared into the dancing flames of our fire.

I was about to suggest we leave to look for them when the familiar whistle rang out through the night. Turning quickly to look beyond the small circle of firelight, Halvard entered our camp, followed by Einar and then Elric. The look on their faces confirmed what we all feared—Kenrick's men were heading toward the mountains. That was not a good sign.

"Tell us what you saw, Elric?" Thyra asked, thrusting a bowl of food into his hands.

"It is what Einar and Asmund had witnessed earlier. Kenrick's men are moving northwest toward the mountains, though it's hard to tell where their destination will end," Elric said as he took the bowl from Thyra, but he immediately set it back down on the ground. He ran his hands over his face, exhausted.

I helped Thyra pass food to the others, and then we sat down, waiting for their report.

"So, will we be following the soldiers? They might lead us to Jack?" Thyra asked.

Elric gently shook his head.

"I do not think they are heading back to Kenrick. They are still too heavily armed," he said softly. "No, we will rest for a little while and at first light, continue to Vardia. The king and queen must be informed of the Lokrum's movements. With the large number of soldiers and weapons, their goal can only mean more destruction."

"Do you think they are heading to Wynfalle?" I whispered because I knew his kingdom was part of the mountain region.

Elric glanced my way, surprised by my question. He didn't respond, but his look revealed that I understood his thoughts and concerns.

Halvard and the others turned away, aware of what Kenrick's march could mean for Wynfalle's fate. Although the Wood Elves and Mountain Elves were kin, that didn't mean they would help each other. I wasn't sure about the history between the two kingdoms. Elric had only confirmed the solitary life of the Mountain Elves. My eyes scanned every elf until they finally landed on Elric.

"Once we get to Vardia, Ansgar can send warriors to help your people, Elric," I said confidently. "If you believe Kenrick's army is heading toward the Kingdom of Wynfalle, they'll need our aid."

I looked around the circle again. Everyone ignored my statement, not adding their affirmations to help their kin. Elric smiled faintly at me. He stood and took his bedding out of his bag.

"What?" I asked innocently.

They nodded uncomfortably before standing to unpack their bags, leaving me watching their retreating backs.

I walked up to Halvard.

"Ansgar and Eydis will send help, won't they?"

He paused and turned with the same faint smile.

"We will ask, Anwen. But we cannot spare many of our warriors at this point," he stated wearily. "Many are away already on various missions. No matter what direction the army is taking, we do not have positive confirmation that they are needed in Wynfalle."

He avoided glancing at Elric. It felt like a knife stabbing my heart.

"But," Thyra walked over to Elric and placed her hand on his arm, "we will not let them fend for themselves. Something will be done if that is the true destination of the Lokrum."

Elric turned to her and shrugged indifferently, but I knew him well enough that his seemingly casual attitude masked his true pain.

"Yes, we shall see," he said, quickly glancing in my direction. "We shall see."

***

I woke up to darkness and the crackling fire. Everyone was asleep except for Elric, who was nowhere to be seen.

Concerned, I searched the camp, looking for any movement in the night. A faint outline of a pale figure near a tree caught my eye. I sighed in relief, recalling that someone was watching over the camp while we slept, but I wondered how long he'd been awake—and I believed it was Thyra's turn to watch tonight.

Carefully and quietly walking between a sleeping Asmund and Halvard, I sat beside Elric. He didn't acknowledge my presence, only continued to stare into the dark forest.

"Are you okay?" I whispered.

The black void of the forest held his attention a few seconds longer. His eyes met mine, and I was stunned by the depth of their sorrow. He turned away and focused on the bow resting in his lap.

"Well, that is a loaded question, isn't it, little one?" His crooked grin showed a hint of sarcasm. I placed my hand on his arm and gave it a gentle squeeze.

"We will send people to Wynfalle, Elric, to check on your people. No matter what the strain is between the Mountain Elves and Vardia, we cannot let them be butchered, not like Arcadia."

I turned away from him, looking up at the sky as the moon's silver light filtered through the empty branches of the tree.

Arcadia.

A shiver ran through me, recalling the Lokrum's devastation of the small, defenseless village. So many needless deaths, all because of Kenrick's plan to lure me away from the protected forest of Vardia and into the hands of the Lucians. It didn't quite go as he had intended.

Elric placed his hand on mine, his thumb gently rubbing circles along the back. I closed my eyes and rested my head against his shoulder. He gently kissed the top of my head and let out a sigh.

"Halvard is right—Vardia can't send soldiers right now. I truly understand our kingdom's priorities, but the feelings I have can't be ignored. Even though my people have turned their backs on me, I refuse to do the same to them. Do you understand, Anwen?" Elric whispered thoughtfully.

I lifted my head to look into his eyes.

"No, what are you saying? Are you leaving?" Anxiety touched each word.

Elric's hand brushed a stray tendril of hair from my cheek.

"Aye, I will leave once we are safely in Vardia. Please understand that I have to do this," he whispered. "You do not need me to guide you anymore." He chuckled with pride. "You are strong and fully capable of leading our people now, Anwen. I have faith in you. Vardia has faith in you."

I couldn't believe what he was saying, so I shook my head in denial.

"No, I need you, Elric." I lifted my hand to his face, gently caressing his cheek. Desperation flared inside me. "We don't even know if Kenrick's men are heading to Wynfalle, so let's not make hasty decisions, okay?"

Elric leaned in and softly kissed my lips.

I wrapped my hand around his neck, pulling his kiss deeper. Elric pulled me onto his lap and wrapped his arms around my back. When we finally parted, we were breathless, our foreheads resting together.

I looked into his pale blue eyes. "Please, let us talk to Ansgar and Eydis and discuss our next moves."

My head gently nestled in the small dip between his neck and shoulder as he held me in his arms. The rapid beat of his heart mimicked mine. He didn't respond to my plea, though.

"I love you, Elric. I want to help you. Please, let me." I whispered into his neck, kissing him softly.

His arms tightened around my waist in response to my plea—I knew he had already made his decision.

***

As I strapped my pack onto Glaesir's saddle, I looked over at Elric and remembered our talk earlier this morning. My stomach twisted nervously at his declaration that he was leaving Vardia—something I hoped wouldn't happen until we knew where the Lokrum were going.

At least, that was just my hopeful thinking.

My hand instinctively reached for my lips. The memory of our kiss lingered—desperate yet passionate. Elric's anguish seemed to seep into every part of my body, clinging to me into the early hours of dawn.

I glanced at the group as they hurriedly packed their belongings. There was a sense of urgency to get home quickly, not only to keep the search alive and find Jack but also with the growing realization that their mountain kin might be in serious danger—and if Wynfalle fell to Lucia, then Vardia could be next on Kenrick's list.

We mounted our horses, our weary bodies already anticipating a long day of travel. Halvard took the lead this time, while Elric covered the rear of the group.

Although I knew he probably hadn't slept at all, Elric's eyes darted around, alert and with his bow ready. I admired and respected each warrior for their tenacity and unwavering loyalty to Elric, especially when they knew one of their own was hurting. You could see it in the remorseful glances they tried to hide from him. It was as if they already knew what the king and queen would say about sending help to the mountains.

The day flowed into early evening when we decided to take a quick break. As we crossed into Rydlyn, we entered wide fields with only patches of tall, small trees. Hills dominated the landscape around us. Our journey would take at least another ten days to reach the Vardia border, even if we maintained our fast pace—something we were all willing to do.

The first few days were silent for everyone in the group. We kept traveling nonstop, only pausing to let our horses rest. By the ninth day, Elric decided to stop earlier than planned, but everyone was relieved—exhaustion took a toll on us.

Thyra and I led the horses to a nearby stream and tied them together at the bank. We sat down on a large flat rock by the shoreline, enjoying the quiet of not being on a swaying horse for a while.

I tilted my head back, letting the sunlight warm my face. But I couldn't relax because of the relentless questions racing through my mind. How will Ansgar and Eydis react to Wynfalle's news? Will we just turn around and head back north? Will we find Jack if we go? Or will we face more death and destruction caused by the Lokrum?

I was so lost in my thoughts that I didn't hear Thyra calling my name.

I opened my eyes again when she said my name. An apologetic smile appeared afterward.

"Sorry, lost in my thoughts," I said with a slight chuckle. "What did you say?"

She smiled understandingly. "I was asking if Elric has talked to you anymore about Wynfalle?"

I bit my lip, hoping that Elric's announcement about leaving Vardia wasn't confidential. I stared at my hands, not really wanting to lie to Thyra either. Maybe she could talk him out of leaving?

Deciding to tell the truth, I told her.

"Yes, he has talked to me," I said somberly, turning to her. "He said he will not turn his back on his family and plans to return to Wynfalle." I silently apologized to Elric for my selfish intentions. I studied her as several emotions flickered across her face. She suddenly pulled her legs up and hugged them to her chest, shaking her head.

"He cannot go back, Anwen," she said with concern. "He was banished a long time ago, and there will be consequences if he returns."

My heart started pounding wildly.

"Consequences? Like what? What would they do to him?"

Thyra shook her head slowly again. "I am not sure, Anwen,

but I know banishment is not to be taken lightly. Even for our kingdom, there have been severe punishments for those who return."

"Then surely Ansgar will allow other soldiers to travel to Wynfalle to check on their situation? He wouldn't let Elric go without assistance." I said confidently, but Thyra's expression remained skeptical. "I don't understand, Thyra. Why is there such a rift between Vardia and Wynfalle? What happened to cause this mistrust? And please tell me the truth. I see how some of the elders treat Elric, especially now that his heritage as a Volun was known. Whatever happened was in the past; why is it still so difficult for everyone to see that it is just Elric, someone they have known for a very long time?"

Thyra stood up and started gathering the water bottles near my leg. I leaned over and took her hands.

"Please, Thyra," I begged. I took the plunge with my next words. "You know how I feel about Elric. I love him with all my heart, and even though Hrafn didn't approve of us being together, I know Elric loves me too. I don't know what to do to make him stay."

Thyra sat back down with a sigh and gently placed her hands on her lap.

"I know, Anwen. I have noticed how close you two have become. Please understand that I wish you happiness, but I must be honest—not all of our people will be receptive to your union. The old disagreements among our kin define us, and you can't ignore the history," she paused, "especially for those who lived through it."

"I understand, Thyra, truly, as the good and bad history pretty much defined many people in my old world. But please give me something here to work with because there are no books that I know of that tell the history between the other elf clans, and Elric will not speak about it," I gave a short snort in exasperation. "Believe me, I have tried to talk to him about it."

Thyra hesitated before turning to me with a strained smile.

"Well, the short history lesson it will be then," she replied and then continued, "Many years ago, all the kingdoms lived in peace . . . or let's just say they at least tolerated each other. But greed and power always disrupt the best of allies, especially when there is already discontent among them, and it can be deadly. It was a dark time in all elf clan history—when some of our people committed unspeakable atrocities against their own kin, their own families. That is how our mountain kin became our enemies in a period we call the Great Purge."

"Yes, I remember Hrafn mentioning this, but he never really talked about it," I replied.

"Most do not talk about it—fearing that if one speaks about the brutalities of the past, they will invite dark magic into our world again," Thyra looked off into the trees, appearing to remember an old memory. "The Volun at the time was delving into darker magic, more so than what he normally invokes. And with the help of the Rock Giants, Centaurs, Goblins, and both Kingdoms of Lucia and Jordanna, the Volun gathered the Woodland and Desert Elves along with their supporters and friends and exterminated them. And while many of the Mountain Elves did not participate directly in the deaths of thousands of our ancestors, they were the scouts who hunted the families, signing their death sentence."

Now I started to understand why many fear, even hate, the Mountain Elves, especially Elric and his magic.

"But Thyra, our people know Elric and have supported his rise in the military, especially the king and queen—their trust in him must validate his loyalty."

"I understand, Anwen, but it will be hard to convince many to help Wynfalle. As you know, our kind live a long time, and many who survived that period, as well as those who were the offenders, are still with us." Thyra gave my hand a light pat and stood up, taking me with her. "Elves have a long memory—what Elric stands for, being a Volun by birth, no matter what he has become in Vardia, only resonates with the times of the Purge and the destruction that his kind, our kin, have brought upon Emberval."

Thyra placed her hand on my cheek.

"Come, let us return to the others. They will worry about us," she said. She wrapped her arm around my waist, guiding me back to the camp.

"But it has to say something when Ansgar and Eydis, as well as Hrafn, knew about Elric and his power and yet, they took him in and cared for him," I said as she guided me.

She gave me a sad smile. "Maybe, Anwen. We can only ask."

Thyra grasped my hand tightly, almost in desperation, as we slowly wandered toward the camp, but I silently shook my head in frustration. Her answer didn't give me the hope I was seeking.

***

My conversation with Thyra kept replaying in my mind as we sat around the fire that evening. Silence weighed heavily on all of us during dinner once again, and I tried to talk to Elric alone, but it never worked out. My desperation must have been obvious. He avoided me for most of the evening, but he was also avoiding the others, too.

I sighed when I saw Elric tossing and turning in his bed, his thoughts, like mine, must be keeping him awake.

Finally, daylight appeared, and we packed our belongings for the trip home.

Our journey was grueling. The day's heat soaked into our skin. Fortunately, we had enough water to last until we finally crossed into Vardia. We halted our horses, glanced up at the tree fortress, and made sure the sentries recognized us as friends, not enemies. With reports of increased Lucian attacks, the king stationed additional soldiers at the wall—Kenrick's army was always on everyone's mind.

We entered the forest, finding some relief from the heat. Since we rode horses, we took a different path into the kingdom; however, the soft tinkling laughter of the fairies greeted us. After several hours, we finally reached the horse corral and stables. As we dismounted, a young stable hand ran toward our group, clearly excited.

"Princess Anwen, Commander Elric, we have been waiting for your return. Bless the gods, but we have great news!" he said as he clapped his hands together.

I looked at the others to see how they reacted. My heart started pounding faster. What was happening?

"Master Jack, he is back! He has returned!" The stable hand could hardly contain his excitement. "He is in the castle."

"What? How?" I exclaimed as I grabbed Thyra's hand.

Without saying another word, I sprinted from the stables and skipped every other step on the stairs, rushing up to the castle as fast as I could. I didn't slow down for the others because I could hear them right behind me. My legs kept moving until I was standing right outside Jack's old room, the one he had before he moved into Thyra's tree house.

My heart pounded loudly with every ragged breath. His door was half shut—voices muffled behind it. I gently pushed it open, still not quite convinced he was inside. But there he was in his bed, eyes closed and looking unnaturally pale.

Thyra stood beside me, and I could feel her hesitant reaction too. We entered the room and knelt by his bed. I took his hand and brought it to my tear-streaked face.

"Jack? My sweet Jack," I said through my tears. "Can you hear me?"

He didn't react to my words. I saw Eydis and Sulwen standing at the foot of his bed. Eydis opened her arms for me, and I quickly ran into them, crying tears of happiness.

"How is this possible?"

Eydis pulled away from me without saying anything, her eyes darting toward the fireplace. Thyra immediately stood up, looking over my shoulder.

I turned around and saw someone I never expected to see again. Especially in this world.

"Abby?" I whispered in wonder.

FOUR

Recognizing the name, Elric grabbed his dagger from his belt, and before I could stop him, the blade was pressed to Abby's throat. I hurried to his side and placed my hand on his arm.

"Elric, please, let me talk to her," I said.

My eyes stayed on Abby, but terror flashed across her face. We were speaking Skovmal, the woodland language, so she couldn't understand what I was telling him.

Elric hesitated for a few seconds before pulling his dagger away and stepping back from us. His eyes remained fixed on Abby's face as well.

"She tormented you in your past life," he simply stated. "How did she come to be in this world and in Vardia?" He glanced at me. "And above all else, how was she with Kenrick?"

My eyes tracked Abby as she moved away from us, rubbing a spot on her neck where a small bloodstain was starting to form. She looked from Elric to me, then glanced at Jack, who was still unconscious.

"Jo, I really can explain," she pleaded with me. "I was a prisoner just like Jack."

"How did you get away?" Elric asked menacingly in English. His heavily accented words seethed with distrust and hatred. "Kenrick does not release prisoners."

Thyra moved forward, her eyes fixed on Abby's face.

"Elric, let her explain before we jump to conclusions. She brought Jack back to us." Although her words made sense, Thyra's uncertainty about his sudden appearance still lingered.

Eydis cleared her throat, and we all looked over. Elric and the other warriors bowed their heads in respect.

"Your Highness," Elric said. "Forgive me. I have heard about this human and her treatment of Anwen—this Abby was not kind to her. I was only reacting to my emotions."

"Yes, Commander, it is understandable," Eydis said with a heavy sigh, "but let us all leave Master Jack and go to the Throne Room to discuss this latest situation."

Everyone bowed again as Eydis left the room. I nodded to Abby for her to follow Thyra. Elric was about to follow her until I crossed the room and knelt by Jack's bed.

"I will return, Jack, okay? We just need to clear a few things up with Abby," I whispered to him, hoping his eyes would flutter open and reveal the bright blue depths.

But he didn't move and was still so deathly pale. Tears threatened to fall again, but I kept my head held high. My eyes fixed on Elric. His expression reflected mine. We quickly followed the group into the Throne Room.

Hopefully, Abby answered the questions honestly—she

faced a tough audience waiting for her, even if she rescued Jack.

***

I looked down at Abby from the dais. So many questions ran through my mind.

"Explain yourself, Abby—how did you come into this world, and how were you captured by Kenrick?"

Abby looked at all the accusing faces around her and then looked back up at me.

"I—I followed you that night, Jo. I ran after you, yelling, but you probably didn't hear me, and then I saw the light in the strange triangle," she paused and shook her head in terror. "I just had a feeling that you both walked through it, so I did too." Abby looked down at her hands and started nervously twisting them together.

"I passed through and found myself in the forest, not sure where you and Jack were, but I just started walking and calling out your names." She looked up at me with fear in her eyes. "And then a group of men captured me. I was so scared and didn't know what to do. I thought maybe they took you too. We walked for days, and then all of a sudden, everything went black, and I woke up in a cell, chained to a chair."

I flinched slightly, recalling my own experience of being kidnapped by the Mage and waking up chained to a similar chair.

"And Jack?" I asked. "When did you discover him?"

I wanted to believe her, but like Elric, I didn't understand why Kenrick would have released her or how she managed to escape.

Elric crossed his arms, his expression menacing. Abby glanced briefly at him, fear and maybe a little defiance clouded her eyes. "I don't know, maybe a month or so ago. The days and nights seem to blur together when you are stuck in a dark cell . . . but I do remember a lot of crying coming from another room down the hall, and then I heard your name—someone was calling out your name," she whispered, her voice barely audible to everyone except me.

Guilt pierced through my body. I slowly descended the stairs and stood in front of Abby. Elric shifted slightly toward me as if expecting an attack from her. I looked up at him and shook my head slightly, signaling him to stop. Abby noticed the gesture with a curious expression. Her eyes flicked between us.

"And how did you escape?" I asked in the same tone. "What's wrong with Jack?"

Abby's head began to shake, troubled by something only she could see.

"Jack was okay until a few days ago, then several guards took him away. It was horrible, Jo. The man in black is evil and did things to Jack, but I don't know what, and then he . . . ," her voice trailed off, and she started to shake uncontrollably. Suddenly, she collapsed to the ground as severe tremors convulsed through her body.

I jumped back in shock. Halvard and Thyra knelt beside her, grabbing her arms and head. I looked up at Eydis and Ansgar, unsure of what to say or do. Elric dropped to his knees and held her legs until she stopped kicking and lost consciousness.

Quickly kneeling down, I closed my eyes and placed my

hands on her chest, then moved them to her head, hoping to find out why she had the seizure.

Darkness instantly swallowed me. Coldness tightened around my throat. My body felt like I was underwater, lungs aching for air. An ominous presence overwhelmed me. I fought for breath. Through the haze surrounding me, I saw I was in an unfamiliar room. A cloaked figure paced desperately in front of me. His hand rose to my throat, gripping it and choking the air from my lungs. Strange symbols covered his armor. He pressed closer to me. Darkness masked my sight.

I was startled out of my trance by my own screams, crawling away from Abby's motionless body. Elric immediately was at my side, holding me as the vision quickly faded.

"Anwen, what happened?" Elric asked anxiously.

"I—I don't know," I stammered, trying to shake off the coldness saturating my body. "I think I witnessed one of her memories."

I quickly crawled over to Abby's side. "Abby? Can you hear me?"

Her eyelids fluttered.

"Abby? Wake up, you're safe now," I whispered as the memory of what she endured in Kenrick's prison shook through me. The sight of the cloaked figure and the cold fingers gripping my throat, or rather, Abby's throat, made me shiver. With sorrowful eyes, I looked up at the king and queen.

"Is there a room where she can rest?"

Quickly recovering from watching my episode, Eydis waved her arm toward the hall.

"Yes, yes, of course. Halvard, take her to the room next to Jack's for now," she directed.

We followed Halvard into the empty room. He gently laid Abby on the bed. We gathered around her, unsure of what to do next. Was Abby now a prisoner until we found out more? Or was she a friend—the one who saved our Jack?

I briefly glanced at Elric, knowing from his expression that he thought the former. I, on the other hand, wasn't quite sure yet.

***

A guard stood outside Abby's door when I left Jack's room. Jack remained in some sort of sleep state. No one understood why he was still unconscious—but we all agreed that dark magic was likely involved.

Thyra was sitting with him as I decided to check on Abby. I smiled at the guard when he opened her door for me. The room was too dark and a little cold, so I strolled to the hearth, placed my hands on the wood, and lit a fire.

"How did you do that?"

Abby's voice startled me. I quickly stood up and turned toward the bed. She was sitting on her elbows, her eyes wide with surprise and, oddly enough, hostility.

I hesitated before answering her, unsure if I should reveal the truth about my identity. I walked to the foot of the bed and stood with my arms crossed.

"How do you feel?" I asked instead.

She shrugged her shoulders. "Fine, I guess. What

happened?"

I pulled a chair away from the wall and sat beside her bed. I placed my hands on her arm. She sighed and laid her head back on the pillow.

"Am I a prisoner?" she asked with agitation.

"No, not at all," I responded, trying to mask the insincerity of what I said.

"Then why is there a guard outside the room?" she asked defiantly, crossing her arms over her chest. "Look, Jo or whoever you are, I did nothing wrong, and I am not sure why these people are acting the way they are."

"I understand your anger, Abby, but you have to realize that these people, as you call them, are enemies of Kenrick. You showing up after all this time with Jack—who still isn't responding to us—has everyone on edge," I tried to explain. "Please tell me how you escaped and how you knew the way to Vardia?"

Abby sat up and leaned against the backboard, her eyes now cast downward.

"I don't remember much. I woke up in a strange room, strapped to a table and alone. I was there for what felt like hours, but no one came back for me, so I tried to break free. It took a while, but I finally escaped, and when I got outside the room, I immediately found Jack down the hall, in another room, also strapped to a table. He wasn't moving, but I loosened the straps and then carried him away," she looked up with desperate eyes. "I know it sounds unbelievable, but I swear, Jo, we were just lucky. I found a way out in the lower cellar near the kitchen, I think, and that was that. It seems easy, but believe me, it wasn't. And then I just kept walking. I don't know how long I traveled. Days turned into nights. I didn't know where I would end up, and then suddenly, I have people shoving arrows in my face. But they recognized Jack and brought us here."

I kept staring at her—not necessarily out of disbelief but with awe. She saved Jack. He was unconscious, but she carried him all the way to the kingdom. So brave, and I had to admit, so unlike the Abby I knew—which raised the question . . . what was in it for her? The old Abby wouldn't have cared to help anyone but herself. But again, being in a strange world can make you do things you normally wouldn't.

"You do believe me, Jo, right? I mean, I know I never treated you right, but I wouldn't let anything happen to Jack . . . or you, for that matter. I wouldn't wish any of this on my worst enemy," she said, sighing with defeat. "Where are we anyway? And who are you?"

"Well, that is a long story, and I am afraid that you need your rest," I declared, standing up. I really didn't want to get into my journey to Vardia with her right now. Distrust was still an unspoken factor. "I will come back in the morning and talk, okay? I promise everything will work out."

Abby nodded and settled back into bed. I quietly closed the door behind me, then turned around to come face-to-face with Elric, who was leaning against the wall, waiting for me.

"So, how is our prisoner?" he asked sarcastically.

I put my finger to my lips and told him to be quiet.

"Please, keep your voice down. I just told her she wasn't a

prisoner," I said irritably.

Elric smirked.

"So, you lied," he stated.

I rolled my eyes and tucked my arm into the crook of his, guiding him away from the room. We walked to the veranda, where he turned me around to face him, his eyes full of worry.

"I don't want you to be alone with her, not until we get the truth from her," he said. "I don't trust her."

I quickly told him what she said to me about her escape, all the while he stared at me in disbelief.

"I can't believe Kenrick and even his Mage would let anyone escape. Her story doesn't add up, Anwen," he muttered as he gazed into the dark forest.

"I understand how you feel. I feel the same way, too, but she is here now, and Jack is safe. She can't harm me anyway," I said with confidence.

He swiftly looked at me.

"You should always be cautious, Anwen. Never let your guard down, even in Vardia, especially now with her here," he insisted. "I have tried to see into her mind, read her emotions. I know you have tried as well. Darkness shrouds her thoughts."

I shrugged my shoulders. "I have tried to read her thoughts with no luck, but that doesn't mean there's something wrong, right? I mean, she has suffered a lot these past months, Elric."

He seemed frustrated, and I knew he was only looking out for my well-being and that of Vardia, but what could she do here? Vardia was the safest place to be right now.

"Elric, please, give her a chance. For me?" I asked as I

placed my hand on his cheek.

He covered my hand with his and closed his eyes briefly. His irritation at me faded away. Our energies briefly connected—our hands glowing within each other. His thoughts entered my mind, and I was overwhelmed by his sadness.

Wynfalle.

I quickly withdrew my hand, still not accustomed to this unique ability to read minds and emotions. And it was intense.

"Oh, Elric. I am so sorry. With Jack's return and the situation with Abby, we haven't talked to Ansgar about sending soldiers to the mountains," I said regretfully. "What should we do? Should we talk to him now?" I was prepared to wake him up if necessary.

Elric offered me a slight smile.

"No, little one. We shall wait. I will not leave you in this unexpected situation now. Not until I feel that the people in Vardia are safe," he pulled me into his arms, "and that you are safe."

I held onto him, silently praying for the Mountain Elves' safety, but also selfishly thankful that I had Elric for a little longer.

FIVE

Carrying a breakfast tray, I approached Abby's room door, nodding to the guard as he opened it for me. I quickly scanned the room and saw Abby fully dressed and standing by the window. She immediately turned around and gave me a faint smile.

"I was wondering when I would see you again," she sighed with frustration. "I was afraid your friend would tell you not to come."

I noticed her drawn-out emphasis on the word friend. I set the tray down on the side table.

"Well, he tried to," I agreed with a soft chuckle. "But I'm not easily convinced that you're out to get me or my kingdom."

Abby sat down at the table and laughed. She picked a few nuts and berries from the plate, slowly placing them into her mouth.

"Well, time will tell," she said softly.

I looked at her, confused by her words. What a strange

thing to say, even as a joke—especially when everyone looked at her with distrust and hesitation. A shiver ran down my spine when our eyes briefly met.

Abby immediately retorted, "I am so lethal, right? I wouldn't even know how to find my way out of Vardia or back home without help."

She let out a sigh and glanced around the room.

"It is nice here . . . very quiet," she said, nervously wringing her hands. "It was never quiet in the prison."

Guilt flooded me, and my distrustful thoughts disappeared.

"I'm so sorry, Abby, for what you went through. I can't imagine it at all, but both you and Jack are safe now, here in Vardia. The elves are wonderful, and in time, they will see that you are their friend."

Abby tilted her head up at me, and for a brief moment, surprise followed by anger flickered across her face. But as soon as I noticed the emotions, they vanished in an instant.

"I know the king and queen would like to ask you a few more questions, but for now, how about I take you on a quick tour of the kingdom?" I asked, hoping a breath of fresh air would lift her spirits.

"They will let me out of this room? With you?" She asked warily.

"Well, yes, why wouldn't they?" I asked, not sure why she would be worried.

Suddenly, I remembered I hadn't revealed my real identity. I started to laugh at her cautious expression.

"Come on, I will wait outside for you to finish eating, and

then I will explain my new life here," I declared.

Abby nodded, her eyes narrowing cautiously at my response. I kept smiling as I opened the door to leave. When I looked back at her, my smile disappeared—the way she handled the food made me think she hadn't had a proper meal in months. The abuse at Kenrick's hands was obvious and made my stomach churn with anger.

I waited outside the room and talked to the guard until the door opened slowly. Abby peeked her head around the corner with a serious look on her face.

"Am I allowed to leave now?" she asked with a hint of sarcasm.

I responded to her with a smile, signaling her to follow me down the hall. She walked past the guard with a skeptical side glance but smiled at me as we went down the stairs.

"I can't believe we are inside a tree," she whispered. Her hand gently caressed the wall.

I nodded in agreement.

"I know. When Elric first brought me here, I had so many questions, but this world . . . ," I paused, "It's amazing. Vardia is beautiful and tranquil—an incredible city in the trees."

We paused outside in front of the castle when Abby saw the large carving of an hourglass. She looked at me with questions in her eyes.

"Jo?" she asked as she looked at the carving again and then back at my necklace. "Your charm . . . why is it carved into the door?"

I laughed, holding my amulet.

"Yes, about that . . . " I said hesitantly. "Well, now is a good time to tell you, I guess."

I held my hands out in front of me. A golden ball of energy hovered a few inches above my palms and then turned into shimmering, wispy strands, looping through the air in front of us.

"I am from this world, Abby. My mother was Princess Eira of Vardia, and she was a magical Healer," I paused again as I let the information sink in. "And I am a Healer as well. My real name is Anwen."

Abby's mouth moved silently up and down, attempting to form sounds and words. Concerned that she was going into shock, I lowered my hands in front of me, extinguishing my energy, and walked toward her.

"No, don't touch me," she hissed, backing away from me. "How can you be from this world? And you're a witch?"

I started to shake my head at her. "No, no, Abby, I am not a witch, I mean, I have powers, but I am so much more to my people."

"Your people?" She tilted her head in confusion—her eyes scanning my face cautiously. "But you don't have ears like them . . . and why were you in my world?"

My mouth went dry, and suddenly I felt very exposed—the truth was stuck in my throat, refusing to form the words to explain my situation. My senses tingled with danger—the idea that something bad could happen if she found out the truth. I couldn't shake the feeling of dread when I looked at Abby's face. But what would it matter if Abby knew my heritage?

"I am half Wood Elf," I paused, the dread easing but still prickling my mind. "My father was a Lucian."

I looked out over the clearing. People passed us with curiosity. I hesitated to continue my story. But I knew she would find out the truth anyway, so I delved into the one subject I hated to think about—my family's murder. I lifted my chin and continued.

"My father was Prince Garrick of the Kingdom of Lucia, Abby. Kenrick is my uncle. He killed his own family, my family. My mother sent me into another world to keep me safe from him."

There. I said it—the truth was out. The words slipped easily from my mouth, but the feeling of dread lingered. Something in Abby's eyes changed, making me pause. A cool, dark stare looked back at me—chaotic and intense. Then her gaze suddenly dropped to the ground. When our eyes met again, everything seemed normal. Chaos was replaced by calmness, peacefulness, and acceptance. The sudden shift was confusing and unsettling.

"I am so sorry, Jo," she hesitated, "I mean, your family was murdered. How horrible. And you have magic? Wow . . . that's so weird. You know?"

Abby turned away and went down the stairs, stopping at the bottom. Her eyes followed me as I walked down the steps to stand beside her.

Was she being genuine?

"So, you're not going to freak out on me, are you?" I asked with a wry grin. Guilt and shame flickered inside me. Was I imagining the darkness surrounding her?

Though her smile was weak and slightly strained, she shook her head.

"No, I think the shock has passed, but I'm curious, though, about you and Jack being here and how you came to be in Vardia. I mean, did you stumble into the kingdom as well?" she asked with a slight, sarcastic tone. "Were you taken as a prisoner, too?"

Abby started walking away from me again, her back stiff.

My annoyance at her attitude began to rise. Typical Abby—always trying to control everything. The guilty feeling started to fade.

"No, Elric and a few others were scouting the area around the portal, and they found us," I stated. Her questions raised a red flag for some reason. She didn't need to know the whole story—that we were actually kidnapped at first. "And during our journey to Vardia, Elric discovered that I was Anwen."

"Wow, that was some great luck, Jo. I mean, Anwen," she said with a bored tone.

I glanced over at her, and my internal alarm went off. She appeared a bit bothered by my background and how I ended up in Vardia. Was she jealous?

I was about to ask her if she was feeling okay when she stopped and turned towards me.

"So, who is this Elric?" she asked, with her hands on her hips, her tone filled with accusations.

"Well, he is a good friend," I said irritably at the sudden bluntness.

She looked at me for a few seconds, then rolled her eyes,

laughed, and threw her arms around my shoulders. I was left speechless and cautious of her unpredictable behavior now.

"I was just kidding, Jo," she said while laughing.

I cautiously smiled at her strange reaction—her completely bizarre behavior.

"I think he likes you," she declared, "and I know you like him. I can see it every time you look at him. I mean, he was like a rabid dog when he lunged at me. Like I was going to hurt you or something."

I stepped back from her grasp. Something felt wrong about her now. Even though this was typical Abby talk, it just seemed off.

"Well, let's head back inside for a while. The king and queen, along with their son, General Vidar, would like to ask you a few more questions about the location of Kenrick's new hideout," I said with authority, turning away from her and heading to the stairs.

I refused to look back to see if she was following me, but I felt her anger. Eventually, I heard the pitter-patter of her feet as she ran to catch up.

Yes, tonight should be interesting, to say the least. I had to hold back a smile when the thought of Vidar questioning Abby flashed through my mind—his intimidating presence and her cowering before him. I'm not a vindictive person, but the idea of seeing Abby falter in front of the elves pleased me.

Guilt started to surface—my sneaky thoughts felt trivial. But as I was leaving Abby's room—her pouty face and defiant stance—I quickly reevaluated that feeling.

I smiled as I headed to my room to change into one of my beautiful dresses.

***

I visited Jack before dinner. His room was illuminated by the orange glow of the roaring fire. A lump formed in my chest when my eyes landed on his unmoving form. I missed his infectious laughter and funny banter.

I assumed Thyra was taking a quick break from her constant vigil beside him. She was never far from the bedside, holding Jack's hand while reading one of her favorite children's books to him, hoping that the steady sound of her voice would wake him up.

I walked over to his side; the silky dress made a soft swishing sound as I knelt by the bed.

"Jack? Can you hear me?" I asked, holding my breath and waiting for a hopeful response. My eyes misted over. I took his hand in mine and brought it up to my cheek.

Closing my eyes, I tried to read his emotions again—anything that would give me a sign that he was still in the small shell of his body. But all I felt was darkness—and loneliness.

"I promise, Jack, that I will find a way to reach you. We miss you so much," I whispered into his hand, placing a quick kiss on his palm. I gently laid it down by his side. "I will be back later tonight. Thyra should be back soon."

I turned around to leave when I suddenly came face-to-face with Abby. We just stood there, looking at each other, almost sizing each other up. For whatever reason, whether it was from our past history or our most recent outing, we both remained cautious around each other.

When she looked at Jack, a wave of tenderness appeared on her face. But when she looked back up at me, hatred briefly took over her. The range of emotions, no matter how quick, surprised me.

"How did you leave your room unescorted?" I finally asked.

"I opened the door, and no one was there, so I thought I'd check on Jack," she said nonchalantly, as if it was no big deal.

She brushed past me and took Jack's hand in hers.

"Hey, Jack, it's me, Abby," she whispered. "You will get through this, I promise."

The way Abby spoke to Jack put me on edge. How did she know he would recover? That he would get through this? Anyone else muttering those words would have been sincere, but she was harsh and overly confident—as if she knew exactly what was going on inside his small, defenseless body.

"Well," I interrupted, "let's head to the veranda. We'll come back and say goodnight later."

I didn't know what else to say to her. My emotions were just as confused; I wanted to trust her, but something about the whole situation didn't feel right. There was something strange about her, but I couldn't quite put my finger on what it was.

She turned around and put her hand on my shoulder like we were old friends.

"Yes, let us not tarry," she said confidently. Her words carried a hint of a strange accent—enough to make me pause.

Hopefully, Abby's questionable intentions will be revealed

tonight.

***

I scanned the faces around the table— the mood was somewhat relaxed, but a sense of urgency still filled the air. I sat next to Eydis and Elric, while Ansgar, Vidar, and Halvard sat across from us, along with Abby, who seemed more comfortable as the night went on. She repeated that she had no idea where Kenrick was hiding now; she only remembered that the air around her was thick and hard to breathe.

Vidar and the others agreed that he must be hiding within the mountains, but again, this was just speculation. Where in the vast mountainous area could it be? Was his hideout still within the Solemn Mountains? We were no closer to him than we were months ago.

I glanced over at Elric. His hand brushed mine under the table. He furrowed his brow when Abby answered most of the questions from the king and queen.

I knew he still didn't trust her, and I could feel his emotions swirling in his mind as he tried to figure out, like me, what was different about her.

Suddenly, Eydis placed her hand on my shoulder as a loving gesture.

"Abby, I believe Anwen has told you how she came to be with our family?" she asked. Eydis looked at me with tender eyes. "We are so blessed to have her with us again."

Abby's eyes slowly moved from Eydis to me. And it was with me that she kept her gaze.

"Yes, she has told me," she replied with a hint of annoyance.

I bristled at her tone, then glanced at the others, hoping they could see the change in her, but they seemed oblivious. The coldness I had felt earlier returned. Her emotions spiked, sending my senses into overdrive. Abby kept staring at me, and for a brief second, her irises shifted color. My eyes widened in surprise.

My hands gripped the edge of the table. Elric's brow furrowed with concern at my sudden movement. His eyes shifted to Abby—he could sense the change as well.

Abby suddenly pulled away from the table and stood up.

"I am so sorry, but I am not feeling well," she said quietly. "I would like to go back to my room now."

Both Elric and I immediately stood up, but Halvard went over to her first.

"I will be happy to escort you," he said eagerly. He offered his arm, and her hand immediately rested in the crook.

"Thank you, Halvard," she murmured softly.

I was surprised when the moon-eyed Halvard led her out of the room. Suddenly stopping, Abby looked back at the king and queen.

"Thank you for a wonderful meal," she said, bowing her head. "I hope you believe me when I say that I am happy to be here within your kingdom. You have nothing to fear from me." She briefly glanced at Elric as they turned to leave the veranda.

"Well, that was interesting," I said. I sat back down at the table and looked at Vidar.

"Do you trust her?" I asked, hoping to hear someone else

voice their opinions—more like their doubts about her.

Vidar's gaze drifted over the balcony into the forest and sighed.

"I'm not sure, Anwen. I share Elric's concerns about her miraculous escape, but again, stranger things have happened before. It seems the gods were watching over both of them." He looked at the king and queen. "I think we should leave her be—no more guards outside her door from now on. If she's treacherous, let her plan play out, but until then, she's free to move around Vardia."

Both the king and queen nodded their agreement. Elric had doubt written all over his face, but he would not disagree with his Commander.

I sighed and finally agreed too.

"Yes, I think you're probably right, Vidar. She saved Jack, so we should be thankful and give her the freedom, I guess."

But I wouldn't let my guard down. Something was still off about her, and I was determined to find out what.

SIX

The clang of metal greeted us as Elric and I entered the arena. We had been working all morning in the training room, hoping to find a solution to the binding magic cast on the Lucian soldiers. Nothing in the elven books offered any counterspell to the horrible death curse.

Well, I said nothing about our books in Vardia. Elric hinted that his people might have the answers to what we were searching for—another important reason to travel to Wynfalle, in my opinion. We just needed to persuade Ansgar, Eydis, and Vidar.

Looking around, I still felt sad about Jack's absence. Although I knew he was now safely inside Vardia, I couldn't shake the feeling that he was still in danger. I couldn't forget the Mage's warning that Kenrick had other plans for him.

Those 'other' plans still haunted me.

Scanning across the field, my eyes finally landed on Halvard and, ultimately, his sparring partner. Surprisingly, it was Abby.

Elric and I both noticed her at the same time, eyes locking with bewilderment. We stood beside the training circle, watching Abby as she moved around Halvard. She was confident and very comfortable wielding the sword.

The way she countered his move for move was both surprising and a little intimidating—like she had trained with swords before. And she was very skilled.

Halvard noticed us for the first time and suddenly stopped. He crossed his arms and nodded in greeting. Elric watched him carefully, trying not to reveal his displeasure.

"Good morning, sir," he said as his eyes drifted to Abby out of concern. "I found our guest sitting outside by the fountain this morning and thought she might like to join me at the training arena."

Halvard glanced at me, possibly seeking reassurance that his actions were acceptable.

I nodded my head briefly, approving that he was right to make her feel more at home. I didn't know what else to say to him—he was infatuated. I kept my suspicions about Abby to myself, not quite sure of her motives to share them with anyone other than Elric.

I observed Elric to see his reaction, but he also gave Halvard a brief, strained, and forced nod.

Halvard noticed and frowned—he knew Elric wasn't pleased with the situation.

"That is great, Halvard," I said, giving him some comfort from Elric's coldness. "Abby, you look like a pro. Have you had lessons before?" My curiosity about her expert handling of the weapon was getting the best of me.

She shook her head as she returned the sword to Halvard.

"No, not at all. I guess beginner's luck, that's all." She briefly looked at me with coolness, almost like the Abby from the past, but she quickly recovered and threw a smile our way, shrugging modestly.

Elric glanced back at Halvard without acknowledging Abby's statement.

"Halvard, please gather Thyra at the castle and meet us in the planning room. Though I know she would rather stay at Jack's side, it is important for her to be at this assembly. She may return to Jack once we are finished."

Halvard nodded and said, "Yes, sir."

He nodded to Abby and then headed toward the castle. Abby's eyes watched him leave—her face flickered with a brief longing.

Interesting.

All of a sudden, Elric turned and signaled to another soldier.

"Frey, would you mind escorting Lady Abby to the castle gardens and courtyard?" he asked, turning to Abby. "Frey could give you a tour of our communal gardens if you'd like?"

Abby nodded and then smiled at Frey, a handsome elf with short brown hair and piercing green eyes. "Yes, that would be lovely. Thank you."

Frey bowed and offered Abby his arm. She hesitantly took it and followed him out of the arena. They rounded the corner, out of sight. Abby's tinkling laughter echoed across the clearing as they headed toward the castle.

I turned around, catching Elric staring at me.

"So, when should I talk to Halvard about his feelings for our guest? Of all people, why does it have to be her?" He shook his head in disbelief, throwing his hands up in frustration. We kept walking toward the bunker.

I shrugged.

"I don't understand it, Elric. I want to believe she is harmless and not part of Kenrick's plans, but something holds me back from genuinely trusting her. When I look at her, I see the same distant and scornful Abby, but then I feel something strange inside her that doesn't seem quite right. And just now, as she watched Halvard leave, I see someone who just wants to belong somewhere—to be part of a family."

I placed my hand on Elric's arm. "I know how that feels. I know how she feels."

Elric cupped my face with his hands. "I understand, Anwen, and I agree with you. But I don't want to see Halvard get hurt. And most of all, I don't want Abby to hurt you."

He scanned the arena and quickly pulled his hands away, realizing his men could see us.

"Let's talk after the meeting, shall we? We can meet later by the Great Tree to have some privacy. We have a few important matters to discuss tonight."

His eyes bore into mine. He gently took my hand and brought it to his lips. A shiver ran down my arm from his touch.

I smiled, eagerly awaiting the list of topics we needed to discuss so urgently.

We arrived at the bunker, an octagonal stone building with

a large, thick steel door. One of several non-wooden buildings located within the kingdom.

We headed down the stairs to the main strategy room, where Vidar was already hunched over a circular table at the center—a three-dimensional map of the kingdoms was displayed there. We nodded in acknowledgment and took our seats on the opposite side of the table. We waited for Halvard and Thyra to arrive so we could discuss our next steps against Kenrick.

***

Twilight settled around me as I sat beside the well of our Great Tree, Jilneim. The leafy branches shimmered with tiny blue and white lights. The fairies buzzed through the leaves, guarding their home—the Sacred Tree.

The golden Okri orbs gently floated in the sparkling water. Small bubbles rose to the surface, delicately popping and revealing a soft musical note. I placed my hands over the water, careful not to touch the sacred liquid. My eyes closed briefly as I felt the heavy energy of the Okri intertwining with mine.

My hands began to take on a golden hue as the energy and thoughts of the Okri spread through my body. A small smile crept across my lips.

The past six months, since I returned to Vardia after my kidnapping, I had been secretly visiting Jilneim late at night, linking with the Okri—their connection, their comfort, helped me cope with the loss of Hrafn and Jack.

Calmness flowed up my arms and into my body, eventually spreading to my mind. The soft, gentle voices of my ancestors whispered within me. A sigh of relief escaped my lips as I closed my eyes longer and allowed their soothing thoughts to surround me.

Hesitant footsteps entered the clearing. I slowly opened my eyes to see Elric's surprised expression. I was standing now, and when I looked down at my hands, the mysterious markings and glowing hue gradually faded.

Elric silently approached me, his eyes never leaving mine. He finally found his voice.

"How did you do that?"

My eyes shifted to the Okri. They continued to drift in the water as if nothing had bothered them.

"I don't know," I said quietly. "I've been visiting Jilneim for months, communicating with the Okri, but I guess I never really noticed anything out of the ordinary."

Elric took my hands in his, and we sat down on the well wall. His admiration for me was clear.

"You never cease to surprise me, Anwen. Your abilities are one of a kind, unlike anything in our world, even compared to Hrafns. I don't know how to describe many of your skills," he said.

I studied his hand in mine, his thumb gently rubbing circles along the back. He lifted his right hand and touched my silver brooch—his energy linked with the magic inside it. He created the special gift so I would always stay connected with him. This brooch saved me from Kenrick when I was kidnapped. Elric knew where to find me because of the power it held—a power I couldn't yet understand.

Like a hammer hitting my chest, I felt his sorrow and pain radiating from his energy.

"I am so sorry, Elric," I whispered, tears welling in my eyes. "I tried to convince Ansgar to let you go to Wynfalle to keep your people safe, but he can be so stubborn sometimes."

Earlier in the evening, Elric approached the king about leaving for Wynfalle, hoping to warn his people of a potential attack. But, as Elric predicted, Ansgar wouldn't permit him to go. I imagined he knew Elric's banishment would cause trouble and, more than that, the likelihood of harsh punishment when he returned to the mountains.

But I also sensed fear in my grandfather.

When Elric wasn't practicing his magic, everything was fine; he was one of the king's warriors. But now that Elric was my teacher and using his powers again, I felt the fear inside Ansgar. Like many Vardians, he feared the Volun growing within Elric.

Elric looked up into the tree, silence all around us. He sighed in frustration.

"Anwen, I knew they would refuse my request to leave," he looked back down at me. "Just like you knew as well."

He stood up and walked away from me. I quickly followed and turned him around to face me.

"You're still going, aren't you?" I asked accusingly, not believing he would defy Ansgar. "You can't! Not only will you face punishment by your people, but you are risking banishment here, Elric. I can't bear to lose you."

He grabbed my shoulders, his hands pressing down hard in desperation.

"You of all people should understand the importance of family, Anwen. If I don't do this, it will haunt me for the rest of my life," he released me and turned toward the dark woods. "I will risk everything for a clear conscience . . . that I may save my people from being another of Kenrick's extinct race of beings."

He lowered his head in sadness.

"Jack needs help, Anwen. I can gather information from our Seer; she can help identify the dark spells surrounding him, and she alone can help cure him."

He turned back around to face me. "I shall return, I promise, but you need to understand why I need to go."

I quickly pulled him into my arms, my hands clutching his neck in desperation.

"I know, Elric, I know you need to do this," I said as my voice broke. "That was never a question for me."

I pulled away from him and gently touched his face. Tears threatened to fall as the premonition I had in Arcadia flooded my thoughts. A feeling of foreboding took hold.

He pulled me toward him, kissing me deeply and with such emotion, leaving me breathless. Wanting more, I intertwined my hands in his hair to draw him closer. When we finally broke apart, Elric rested his forehead against mine. His breathing was heavy.

"I love you, Anwen. Never forget that," he whispered, his voice trembling with desperation.

I murmured softly, a slight smile on my face, "I love you more."

He chuckled softly and huskily when I kept up with our

daily affirmation game.

"I do not think so, my dearest, because I love you most," he whispered again. His lips brushed across my neck and up my jaw until finally finding my lips again. Soft and slow, but then deepening in desperation.

A loud clapping noise sounded across the clearing. We quickly stepped back, our bodies and hands instinctively reacting in defense. Abby stood to the side, her hands slowly coming together, making a sound like lightning.

"Well done. That was touching," she sneered, stopping and folding her hands into clenched fists at her sides. "It is quite numbing to see you both declare your love for each other."

She slowly walked along the edge of the clearing, heading toward the well. "It is so, how should I put this . . . repulsive to know that with people dying and facing horrific death in all the kingdoms, that you two have found true love."

Both Elric and I watched her every move, always keeping our eyes on her.

"Abby," I said cautiously. "What's wrong?"

She started to laugh, but it wasn't her usual laugh. A deep, guttural sound burst from within her—not a human noise, something I'd never heard before. The energy coming from her was heavy, and the intense feeling of hatred overwhelmed me.

I quickly looked at Elric, and his reaction was the same. This was not my Abby.

Sensing danger, Elric threw up his hands and released his energy toward Abby. In an instant, she reacted by pointing her hand at Elric, knocking him backward against one of the oak trees surrounding the clearing. He was slow to stand up, struggling to breathe from the force of the magic. I turned and fully hit her with my power.

But at the same time, she did the same, pointing her hand at me.

I was pushed back against the well wall, shockingly unable to move to defend myself.

Abby leaned over me, lips curling into a hateful smirk.

"How dare you flaunt your new life, how you think you are better than everyone, that you are special," she hissed, "because you know nothing about this world—the suffocating evil and deception of the elves and what needs to be done to protect it from them."

"Abby," I said, struggling to speak. "Who are you? What happened? Why are you doing this?"

"You, Anwen, I am doing this because of you," her eyes scanned the clearing. "I am doing this because of what the elves did to me, and what Kenrick can offer in exchange for the destruction of your people, for the eradication of all elves within Emberval. I have watched you in both worlds, disgusted by you—vengeance is what I want," she spat out.

Without warning, Abby changed before my eyes. Like a domino effect, her skin rippled with tiny scales, a dull gold color with a tinge of black at the tips. Her clothes fell to the ground as her entire body transformed into a dark creature. Her hair was the same color as her scales, gold with dark streaks, and her eyes were black as night, shimmering with gold flecks.

Her eyes shifted from me to Elric, hatred and loathing

boiling within her.

"By the gods," he struggled to speak. "You are a Lirrean. But how can that be?"

Abby hissed at him, crouching low—ready to pounce.

"Yes, elf. Because of your repulsive people, I am the last of my kind." She leapt up and knelt beside me once more. "And you! For once, I agree with Draugr. Even though Lucian blood runs through your veins, you are nothing like my Master; you're just a filthy elf. A traitor to your own kind!"

I tried to move my hands again, but it was no use.

Abby laughed at my struggles.

"Try harder, *Jo*," she spat out my old name with such hatred. "For you are no match for the spell I placed on you."

She tilted her head with disdain. "How fun it would be to play with you a little more. Watch you twist and scream in pain." Her laughter sent chills down my spine. "But I have my mission, elf. Watch me destroy your kingdom—your people, Anwen. Watch as I destroy everything you have come to cherish."

My eyes followed her as she quietly walked to the well. To my horror, she reached into the water and grabbed an Okri, pulling the glowing orb out.

Elric yelled at her. She raised the orb high in victory.

"So small and gentle-looking, yet holds so much power and chaos." She tilted her head in contemplation and wonder.

"Abby, please put her back," I begged as I felt the orb's energy fading. "You are hurting her."

She gazed at me with her dark, cold eyes.

"I don't want to hurt *it*, Anwen. We have other plans for

it—for all of them."

I watched in horror as her mouth unnaturally opened wider than normal, unhinging at the jaw, and swallowed the orb.

Pain shot through me. The orb's scream echoed inside my mind.

Abby plucked a second orb from the well, then another, then another—swallowing every last one of them. Agony and heartbreak flooded through me. My body thrashed on the ground.

Elric called my name, but I couldn't speak. Everything around me started to fade. Darkness filled my vision. Elric shouted something at Abby, but his words were unfamiliar to me. I could barely open my eyes—Elric's face twisted as he cast the spell. I felt his magic spreading through the clearing. A sudden burst of heat throbbed in my chest. My brooch vibrated and glowed, pulsing along with Elric's words.

Abby screamed at him and wavered in her steps. She tried to counter his spell with her own. I could barely keep my eyes open. I fought through the pain, hoping I wouldn't pass out. My vision blurred at the edges.

Suddenly, Abby twirled into the air. Black feathers burst around her as she transformed into a strange bird—a creature I had seen before. The bird shot straight upward and disappeared with a high-pitched shriek.

Within seconds, Elric was by my side, trying to stop the uncontrollable trembling rushing through my body. The Okri's screams echoed inside me. My hands, now able to move again, quickly went up to cover my ears.

"Anwen, look at me," he whispered calmly. "Listen to my voice. You have to focus. The Okri are frightened, but you need to calm them—communicate with them. Assure them that we will find them."

I opened my eyes slightly and tried to focus on his face. His words. Silently, I called out to the Okri, letting them know I could still hear them—letting them know I would find them.

Gradually, they ceased their cries.

Ansgar, Eydis, and Thyra ran into the clearing with an increasing number of Vardians. All were pointing and staring at Jilneim in shock and terror. Elric and I followed their gaze.

Lying on the ground, and still falling, the tree fairies toppled from the branches—one by one—dropping with a soft thud. Dead.

SEVEN

Silence and shock filled the clearing. Everyone noticed the darkness covering the Sacred Tree—the fairies who survived were gathering the bodies of their loved ones from the ground. The absence of the Okri was felt by all. Questions arose as they began shouting and crying out in despair.

Elric jumped up from where I was on the ground, running towards Ansgar and Eydis, who were both standing in the center of the clearing, confused by the events.

"Your Majesty," he said urgently. "We need to act quickly. We are losing Jilneim."

Elric watched me with concern. Thyra helped me onto the well wall. My trembling hands waved in horror at the dead fairies littering the wall and floating in the water—now dark and cold.

I felt my heart falter—the agony and loss of the Okri unbearable. My hands clutched my chest and twisted into the fabric of my dress. Feeling nauseous, I dropped to my knees and vomited. Thyra held my hair back and looked up at Elric.

"She is in distress, Elric. What is wrong? What shall we do?" she asked urgently. Vidar and Halvard rushed to Thyra's side, fear evident on their faces.

Eydis understood what was happening to me and rushed to my side.

"Anwen, you're in shock. Try to calm down and let your energy flow through you. Let it help you," she whispered in my ear.

I tried to concentrate on her words and let my energy mask my grief and anxiety. The loss overwhelmed me. The Okris' faint voices cried out, filling my mind with their fear. Tears began to fall uncontrollably as another wave of nausea swept through my body with intense force.

Elric knelt beside me and grasped my face with his hands.

"Look at me, Anwen. Focus on my voice. I am going to merge my energy with yours, let it help you overcome your pain—recover from the loss—so that you can think straight," he whispered. Anguish radiated from his voice.

I tried to focus on his eyes, but my vision blurred in and out. I closed them immediately.

Suddenly, a slow tingling sensation moved up my arms, into my chest, and down through my legs. The pleasant feeling calmed my thoughts and eased my heartache. I let him merge with my energy. It overwhelmed my senses; unlike when Hrafn was transferring his magic to me. Elric's energy enveloped my magic, caressing it in a very intimate way. Peacefulness and calmness flowed through my body.

I opened my eyes again and saw Elric's worried face

looking down at me. After blinking a few times, I started to collect my thoughts, and the pain finally eased. The voices were now a faint whisper, still present, but I could feel my body regaining control.

"Can you hear me?" he asked. "Can you understand me?"

I nodded my response, unable to speak just yet. His voice sounded like an echo in a tunnel. I shook my head, trying to focus only on his words.

"Can you stand?" he asked.

I nodded again as he held my waist and helped me to my feet.

"I am fine, Elric," I managed to mutter, my hands gripping his around my waist. "Thank you. I am better."

My attention was focused on the elves in the clearing.

"The Okri are gone," I whispered, the seriousness of the situation clear in my voice. "But they are communicating with me."

Surprise registered on everyone's face at my statement. Ansgar walked over to my side and placed his hand on my shoulder.

"How is that possible, Anwen? What has happened here?" he asked.

Eydis joined him.

"Who did this?"

Elric surveyed the clearing and saw all the frightened faces staring back at him.

"We have been betrayed by Abby," he stated. "She is a Lirrean . . . and she took the Okri from Jilneim. That is why death has overtaken the fairies."

Angry gasps rang out. Protests echoed through the trees.

Elric's eyes met mine.

"We tried to stop her, but she has considerable strength. Strange spells immobilized us so she could steal the Okri," he continued. "And she was here on Kenrick's orders."

Vidar addressed his parents. "We need to take Anwen back to the castle and discuss our next steps."

Agreeing, everyone hurried from the clearing. Elric wrapped his arm around my waist, holding me as we made our way down the path.

I glanced back at the Sacred Tree, which now looked withered and unwell. The absence of lights and the whirl of fairy wings pierced my heart and soul. Darkness and despair surrounded Vardia.

***

Elric led me to a chair. Everyone gathered around the platform. Eydis kneeled beside me, holding my hands with concern.

"Anwen, how is it you are communicating with the Okri?" she asked with wonder.

I explained to her and everyone gathered around me about my nightly visits to the tree over the past few months. How it was the Okri who first reached out to me, asking me to visit and talk with them. I didn't think much of it until tonight, until they were taken and I realized how strong our connection had become.

"Anwen, no one has ever communicated with the Okri like

this," Ansgar admitted, "what you are telling us has never happened in our kingdom."

He collapsed onto his throne, his hands covering his face in exhaustion. He looked up to his people with distress, something I had never seen on his face before.

Eydis approached him and placed her hand on his shoulder. "Ansgar, what should we do?" she whispered so only Vidar and I could hear.

Elric started pacing in front of the platform.

"The Lirrean said she was the last of her people and that the Okri are part of a larger plot," he paused briefly, but then continued. "Kenrick and his Mage are preparing something destructive for Emberval, and with the possession of the Okri, he is one step closer to fulfilling that plan. Many years ago, my father told me of a legend—a dark tale of using the ancestors' magic to end the gods' power. I was a young boy, and my memory has faded, but the story and the recent events align with the legend. The fall of the gods and the rise of chaos were the outcome."

"Then what shall we do, Elric?" Vidar asked. "Is Anwen in danger? It seems she is now directly connected and communicating with the Okri, so what will happen if they perish? What if Jilneim meets the same fate? We are at a loss for what to do. This is beyond anything that we have prepared for in Vardia."

Elric ascended the dais and turned to all the elves; the anticipation and need for him to have the answers were evident on many of their faces.

He finally faced the king and queen. "The Okri are only one part of the puzzle to fulfill the prophecy," his eyes flickered to the crowd before landing on the king and queen again. "Kenrick needs the Orbs of Urora from the Sacred Spring in the Wynfalle Mountains and the Auras from the Sacred Well in the Sorayn Desert."

The crowd began to whisper in shock, but Elric kept going.

"With your permission, I will travel to Wynfalle, not only to warn them of Kenrick's intentions but also to seek the Seer—to attempt to thwart the dark magic. What better way to combat this darkness across our kingdom than with the help of the one person who was blessed by Odin himself with the knowledge of the Shadow Magic—she will know the prophecy . . . she can help us."

Now the whispers turned into raised voices of protest. Many still didn't trust their mountain kin.

Elric looked at Vidar, dismissing the objections.

"General, I see no other option but to go to the mountains. I will do whatever it takes to save Vardia," he said with heartfelt conviction, then looked at me. "I will do anything to save Anwen."

Struggling to stand, I shuffled next to Elric and slipped my arm into his.

"I will travel with Elric to Wynfalle," I pledged with the same passion. "Vardia needs Jilneim and the Okri, and we must do everything we can to save them."

I turned to Ansgar, Eydis, and Vidar. "If what Elric says about a prophecy is true, then the Mountain Elves need to be warned; they need our help just as much as we need theirs." I looked at Thyra and continued. "They might be able to help Jack because something tells me he could be part of this plot as well."

I searched the faces of the crowd—hoping to find understanding and agreement with my next words.

"We need to put aside the past and our differences during this time of need. Not only for Vardia but also for Wynfalle. Our connection to the Ancestors is essential—a core part of who we are as a community and a kingdom. Vardia will fall if the Okri are not rescued and brought back."

My legs nearly gave out until Elric grabbed my waist. I looked back at my family again.

"We will need to act quickly with our decision because I am unsure how long we have before Vardia feels the repercussions of losing the Okri. Hrafn warned of losing Jilneim," I paused, "and the Healer if something like this happens. We are facing devastation not just in Vardia but for all the people of Emberval."

My family jumped off the dais and pulled me into their arms. Their fear and concern washed over me—along with their love and understanding.

Moved by our sincere statements, Ansgar moved away from us.

He raised his hands to Thyra, Halvard, and a group of elven warriors waiting anxiously for their orders.

"Thyra, you will lead a small group of soldiers along with Ambassador Sigurd to the Kingdom of Sorayn, where you will meet with the combined clans of the Sand Giants and the Desert

Elves. Here, you will request their support as allies against Kenrick and his forces. Queen Gamila must be warned of an imminent attack on their sacred Auras."

Next, Ansgar turned to Vidar. "My son, you will travel with several of your best men to the Rock Giants in the valleys of Wynfalle. There, you will have the dangerous task of negotiating with King Grannir for the support of his clan."

Vidar began to protest, but Ansgar raised his hand to halt him.

"I understand your concerns, Vidar, but we must try to gain his support, even though he's currently struggling to prevent his own soldiers from betraying him and siding with Kenrick. Sedition is widespread in his ranks, but if the king pledges allegiance, all we can hope for is that the rest of his people will follow."

Ansgar faced Halvard.

"Halvard, you will accompany Elric and Anwen to the Wynfalle Mountains. With this task, you will personally escort Ambassador Ragnhild during the negotiations with King Torvald."

Gasps and dissatisfaction swept through the crowd.

Ansgar raised his hands again to silence the elves. His eyes moved over their scared faces.

"Anwen's observation and statement are indeed correct. We need to set aside our differences, our anger, and our misgivings with Wynfalle. We need to focus on saving Vardia and protecting our Great Tree," he nodded with newfound determination as his eyes settled on Elric and then slowly moved to me. Turmoil flickered across his face as he made his decision, but only briefly. As my king—not just my grandfather—he understood the slim chance of success, but we had to try regardless of the outcome.

"I believe our greatest chance of survival depends on King Torvald and King Grannir. Both Elric and Anwen are right; we need our mountain kin now more than ever." He raised his arms to the side. "We will prevail against the evil that has fallen upon our kingdom! Vardia will rise to the challenge, and we will contain and crush the evil spreading throughout Emberval. Vardia forever!"

Loud cheers erupted from the crowd, chanting our names and celebrating Vardia's victory while condemning Kenrick's destruction and death. My stomach twisted at the thought of our perilous journey to Wynfalle. A storm of emotions raged inside me. I swallowed hard at the sudden tightening in my chest.

Eydis placed her hand on Elric's shoulder and put her other hand in mine.

"Let us wish you a safe journey, for tomorrow marks the start of a new era with our mountain kin, one welcomed with kindness and acceptance."

I looked out at the optimistic crowd—enthusiastic and confident about our imminent success. Our quest will determine the victory or downfall of Vardia.

No pressure, right?

I looked back at Elric and realized he will be in double the danger on this journey. I felt scared for what might happen to him once we faced the King of Wynfalle. My premonition from Arcadia haunted me; the dark shadow that covered Elric scared me. Truly, this journey will change many lives. Failure cannot be an option.

EIGHT

The night was sleepless and painful. The distant wail of the Okri kept me on edge—it broke my heart. I felt connected to them in every way; their pain was my pain, their fear was my fear, and there was no resolution at this point. Not until we rescued them from Abby, wherever she took them.

Glaesir suddenly lifted his head. A stream of air puffed from his nose, drawing my attention away from the distant voices still crying in my head. I leaned down and patted him on the neck.

"I'm okay, boy, don't worry," I assured him. "I'll be fine."

We just entered Rydlyn as we traveled the long road to Wynfalle. I glanced back at our small group of travelers, and my eyes settled on Halvard. His silence was thick in the air. Abby's betrayal must have weighed heavily on his mind—and his heart. I imagined he was trying to process both her deception and its impact.

I quickly looked away from him, realizing that even I, who had known her in my old world, never would have guessed she would do something like this—that she could be someone completely different. But I couldn't deny that the way her body transformed into her true form was incredible. She looked like someone right out of a comic book from my old world.

I glanced over at Elric, who was in his usual warrior mode now, scanning our surroundings in anticipation of an ambush. Lyfir's gait was steady and cautious. I didn't want to disturb him now, but I planned to ask him about the Lirreans when we stopped for the night. I was curious about the history of these strange people, wondering how Kenrick managed to find a race that was supposedly extinct.

My gaze finally shifted to our fourth traveler, Ambassador Ragnhild. A regal aura surrounded her, even as she rode her horse. Considered one of the elves' Elders, she was held in extremely high regard, almost as much as the queen. Her long white-blond hair was pulled up into a delicate bun with small braided loops hanging from the sides—a sharp contrast to her dark brown skin. Her very appearance demanded attention. I felt intimidated by her, and I believed she knew it—and took pleasure in it.

I turned back around, brushing stray hairs away from my face. The day was already very hot and humid. I fanned the air around myself.

We rode for the rest of the day until the tall trees finally blocked the last rays of the setting sun. Elric led us to a quiet spot along a small creek for the night.

"We will rest here and leave at first light," he proclaimed. "Our pace today was adequate, but we must do better tomorrow to reach the Wynfalle border in a reasonable time."

We all nodded in agreement. Looking at Elric's map, we had a few more days of travel in Rydlyn, then we would head west and cross into Jordanna. From there, we go north into one of Wynfalle's valleys, just before the long climb up the mountain to the kingdom.

Or I should say a fortress. Elric's description sounded almost haunting when he spoke of his homeland—how the elves rarely left the mountain or socialized with the other kingdoms. Shivers ran down my spine as I thought about how cold it must be there—and how lonely and isolated.

We dismounted from the horses and led them to a spot near the stream. Halvard took the reins from the ambassador and led the horses to a lush, green area by the water. She grabbed her pack from the saddle and headed toward a small group of trees, a place noticeably separated from the rest of the group.

The ambassador watched Elric cautiously as she passed by him. He didn't notice her actions, but I did, and it made me angry. Especially now, as we head toward an uncertain future with Wynfalle. She could at least show a little compassion, especially since she knew he would be punished by his people.

Sighing in frustration, I turned back and stroked Glaesir's neck, trying to ignore the heat of anger. Although Elric seemed resigned to being treated like a villain, I couldn't stand it. I was about to walk up to Ragnhild and confront her narrow-mindedness when I suddenly felt a presence beside me.

Elric placed his hand on mine as I absentmindedly tangled it in Glaesir's mane.

"It is fine, Anwen," he whispered. "I know you mean well, but the ambassador has every right to behave the way she does around me. Her parents were murdered because of the Volun in a war that still has deep roots in many of our people's minds. I cannot fathom the painful memories that surface when I am in her presence."

I was about to argue with him when he gently brought my hand to his lips.

"Let it pass, Anwen," he murmured into my palm. My breath caught in my throat as his cool lips pressed against my warm skin.

"Fine, but only this once," I conceded. "You are not your ancestors, and she should understand the sacrifice you're making by returning to your people."

Elric quickly pulled my hand away and turned his back to me. But not before I saw his expression; one I had never seen before crossed his face.

Fear.

And a sadness that I didn't think anyone could ever understand, not even myself. He hadn't seen his family since he was a kid, over two hundred years ago.

I watched him go back into the campsite, gathering his bow and quiver to hunt, and left quietly. Sadness for his dilemma weighed heavily on me. I wanted to follow him and hold him close, assuring him I would never let anyone harm him. But I knew he would only pull away more. I sensed his pain, and deep down, I knew he believed he deserved the punishment awaiting him when we reached Wynfalle. I wasn't sure how to help him, and that frustrated me—especially when he refused to accept any good intentions.

I led Glaesir over to the other horses and tied him to the makeshift corral.

I picked up my pack and moved toward camp, placing it near the ambassador's bedding. I wanted to make it clear to her that she wasn't isolated, so to speak, but that we were all in this together, especially Elric.

So, guess what, Ms. Elder Elf, you have a close companion for the night.

I smiled when I saw her eyes squint slightly in annoyance at my closeness. Ignoring her, I began to prepare my bed.

When Halvard arrived with firewood, I quickly built a fire, hoping Elric had brought back a nice, fat, juicy rabbit—meat I really enjoyed. He didn't disappoint, walking into camp with several strange-looking rabbits for our dinner.

As he filleted them and laid them on a spit over the fire, I prepared a few of our vegetables I'd brought from home and roasted them over the flames. By the end of the night, with full bellies, we sat around the fire and relaxed—or at least tried to.

Elric and Halvard lit their pipes. I watched the white wisps of smoke swirl and twist in the air, reminding me of my energy—the tendrils curling around their heads before vanishing into the night. I stole a glance at the ambassador, who gazed into the dancing flames. The golden light reflected in her wide eyes. She stayed silent and still—as if in deep meditation.

Both Elric and Halvard were also lost in their thoughts as they absentmindedly stared into the fire. I cleared my throat, thinking it might be a good time to ask a few questions.

"Elric, can you tell me about the Lirreans? I remember you saying a while back that there was only one other race that could handle the Okri . . . did you mean the Lirreans?"

Elric, still staring into the fire, nodded. "Yes, but no one has seen a Lirrean for thousands of years. Legends say they were wiped out by a civil war within their clans."

"So how is it that Kenrick has kept one hidden all this time? Surely, someone would have heard about her existence," I asked, noticing that the ambassador's attention was now focused on our conversation.

"I am not sure, Anwen. Any chatter or sign that a Lirrean existed and served Kenrick would have definitely spread through the kingdoms, but news never reached our scouting missions. Hrafn, in particular, would have known, even if it was just a rumor," Elric paused. "But there is one person who knew a Lirrean during her long life—the Seer Herja. She will know how to handle Abby; she will know how to help us."

Silence once again surrounded us. The flickering flames hypnotized us. Waves of orange and red flickered across the wood.

"It is said that our all-powerful gods first created the Lirreans as Keepers of our world," Ragnhild said unexpectedly. Her words were soft and deliberate, as if emphasizing the importance of what she was telling us.

We looked up, startled, but still, we didn't make a sound. Her deep voice commanded our attention.

"They were the original guardians, tasked with watching

over all life in our world. Their essence was nearly as powerful as that of the gods, and they knew it. They exploited the gods' grace and began to defy them—prayers ceased, sacrifices stopped—until the gods finally grew tired of their rebellion and created the elves. Just one race of elves, with no division or difference," she glanced at Elric. "Our ancestors lived in harmony with each other and with the magic around them, so the gods rewarded them with the Okri, the Urora, and the Auras—making them the Keepers of all living energy passing into the afterlife. But this angered the Lirreans, and some clans among them turned violent, declaring war on the elves—and, by extension, on the gods. The clans opposed to war and destruction begged the gods for support, but they refused. In the eyes of all Lirreans, the gods turned away from them—their firstborn—leading to a civil war among the clans. Their relationship with the gods and the elves was forever strained. Peace dwindled within the Lirrean clans—war raged across the land—and that persistent unrest and anger ultimately destroyed them. Or so we believed."

Ragnhild glanced briefly at all of us, a faint smile forming. "Though our great Okri has been taken and our world may soon fall into chaos, one cannot deny that the discovery of a living Lirrean is something important to consider," she looked back down into the flames. "And, yes, Commander Elric, Herja will be able to tell us much about the Lirrean race, and for that, I am eager to converse with her."

Ragnhild suddenly stood and bowed to us. "It is late, shall we start before the sun rises, Commander Elric?"

Her question for Elric felt more like a command to me, but both Elric and Halvard quickly stood up and returned the bow.

"Yes, ambassador, of course," Elric said in an equally commanding voice. "Before sunrise, indeed, for the day will be a long one as we continue through Rydlyn."

Ragnhild looked at me. An eyebrow raised at my lack of manners, I suppose. I stood up and bowed.

"Rest well, ambassador," I said softly but with a touch of irritation.

Ragnhild's brow furrowed slightly, but then she slowly smiled—a smile that didn't quite reach her eyes.

"Yes, you as well, Healer Anwen," she whispered, emphasizing my title with a hint of sarcasm as she turned to her bed.

I turned around to sit down again when I noticed both Elric and Halvard staring at me. Their expressions showed confusion over our strained exchange. Elric frowned but didn't say anything. Instead, he mumbled good night and turned to his bed. Halvard nodded at me and did the same, leaving me all alone and a little upset.

There was nothing else for me to do but follow their lead, so I stoked the fire and went to my bed next to the ambassador. I could tell she was trying to steady her breathing, anger clear on her face. Her energy radiated from her. Maybe putting my bedding next to hers wasn't such a good idea. I felt on edge. My thoughts whirled inside my mind. Sleep was out of the question.

And to make matters worse, the Okri started resonating in my head—softly at first, but soon the noise grew louder. I tossed and turned, hoping to find a comfortable position. I tried different breathing techniques to quiet their cries, but nothing worked.

The voices kept me awake last night, which I didn't tell anyone else, not even Elric. They would just worry. But I knew another sleepless night would only slow down our travel plans for tomorrow.

After spending an hour just lying in my bed, I decided to visit Glaesir. Maybe his presence would help soothe the distraught orbs.

As I started to stand, the voices became overwhelming. I stumbled, the deafening sound overtaking my senses. A cry escaped when my vision blurred. My hands fumbled along the ground, needing something to hold onto as the pain increased. Suddenly, a hand encircled my waist, startling me.

"Anwen, are you okay?" Elric's soft voice whispered in my ear.

"The . . . the voices," I stammered in panic. "So loud . . . the pain . . . I can't see."

"Okay, let me help you," he said as he led me back to my bed. "Let us lie down and meld our energies again, Anwen. Okay? That helped you, did it not?"

I nodded, hysterical voices echoing in my mind. Tears streamed down my face, the pain now nearly unbearable. My hands instinctively covered my ears, flinching as the cries of fear from the Okri reverberated through my head. What was Kenrick doing to them?

Elric guided me onto my bed. He gently took my hands and

placed them on his chest. His hands caressed my face, wiping away the tears. His energy flowed from his body into mine. The familiar and intimate sensation of our energies merging calmed my nerves and quieted the voices to a faint whisper. He drew me closer, nestling my head against his chest as his arm wrapped around my waist.

Sighing with sudden relief, sleep took over me.

NINE

I felt Elric move away, so my hand instinctively reached out to bring him back. When my hand grasped empty air, I opened my eyes and saw Elric walking to his own bedding and packing up his belongings. Halvard kneeled next to me. His hand pulled back from my arm when he saw I was awake. Surprised, I looked across to find Ragnhild staring at us, frowning and shaking her head.

"Did we oversleep?" I asked Halvard, not really caring about the ambassador's disapproving look. I quickly glanced at Elric, noticing that he was avoiding my gaze.

Was he embarrassed that Ragnhild caught us together?

"No, Anwen, you are fine," Halvard assured me, also noticing Elric's distant behavior. "But it's time to continue with our journey. The ambassador is ready to go."

I quickly looked up when I heard the sadness in his voice. Our eyes met, and it was then that I finally understood Thyra's words of caution—how many of the elves disapproved of Elric and me being together. Halvard knew this and felt sorry for us.

I shook my head to clear my thoughts. The Okri began to chatter again. Judgments aside, Elric helped me last night. Didn't they realize that?

Slowly standing, I tried to focus on controlling my breathing, talking silently with the Okri through my thoughts. Though Elric's energy helped me tremendously, I needed to manage them on my own, just in case he was not available.

I stood with my eyes closed, breathing deeply to soothe my energy and calm the voices—they were scared and kept calling out to me. Once the voices were under control, I opened my eyes and saw everyone staring at me again. Elric looked like he was about to drop everything he was holding and rush to my side.

I smiled at him, thanking him for last night with my thoughts. A slow, sensual smile spread across his face, causing my heart to stutter.

Ragnhild gave me a quick nod and kept packing her things. I took Halvard's hand and gave it a gentle squeeze.

"I am fine," I reassured him. "The Okri are pacified for now."

He smiled, then collected his belongings and headed toward the corral.

When we finally mounted our horses, everyone looked around the camp for anything left behind—enemy scouts could be tracking us. We resumed our journey once more.

Hopefully, our day will be as uneventful as yesterday. Could we be so lucky? Again, my magic was excellent, but foretelling the future? Not so much.

***

Traveling through Rydlyn took longer than expected. The heavily forested kingdom offered no discernible paths through the overgrowth. With the amount of untouched vegetation, we all believed—or rather hoped—that the Lokrum had never traveled this way to the mountains.

On the other hand, the chance of running into the Forest Giants was quite high and could be just as dangerous. However, their presence still remained unknown for some reason. Something was wrong, and the ambassador was the first to voice her concern.

"Commander Elric, we should have been greeted by the giants by now, don't you think?" Ragnhild asked. "Perhaps they have taken refuge somewhere else?"

Elric shook his head, disagreeing with her assumption. "No, ambassador, the giants would not have left their home defenseless, just as we would not have left ours unprotected."

He looked around again at our surroundings. "No, they are still here, just not showing themselves to us quite yet."

Though his words soothed the ambassador, I could tell he was nervous about the situation.

Nonetheless, both Halvard and Elric placed their bows across their laps. The Forest Giants were aligning their allegiance with Vardia, but it didn't hurt to be prepared.

I looked at Elric when he signaled for me to get ready too. Just as I swung my bow over my shoulder, an arrow suddenly struck the tree in front of me.

A scream escaped. I leapt off Glaesir's back and took cover behind a fallen branch. Elric jumped from Lyfir to the nearest tree. Swinging up and over, he hid among the leaves to locate the enemy archer. At the same time, Halvard dismounted, grabbed the ambassador, and threw her to the ground for cover.

I nocked an arrow, raising my head slightly above the branch. A sense of déjà vu flowed through me. I definitely didn't want to be a target again. I quickly turned around when Halvard, behind another tree with the ambassador, signaled to me and then pointed to the far left where a rock formation rose from the ground.

I jumped up and sprinted toward the next tree, heading for a gap in the boulder. Elric watched my movements with his eyes. My eyes scanned the row of trees—darkness concealed our attacker. I held my breath, waiting for any sign of movement.

I looked up to find Elric's location in the trees but could no longer see him. I peered around the corner, placing my hand on a ledge jutting out from the formation.

Suddenly, my hand slipped inside the side of the rock, fully immersed, as if the wall was made of sand. My scream was silenced by something cold and gritty covering my mouth. A cold blade pressed against my throat.

"Ye do not think to scream, my lady, or use some of that magic on me, ye hear?" said a low, grating voice from behind.

Elric fell from the tree. His arrow was aimed above me.

"Let her go," Elric commanded with a deadly tone. "Now."

Halvard and even Ragnhild stepped beside Elric, with bows

pointed at my mysterious captor. All I sensed was cold rock against my back, unsure of who or what was holding a knife to my throat.

Before I had a chance to think further about my predicament, the rock formation started to move. Surprised, I stumbled forward. Instantly, something hard caught me and grabbed me around the waist, lifting me off the ground with my feet dangling and pulling me closer to the now-moving rock wall.

A surprised look appeared on everyone's faces. My captor lifted me high off the ground.

How tall *was* he?

"Put down yer bows, ye raggedy lot, or I will slice her open clean to the bone, I will," my captor muttered impatiently.

Elric tilted his head to the side. Something in my captor's voice made him lower his bow.

"Barik?" Elric asked cautiously. "Is that you?"

The figure lowered his head slightly to my level and looked more closely at Elric.

I looked to the side and caught a glimpse of my captor. A scream escaped behind his rough grip. It really looked like a rock formation come to life—almost a human face but with gray, pebbly skin and a bald head. What a terrifying creature!

The rock man hesitated, but then straightened up and held me closer to his body, never letting the knife waver from my throat.

"Who ye be, elf?" he scoffed. "How do ye know my given name?"

Elric swung his bow over his shoulder and stepped slightly

forward, his hands extended in front of him.

"I know it has been a very long time, my old friend, but don't you recognize me?" Elric pretended to be hurt as he brought his hand to his chest. "I am Elric, son of Brynjar, Volun of the Mountain Elves."

Suddenly, the rock man dropped me to the ground. The quickness of his actions and the long fall stunned me and took my breath away. I turned around on the ground and looked up at my captor, and I couldn't believe that peering down at me with the most piercing gray eyes was a giant. I scrambled back quickly and stood next to Elric, who now seemed completely at ease.

Halvard and Ragnhild lowered their weapons and stared at this massive stone being.

"Elric?" The rock man squinted his eyes as if trying to confirm it was indeed his friend.

He stayed like this for a minute, dare I say, completely still as a rock, until he suddenly leapt forward and hugged Elric tightly. We all pointed our bows back at the creature until we heard Elric laughing, though the squeeze made it hard to tell if it was a laugh of happiness or a grimace of pain. My bow stayed raised, but Halvard and Ragnhild lowered theirs.

"Yes . . . humph . . . yes, Barik, it is I, Elric," he stuttered out in brief puffs of air.

"Elric, my long-lost friend," Barik shouted. He lowered Elric and stepped back, inspecting him. "You are not so pale, my friend. And look at your hair—you're almost bald! You look terrible."

Elric shook his head, running a hand through his short hair.

Laughing, he patted Barik on the arm.

"I do not live in the mountains anymore, or have you forgotten?" Elric said.

Barik's face grew serious.

"No, no, my friend, I haven't forgotten," he said sadly. "We would never forget."

Elric's smile wavered briefly but quickly returned as he faced us. Noticing my bow was still raised, he crossed over and smiled warmly.

"Anwen, you may lower your bow now," he said softly. "Barik is an old friend of mine." Elric turned to Barik and introduced us.

"Barik, please meet my friends—Ambassador Ragnhild, daughter of Lord Frey and Lady Eir of the Wood Elves, and Halvard, son of Lord Hjalmar and Lady Arnborg of the Wood Elves," Elric said as each member bowed.

Barik looked at me with wonder. He knelt down, face-to-face.

"And who shall this one be?" he asked.

Elric reached out for my hand.

"Barik, this is Princess Anwen, daughter of Prince Garrick of Lucia and Lady Eira of the Wood Elves," he said with pride. "She is our Healer."

Barik kept staring at me with his stone-gray eyes, smiling.

"Ahhh, yes," he whispered so only I could hear. "But ye are so much more, aren't ye, Healer Anwen?"

My brow furrowed at his confusing question, but he suddenly rose to his eleven-foot height and clapped his rubble-like hands together. Shivers ran up my spine at the cringeworthy, grating sound.

"Well, good day," Barik said. "And let me introduce myself: I am Barik, First Warrior to King Grannir, and you should turn around right now and head back to Vardia."

Elric shook his head, surprised by Barik's candor.

"And why do you say this, Barik?" Elric asked.

Barik shook his head sadly. "Because, my friend, ye will only find death where ye go, nothing more."

We glanced at each other. Fear washed over our faces.

Are we too late? Has the Lokrum already invaded Wynfalle?

TEN

Elric approached Barik, a look of worry and dread on his face.

"What has happened? Where are Menglad and her forest people?"

Barik shook his massive head in surprise.

"Ye don't know, do ye?" he asked. "Aye, she was forced to move her clan further east—to the Outerlands. Several of her kin were captured by Centaurs and trampled to death. Her mate included."

"Centaurs?" Halvard asked, confused. "The Centaurs have always kept to themselves, never taking sides. They rarely leave their homeland. Rydlyn would be too far east for them to travel."

Barik shrugged.

"Many Centaurs pledged allegiance to Kenrick," Barik looked down at the ground with sadness. "They are in turmoil like my clans are, not sure who to trust. They have seized the City of Myrar."

Halvard looked at Elric with concern. Elric also seemed

worried. I remembered meeting a Centaur when I first arrived in this world. Though it was clear he didn't view elves kindly, he still told Elric to protect me.

"What does this mean?" I asked everyone.

Elric sighed.

"It means that we have to bypass the city and head farther west, adding more days to our journey," he said unhappily. "Barik, we can't turn back, no matter the warnings you gave us. We have an important mission, critical to Vardia."

Barik looked at Elric intently, then nodded, showing he agreed with his plans.

"If ye don't mind, I shall follow ye for a while up north," Barik suggested.

Elric rested his hand on Barik's strong, muscular arm.

"Of course, Barik," he said. "You may join our group. Always, my friend."

Barik smiled at us—a strange contrast with his deadly, sharpened teeth.

I couldn't stop the smile from spreading across my face—Giants weren't as cruel as I once believed. Watching Barik interact with Elric only reminded me how little I knew about this world.

We quickly mounted our horses. The sun was nearly at the horizon. Nightfall was almost upon us. Barik led the way—his long-legged strides kept us at a steady pace. Everyone stayed silent for the rest of the day as we headed west. The relocation of the Forest Giants and the turmoil within the Centaur clans weighed heavily on everyone's minds.

How will this impact all the other kingdoms in the fight against Kenrick?

As far as I knew, Ansgar hadn't sent anyone to negotiate with the Centaurs. I glanced at Ragnhild, who looked worried, with her features stiff and unmoving. I could only guess what she was thinking—what this new revelation meant for Vardia and her role in negotiating with King Torvald. I understood that the more allies Kenrick gained, the more difficult it would be for the rest of us.

The need to ally Vardia and Wynfalle had become more urgent in the fight against Lucia now. If we fail, Vardia will be lost.

***

We continued through the evening, darkness covering the path as we navigated the thick foliage. Large hills now surrounded us. Barik didn't argue about our journey through the night. He quietly pushed aside tree branches and overgrown brush without questioning us. He seemed to understand our sense of urgency.

I couldn't help but wonder how Elric and Barik became friends. This odd mystery only heightened my awareness of Elric's past in Wynfalle. I knew it was an important part of him, even before the trauma of his banishment. Determination surged through me—my main goal was to learn more about his people and family.

Elric raised his hand to signal us to stop as he dismounted from Lyfir. Barik looked around cautiously but quickly turned back and motioned for us to dismount as well.

Elric turned to us. "We shall stop here for the night. There's a lake to our left where we can freshen up and water the horses."

The spot that Elric mentioned was hidden behind a few larger trees and some bushes, but it was perfect to accommodate all of us for the night, even Barik with his large frame.

As we set our packs in a circle, Halvard decided to look for our dinner while Ragnhild and I gathered firewood. Silently agreeing, we gave both Elric and Barik some time alone to visit.

Ragnhild and I walked away from our camp into the woods. I glanced back to see both Elric and Barik embrace, laughing and surprised to find each other again. Regret washed over me because of what I would be missing—I wanted to know everything about Elric and his past, even more about Barik and his people.

I sighed in defeat. My time will have to wait. Once again, the patience thing was really starting to bug me.

Ragnhild probably guessed my mood and what my sigh meant. She chuckled softly.

"I understand your curiosity, Anwen, when it comes to the lives of other beings within our world," she observed. "Patience is a divine trait that I know is running thin for you."

I looked away from her, slightly annoyed that she said out loud what I was thinking.

She halted mid-step and grinned at me.

"You do remind me of Princess Eira," she whispered. "Your mother was a contradiction; one minute she would be the epitome of a strong and commanding Healer, and then the next she could literally dissolve within herself, questioning her talents and worth to our people, especially when she married an outsider."

I stood in my spot, wondering where she was taking this conversation.

"So, ambassador, are you doubting my confidence in helping our people? And questioning my loyalty because of Elric?" I asked coldly.

She looked surprised that I reached that conclusion.

"No, my dear, I loved your mother dearly, just as I know Hrafn did," she said, pulling back in shock. "My observation was not made with malice towards you," she paused, "or toward Commander Elric."

She began walking again, making me follow her, but then she immediately stopped.

"You must be wondering why I have been somewhat distant with you, Anwen," she stated, barely looking me in the eyes. "I made that observation because I know the veil of love can muddle the important decisions that we have to make in our lives. I know, my dear, because I have been in the same situation."

Ragnhild held her chin up. "I loved Hrafn with all my heart and soul, Anwen, and I want to believe that he made the right decision in trusting you. But, please, forgive me if I can't quite reconcile the fact that you are here and he is not."

She started to walk ahead of me again, leaving me to ponder her honest declaration. I was shocked by her confession—but also saddened. She loved Hrafn. And now, seeing me here, alive, taking his place . . . I couldn't imagine the heartache.

Guilt over my behavior grew inside me.

I followed her, absent-mindedly gathering firewood. We didn't speak anymore. I figured she had said enough at this point. At least now I understand the reason for her behavior toward me—and maybe even Elric. Hiding our feelings for each other hadn't been a focus on this trip.

When we couldn't carry any more firewood, we headed back to camp. Elric was helping Halvard with the five squirrels he caught.

Barik was nowhere to be found. Elric noticed my confusion.

"Barik decided to hunt for his dinner," he said with a soft chuckle. "Squirrel would not satisfy his hunger."

Halvard snorted in irritation. "Well, I could not find anything bigger for him to eat, so let him find his own food."

Elric laughed even louder, and soon everyone was joining in, making the mood more cheerful.

Barik didn't return until long after our dinner was over. He strolled into our camp, clearly full from whatever he caught. We finished packing up our dishes, and both Halvard and Elric took out their pipes.

I strained my neck just to look up into his face.

"So, you found food, Barik?" I asked, smiling. "I hope it was enough?"

Barik chuckled deeply and placed his hand on his stomach. "Yes, I believe several deer don't need to roam these parts anymore . . . well, not on their own legs, that is!"

My eyes widened like saucers—how could he have caught two deer and already eaten them? Elric laughed at my surprise.

"You should see his clan eat during a feast, Anwen," he said. "It is an event that one does not witness very often, and I am sure they would never venture to watch again."

Barik chuckled and nodded. "So true, my friend, so true."

Everyone snickered softly at their familiar banter. I noticed a different side of Elric that I was really enjoying. He seemed so much more relaxed, and this realization prompted my next question.

"Barik, why were you roaming the forest of Rydlyn? Why were you away from your people in the valley?"

Barik didn't reply immediately, and his mood shifted.

"I was on a mission, watching over a few of my kin as they traveled from the valley into Lucia. I was to report on their actions with the Lokrum," he said grimly. "I found them talking to the ghost man, the one who defies death, and that's when I knew my own kin were traitors. So, I am heading back to the valley to update the king."

Elric's back stiffened. "Ghost man? Do you mean Draugr?"

The mention of his name sent shivers down my spine.

"Yes, that's what he calls himself," Barik said. "He is evil; he commands the walking dead—that's what he does. And he's taking the restless young'uns with him. They're leaving the valley."

Elric threw a stick into the fire angrily. "No, Barik, Draugr is just a man, and one day, I will face this human monster and take retribution for all the pain he has caused across the kingdoms. That day can't come soon enough."

Silence pressed down on us. The fire flickered and crackled, mirroring the emotions inside of me.

Ambassador Ragnhild looked up and asked Barik another question, continuing her role as a dignitary.

"Barik, do you believe that King Grannir is still neutral in his stance with Kenrick? Do you think he would accept a hand of friendship and allegiance to Vardia to defeat the Lucian army?"

Barik stared into the fire, pondering her questions. We waited for his response with bated breath.

"Well, yes, I believe that King Grannir would be quite open to talks with Vardia," he said as he leaned back against the massive rock behind him, the grinding of stone-on-stone sending tremors through my skin.

Ragnhild nodded. "Good, because we have General Vidar and several of his warriors heading to your valley now, hoping to secure your king's support against Lord Kenrick."

Barik sat back up and looked at Elric in surprise. "And where are you headed? Not to the valley?"

Elric looked away from Barik's intense stare.

"No, we are headed to the Wynfalle Mountains to talk to King Torvald," I said. "Vardia hopes to rekindle a relationship with Wynfalle."

Barik shook his head slowly, never taking his eyes off Elric, who still refused to meet his eyes.

This worried me even more. Barik knew the danger of returning to a place that banished you, but he didn't say anything else to Elric, only shook his head in disbelief.

"Well, that should be interesting," was all that Barik said to him.

He turned his gaze to Ragnhild. "I shall go to the valley and meet the general. I will let my king know that we need to be allies, we need to defeat Ghost Man and Kenrick."

Ragnhild nodded, smiling at his decision to help Vardia. Barik turned around and, without another word, went to sleep, signaling that he was done with the conversation. Halvard and Ragnhild also shared the same idea and bid us goodnight. Elric and I were alone, lost in our thoughts. The silence persisted. Nothing moved in the night.

I was upset about Barik's answer regarding Elric's return to Wynfalle. What did he know about the punishment? I wished Elric would talk to me.

As I watched the crackling fire, the Okri began their nightly whispers. My brow furrowed at the intensity of their cries. It quickly escalated into screams of pain—screams for my help. My hands clutched my head in pain. Nausea overwhelmed me. Nighttime was the worst for their cries and hardest to control.

I suddenly felt Elric at my side, clutching my hands and lifting me off the ground. My legs buckled as the pain overtook me. He picked me up and placed me on my bed. I felt his body wrap around mine. At first, our energies collided with such intensity that they took my breath away. But soon, a gentle calmness surrounded me. I curled into his warmth and solace.

"Go to sleep, my love," he whispered softly in my ear. "I will always be here."

I felt the darkness of sleep pulling me under. Elric's clean scent intoxicated me into a blissful dream.

ELEVEN

My eyes slowly opened. Darkness still surrounded us. I glanced to my side at a sleeping Elric, his arm around my waist. I gently lifted his hand away and laid it beside him. Pushing up on my elbows, I looked around to see what woke me. I sat up and rubbed my eyes, listening for the voices, but the Okri were pacified for now.

Halvard was supposed to be on guard duty. I leaned to my left and saw him by a tree, standing upright but with his head tilted to the side, asleep.

I turned my gaze toward the lake, feeling a gentle tug. A faint voice echoed in my mind. Not the Okri this time, but someone else.

Elric continued to sleep, undisturbed by the new voice echoing in my head. My eyes drifted back to the lake—a faint light shimmered in the distance.

The sound was coming from the water.

I made my way through the trees, no longer afraid like I was the first time I had an encounter with water spirits. It felt so long ago that I met my mother for the first time.

I finally reached the edge of the dark water, but the voice vanished.

"Hello?" I whispered into the night.

The silence and complete stillness unnerved me, but I waited a few seconds longer.

"You called for me?" I asked a little louder.

A gentle splashing sound caught my attention, but then the water near the shoreline started to slosh back and forth. The waves collided violently—like buckets of water crashing into each other. The water merged with each splash, building upon itself, crashing repeatedly until a tall column of water formed—standing alone and reaching toward the sky.

I stepped back from the water, unsure of what would happen or who might emerge from the dark column of water.

Suddenly, the pillar fell down and out, forming a figure. When the water began to turn red at the top, creating long hair, my breath caught. Could I be so lucky as to talk to my mother again?

Bright turquoise eyes opened, shining with anticipation.

"Anwen, my love," she whispered. Her water body now complete as she stood before me in the same yellow dress, shimmering with a golden hue around her.

"Mother," I said breathlessly.

She smiled at me, knowing that our last meeting had caused me to deny her as my mother.

"The gods have blessed me with seeing you again, my

daughter," she declared.

"Am I dreaming again?" I asked cautiously. My eyes narrowed as I scanned the darkness around me. "I don't feel like this is a dream."

"No, darling, you are awake, for the gods have an important message for you," she said hurriedly. "We know of your mission, Anwen, and the dangerous tasks ahead of you."

"I don't understand. A message? Can't I talk to the gods? I have so many questions for them."

Eira stepped closer, just a few feet away from me. She reached out and gently touched my cheek, then smiled, knowing my impatience.

"I understand you have many questions, Anwen, although I don't have all the answers for you right now," she said with some hesitation. "But I do know that the gods trust you and think you are a brave woman for enduring the Okri."

She touched my cheek again, with a sad look in her eyes. "I am proud of what you are doing for our people, Anwen. I know you have been in pain because of the Okri connection, but please know that it is a sacrifice that is not unnoticed by our gods."

I looked away from her, uncertain how to acknowledge her statement. Why wouldn't the gods help us then? Why let me suffer like this if they knew what was happening?

Eira smiled faintly, as if reading my thoughts.

"You are special, my love. Powers given to you by the beloved goddess Freyja. Gifts bestowed that only she can explain." Eira stepped aside and raised her hand toward the middle of the lake.

A pulse of light appeared just beneath the water, the rhythm pounding faster and the light enlarging as it moved closer to the shoreline. My mother smiled and then bowed her head. A gold light shone brightly for a moment before dimming. A figure materialized.

An attractive woman with long, flowing reddish-blonde hair, wearing a long green robe with a large gold belt, stopped a few feet away from me. Her bright blue eyes twinkled as she looked me up and down.

"Anwen," she said breathlessly. "How you have grown into a lovely young lady."

She kept walking toward me and placed her hand on my cheek. A wave of familiar energy radiated from her touch.

"You are beautiful, young one," she said with a lop-sided smile, "and very strong-minded. I feel your energy. It is quite impressive as it grows stronger."

She pulled her hand back and looked over at my mother.

"Eira has been talking about you for so long, it feels like we should be old friends," she said matter-of-factly, shrugging.

I was stunned and couldn't speak. Was I really talking to a god?

"I—I don't know what to say or what to call you?" I asked. "Please forgive me for not saying the right words."

She laughed and took my hand.

"Please, call me Freyja, Anwen," she said tenderly. "For we have been together for almost seventeen years now."

I nodded my head, still speechless. I glanced at my mother and noticed the sadness in her eyes.

"I am honored to be in your presence, Freyja, but I have so many questions for you," I said quickly.

Freyja raised her hands to silence me.

"I understand, Anwen, but please, I don't have time to answer all of them because I have an urgent task for you," she said hurriedly. "Fólkvangr and Valhalla are in danger. Your ancestors and the gods' realm are at risk. We need your help, Anwen."

"I don't understand," I said, bewildered. "How can I help you?"

"Because you are the key they are looking for, and we need to stop them."

"Key? Stop who?" I asked, shaking my head in disbelief. I looked back and forth between the two figures.

"I am sorry, but I don't have time to help you right now. Our people need my help; the Okri need to be saved, and Kenrick needs to be stopped. We must travel to Wynfalle as quickly as possible to ask for their help, but also to warn them of an impending battle with the Lokrum," I shook my head at Freyja. "So, I am sorry, regardless, I am helping my people first."

I was hoping she wouldn't strike me down in anger for defying a god, but I stood there, defiantly staring at her.

Surprisingly, Freyja began to laugh.

"You are definitely the daughter of Eira," she laughed, then turned serious. "I understand, Anwen, and I commend you for standing up to your goddess, but putting that aside and speaking with urgency, your journey to Wynfalle is twofold, my dear, because what you seek from Herja is also what I seek—her help and the special knowledge she keeps close."

"Why not seek her help in person? Why me?" I asked, still not understanding my role.

"It is essential that the gods do not interfere in the lives of this world. But the markings that appear on your body, Anwen, were crucial to our survival at one time; but now, unfortunately, they are the means to our destruction," Freyja whispered as she turned away from me and walked toward the lake again.

I stood on the shoreline, puzzled and stunned.

"Wait," I yelled out to her, but she didn't stop. "You can't leave like this! You can't tell me something like that and just walk away! Stop, I tell you! What do I ask Herja? What do my markings mean?"

Freyja turned and raised her hands toward me.

"He calls for me, Anwen, I need to leave you now," she said, "but I will return. I will answer your questions, young one, soon, I promise. But for now, talk to Herja, understand the origins of the Shadow Magic—gather the knowledge that will guide you in the fight against Kenrick and his Mage. Herja is a peculiar one but extremely powerful—earning many of the gods' admiration and respect. But they also fear her. Do not underestimate her strength, and when combined with yours and the Volun's powers . . . I have to admit that a few of the gods are fearful of your alliance—but those fears need to be set aside for now."

Freyja hesitated, wanting to tell me more. A look of determination flashed across her features.

"Kenrick and his Mage explore dangerous and uncontrolled

magic with the help of one of our own—a vengeful god who has chosen this alliance as a means to an end. The downfall for the rest of us and the total destruction of this world. The gods are angry with him. When we stop our brother, we stop Kenrick."

Freyja started to dissolve into the water, disappearing suddenly and leaving faint ripples on the surface. The glow disappeared, and the water darkened again.

Panicking, I turned to Eira, hoping she wouldn't disappear like Freyja. Not yet.

"Mother?" I asked softly. "Do you know anything about what she said? Why is a god involved?"

And how am I supposed to defeat him? Why am I the key to destroying all the gods?

Eira moved toward me, her hands reaching out. She wrapped her arms around me, holding me close—her warmth and strength took me by surprise.

"I wish I could tell you everything, Anwen. I truly wish I could reveal what your destiny holds for you," she pulled away and wiped a stray tear from my cheek.

"But I am bound to the gods—I cannot disclose what is not mine to reveal. Please believe me when I say that Freyja and the others are worried and are only holding back from you until you are ready to fully understand your role in this troubling time."

"So, I continue to Wynfalle as planned, but then what? How do I know what to ask Herja? What about the Okri and Vardia?" The tasks kept piling up, and the success rate was dropping.

"You will know when you meet with her. Even though Seer Herja is one of the oldest elves in Emberval, she is quick and sharp—she will help you. But also keep your wits about you. Close your mind to her until you know when it is right to let her in," she said, and after a slight pause, she added, "Anwen, please be careful when you are in Wynfalle. I feel your emotions running high because of your feelings for Elric."

I pulled away from her arms.

"What do you mean?"

She lowered her arms to her sides and started to step backward.

"Where are you going? Don't leave yet, please, mother," I begged, reaching out to her.

"Hide your feelings and power from King Torvald, Anwen," she said. "Be cautious around all the elves in Wynfalle. They are in a perilous state. Do not be quick to judge, but do not trust blindly."

"Mother, please, don't go," I yelled again. "What do you mean?"

Eira's body sank back into the water. She raised her hand to say goodbye.

"I will talk to you soon, Anwen, I promise," she said, her voice fading. "I love you, daughter."

And then all was quiet.

What remained of Eira was now a still, dark surface. I couldn't look away from the lake—where she vanished. Confusion overwhelmed me from both Freyja's and my mother's words.

My legs buckled as I fell to the rocky shore. What just happened?

I was in disbelief talking to a god—Freyja, who gave me this power. But she didn't answer any of my questions; she just added more to think about and mull over in my already overloaded brain.

Traveling to Wynfalle involved many aspects—not just saving Vardia, but also saving the entire world . . . and saving the gods as well!

Seeing my mother again was wonderful, but her added warning about the Wynfalle elves only confused me further.

Yes, I knew I had to be cautious around them, especially because of the past history between the two kingdoms, but how can I help Freyja, the gods, and even Vardia if I couldn't rely on them? If I couldn't fully trust them, how could our mission succeed?

And Herja? I had to learn her Shadow Magic to help the gods. And what about Elric? Did my mother's warning also include him?

I raised my head and looked up at the light beginning to appear across the sky.

"So, what I have learned tonight is absolutely nothing that can help me!" I yelled to the fading stars.

Frustrated, my hands dug into the rocky sand. The Okri began to whisper again, so I closed my eyes, calming my breath and waiting for the new day to rise from its sleep.

TWELVE

The horses were nervous, stomping the ground and moving nervously to the side with jerky motions. We had been traveling for three days, and with the cold weather and everyone's tension, I didn't blame the horses. Wynfalle was nearby, and we were all anxious about what that might mean.

I hadn't told anyone about my night visits, not even Elric. I felt guilty hiding such an important secret from him, but for some reason, my mother's warnings kept echoing in my mind.

And of course, include the nightly Okri disturbances, which seemed to be getting more intense. I was about to jump out of my skin with any slight movement. I didn't need the extra inquiries and questions that I just couldn't answer yet.

As we drew closer to our destination, Elric grew more distant, not just with Ragnhild and Halvard, but with me as well. He refused to discuss his banishment now or what would happen when we faced his people. I tried to talk to him, but he always changed the subject.

I felt frustrated and apprehensive, but also confused and lost; every emotion imaginable flooded my mind. And to make things worse, I would catch him staring at me across the fire late at night—his expression a mix of concern and fear. When our eyes met, he kept them locked for a few extra seconds, but when he finally looked away, it left a void in my heart.

The one person I felt made Elric happy right now was his friendship with Barik. They whispered to each other as if sharing a secret. I wasn't sure what they talked about, but I saw Barik shake his head at Elric quite often, possibly reprimanding him for going back to Wynfalle.

Well, at least I hoped that was what he was doing.

It was comforting to know there was at least someone Elric would listen to in our group, even if it wasn't me.

Suddenly, the horses stopped. I looked up from my distracted thoughts and saw both Barik and Elric clasping arms. I hurriedly dismounted Glaesir and approached them, unsure of what was happening. As I got closer, I was surprised by the scene before me.

Wynfalle. We were finally here.

Elric looked back at me and smiled.

"Anwen, we have arrived," he said, sweeping his arm.

"Ye have never been here, Your Highness?" Barik asked.

"No, I haven't, but it is breathtaking." I couldn't take my eyes off the beauty of Elric's homeland.

The mountains, even from this distance, looked majestic and stunning in their size. All the peaks were visible, with not a cloud in the sky, and the fresh white snow contrasted beautifully against the blue sky, making them even more awe-inspiring. And they looked cold, as I pulled my coat closer to my body.

I glanced at the others. The same expressions appeared across their faces. Surprisingly, neither Ragnhild nor Halvard had ever traveled this far north either.

"This is where I shall leave ye, my friends," Barik said with apprehension evident in his voice. He grasped Elric's arm again. "Ye be careful, and if ye need anything, find me, and I shall wreak havoc on those who have wronged ye."

Elric grabbed Barik's arm and gave him a brief hug. Then Elric took Barik's hand and slipped something into his palm. Barik didn't say anything but pocketed the item.

"I will, my friend, and the same can be said to you," Elric declared. "Go to your people and meet General Vidar. Let him know that we have reached Wynfalle and everyone is safe." Elric glanced at me and then the others. "And if we need help, I will sound the alarm. Tell Vidar to wait for my signal before he heads back to Vardia. We might need him if the Lucian army decides to invade the mountain."

Barik nodded in understanding and turned to us.

"I shall meet ye soon," he said. "Good luck and keep each other safe. What may seem like a loss of hope shall only be a test of ye patience with those who need time to heal."

He stared at me the longest and tilted his head toward Elric.

The ambassador approached Barik and extended her hand. Barik looked at it for a moment before taking it.

"Thank you, Barik, for accompanying our group this far and for your faith in Vardia and our mission of solidarity against the evil spreading across these lands," she said. She handed him a small piece of cloth. "Please give this to General Vidar when you see him. It is my insignia and a sign of faith and trust."

Barik nodded and placed it inside his coat.

"Very well, ambassador," he said, bowing.

He started walking across the clearing toward the distant valley, turning to us and waving. His long strides quickly took him away. We then began mounting our horses again. Elric raised his hands.

"Let's rest for a bit and water the horses down by the stream," he pointed to the right. "We should wear more layers, because the cold air will hit us as we move closer to the mountains. It's deceptive here, but it will get extremely cold in the valley."

We tethered the horses near the stream while we rested along the shore. Elric was nervous. He unpacked his warmer clothes and set them aside. His hands trembled as he began to tie extra clothing around his legs and arms. Sensing the mood, we all decided to do the same, dressing in full cold-weather gear.

When I finished, I looked down at my strange fur coat—thick and coarse, like a polar bear's skin but with small black spots. Everyone had the same gear, and when they finished dressing, we looked to Elric for guidance again.

His eyes shifted to each of us, his mouth clenching tightly.

"We will be met by several of the warriors as we approach the mountain. Do not be alarmed, for you will not see them approach. They know we are already here and will only reveal themselves when they see our intentions for entering their kingdom," Elric paused. "Do not fight back, no matter what happens, especially when they see who we are. For whatever you think about them, they think the same about you. They are distrustful of everyone, not just the Wood Elves."

He paused and raised his hand to emphasize a point.

"Also, and this is the most important, block your thoughts. Do not try to communicate with anyone in our group through our minds. It is forbidden in Wynfalle. Anyone—except the king and the Seer—who uses their thoughts will be punished. If your thoughts do wander, quickly block them again. Hopefully, since we are not part of the kingdom, leniency will be granted."

Ragnhild and Halvard frowned with dismay.

"But why, Elric?" Halvard asked.

"During the Great Purge, it was discovered that the Volun used mind control on many of his people. Many atrocities were carried out through his deception."

"And so, the king and Seer Herja can use it, but no one else?" I asked skeptically. "That seems unfair."

"But he is the ruler, and she is an elder," Elric said matter-of-factly. "Many do not question the fairness of it, Anwen."

I shook my head at the imbalance of power. How could the Mountain Elves be happy with this ruling? Who ensured that the king or Herja wouldn't use mind control on their people and cause another war?

"Because we have Herja as our balance, she possesses the power to override our king if necessary. However, she will not wield her power against anyone."

"So, has she overruled the king?" I asked, not caring that he read my thoughts.

"I can recall only a few instances where she took a different stance than the king. But these were minor cases, nothing significant. She is strongly loyal to Wynfalle, Anwen. Everything she does is for the good of her people."

I nodded to him, dropping the subject for now. But I couldn't ignore the issue of his punishment and what we should expect once he was discovered.

"And when the warriors recognize you?" I asked. "What will they do?"

"I'm not sure, Anwen. But don't be alarmed, no matter what happens. They will take me to the king first; they won't harm me yet."

Yet.

I cringed at the thought. I stepped toward him, needing to voice my concerns, but he stopped me.

"Anwen," he whispered to me. "Whatever happens to me, you must give me your word that you won't interfere."

I opened my mouth to protest, but he held his hand up.

"Anwen, give me your word!" he said with force and desperation. "You must do as I say. You need to keep your wits about you and not use your power. Do you hear me? They will know you are a Healer, but they do not need to know how special you are. I will be punished, that is a fact, but think of Vardia. Think of your people. They need you. They need us to succeed and ally with the Mountain Elves. The ambassador needs to win over King Torvald, and I have to tell you, she has an uphill battle before her. He is not a negotiator—he is not the most compassionate and understanding of elves."

My eyes locked onto his, hating the truth behind his words—that I would have to stand by and watch him be punished for something he couldn't control.

"What say you, Anwen?" he asked as my silence persisted.

My head nodded sharply, with my lips pressed tightly together in irritation.

Elric sighed in relief anyway, knowing how difficult it was to agree with his plan. But even with that understanding, I was surprised by how concerned he was about my reaction.

"I will do as you ask, but I will hate every minute of it," I said stubbornly. "If it becomes too unbearable, I can't promise I won't help."

I quickly turned away and stomped back to Glaesir, giving Elric no chance to respond.

Both the ambassador and Halvard followed my lead, grasping their horses' reins. Their downcast eyes and silence confirmed they overheard us.

I glanced at the ambassador, and she gave me a faint smile. I felt sick in my stomach. The anticipation of meeting the elves weighed heavily on me.

The Okri sensed my fear and started to whisper. Not now, I silently begged them. Please, not now.

***

Gray clouds filled the sky. As we drew closer to our mountain destination, the wind howled around us, and the air grew even colder. The horses' hooves crunched through the thick snow, with flakes swirling in the air. Ice formed on the exposed skin of my face. I silently thanked Elric for giving us time to gear up. The furry coats protected us from the biting wind.

We traveled most of the afternoon toward the eastern ridge of the mountains, but Elric soon turned back and headed west.

What was he doing?

"Commander?" the ambassador asked, her voice muffled through her scarf. "Why are you pacing back and forth? We're wasting time with this action, don't you think?"

Elric stopped everyone and pulled his scarf down from his mouth.

"The kingdom is not visible right now," he said. "When the sun begins to set, there is a moment before twilight when the mountain will briefly reveal itself to us."

We all looked at each other in confusion.

"What are you talking about, Elric?" I asked. "Mountains can't move."

Elric smiled.

"This one does, little one," he said. Silver shimmered in his eyes. "Though it has been a long time since I last saw the changing mountain, I believe we will witness its appearance soon enough."

Standing in the snow and looking up into the sky, hoping for this huge mountain to appear, was pointless. Mountains just don't pop out of nowhere. But as soon as I considered how silly it all was, a faint ripple started to flicker in the distance.

I squinted to focus on that specific spot.

And as the sun set, the ripple grew more noticeable. Suddenly, a mountain appeared before us. Everyone gasped at the wonder of it all.

"Welcome to Wynfalle Kingdom," Elric pronounced proudly.

THIRTEEN

I shouldn't be surprised by anything that happens in Emberval, but the appearance of a flickering mountain was probably the most amazing event since being in this world. Everyone was speechless as the mountain grew more stable and solid.

I glanced at Elric, trying to read the many emotions crossing his face: excitement at seeing his home again, mixed with nervousness about what his people would do to him.

I was about to ask what we should do when the same flickering ripples appeared near my leg. Suddenly, someone was standing a few feet away, pointing an arrow at my chest. I saw a dozen other bodies flickering around our group, catching us off guard. We all reached for our weapons.

"Stop," Elric called out, raising his hands in front of him.

We all stopped moving and slowly raised our hands. Elric said something to the elf who was pointing his arrow at him. I didn't quite understand what he was saying because the mountain dialect was quite different. But the other elf lowered his arrow slightly, not all the way, but enough to show he was considering what Elric had said. He responded by motioning for Elric to dismount and then turned to the others. The elves at our feet also motioned to us.

When I dismounted, the elf beside me took the reins from my hands. Glaesir didn't like that at all. He reared up, his front legs clawing at the air. The elf handler pulled hard on the reins to stop him.

"Hey, be gentle with him," I yelled as I stepped toward Glaesir. The elf quickly moved to my side and pressed a black-bladed dagger against my throat.

"Anwen!" Elric shouted. "Stop, let him take Glaesir. They will be leading the horses to the mountain while we walk."

The elf holding the dagger looked at me through dark goggles, a white mask concealing his expression.

"Then let me calm him for you," I said. "He does not like to be handled roughly."

The elf looked at the other person standing next to Elric. They nodded in agreement, and the elf took a step back and handed me the reins.

I handled them gently and stroked Glaesir's nose to soothe him. Once he calmed down, I handed them back to the elf with a slight smirk.

"Be gentle with him," I commanded.

He nodded briskly, leading Glaesir and the other horses aside. Several elves, now holding short, curved swords, surrounded us and started marching toward the mountain.

It was hard not to be impressed by the Mountain Elves.

They truly surprised us and were well camouflaged. I was still awe-struck by the mountain appearing before us, let alone the elves making an appearance in the same way.

What kind of magic were they using? Was this the mysterious Shadow Magic that Freyja was talking about? That I must learn from the Seer?

I noticed one particular elf, the one others looked to for orders, walking quite close to Elric. The elf frequently glanced at him as if recognizing him. I anxiously turned to the ambassador and Halvard. They also noticed the strange behavior.

When we finally reached the base of the mountain, the group with our horses veered off to the left while we turned right—hidden stairs led up the mountainside. Though small lanterns lined the steps, the flickering lights cast ominous shadows along the incline. I hesitated before taking the first step, giving the elf behind me an opportunity to push me forward forcefully.

"Move," he said with a slightly stronger accent than Elric's.

I gave him a harsh frown—even though he couldn't see my face from under the hood and scarf. When Elric stopped and waited for me on the stairs, the commanding elf muttered something to him, which made Elric angry. He responded in the same tone and then took my hand, holding it as we kept climbing. The elf stared at us, and although I couldn't see his facial expression, his eyes showed his true feelings—hatred radiated from deep within.

I glanced at Elric, but he only squeezed my hand to reassure me.

I squeezed back, unsure of what I was offering him. I definitely didn't feel calm about anything at this point.

***

Hours went by as we hurriedly walked up the mountain. My legs ached, and my back trembled. The elf leader kept glancing at Elric, though he didn't seem to notice or didn’t care.

My anxiety increased about what awaited us at the top—what Elric would endure once he faced King Torvald.

Elric squeezed my hand, guessing that my thoughts were about him even though he dared not read them.

Our energies connected. Calmness washed over me, and I smiled, understanding his intentions for calming my nerves.

The elf leader looked down at our hands with agitation, then suddenly pointed the sword at me and said something to Elric.

He suddenly let go of my hand and responded sarcastically to the leader. I could hear the elf's muffled laugh inside his mask. Elric’s eyes grew even colder. My contempt for this elf deepened because of his callousness toward Elric.

A harsh retort formed on my lips but was forgotten when we suddenly stopped. Our path ended at a deep fissure. The elf leader raised his hand, spreading his gloved fingers and signaling forward. The sound of stone grinding against stone echoed through the canyon. A bridge materialized across the abyss. Soon, a door appeared on the other side, revealing a tunnel—its dark opening beckoning us to enter.

When we went into the tunnel, the entrance vanished, momentarily plunging us into darkness until the green glow of torches lit the cavern around us.

More elves joined our group. With their black suits and black hair, they blended easily into their surroundings. But when they faced us, my breath caught—elven skin gleamed. A soft radiance burned from within, giving an eerie glow to their already pale skin.

My steps wavered slightly. Elric tightened his grip on my hand, realizing that from our surprised eyes, he should have mentioned his shining kin.

More elves gathered around us as we continued our descent into the mountain. Small lanterns attached to the walls shimmered with a ghostly glow, reflecting off the smooth, dark surfaces like mirrors. I reached out to touch the strange reflection, silently admiring its beautiful glowing sheen. Symbols, some familiar, decorated several areas along the rock.

My hand reached out to trace one of the runes, but a soldier roughly pushed my hand away.

"Keep your hands to yourself, tree elf," he snarled.

I recoiled from his cold touch and clicked my tongue in annoyance. Elric moved toward the soldier, muttering a warning.

The soldier halted the group and turned slowly to face Elric. Hatred burned in his eyes.

"Do you have a problem, tree elf?" he growled, his face inches from Elric's. A long, bubbly scar marred the right side of the elf's face, his jaw tightening in anger.

Elric looked at him coldly without saying a word.

"Well, what do you say . . . *Merr*," he whispered the strange word menacingly.

I thought the word wasn't a kind endearment when I saw Elric flinch. But he didn't give in to the insult and stayed silent, knowing that anything he said would only make his punishment worse.

The corner of the elf's mouth curled into a sneer. A sharp laugh escaped his lips.

The elf leader muttered a curt reply. He turned away and led our group.

I grabbed Elric's hand, but he didn't respond to my touch. Coldness enveloped me. We were being pushed forward.

We traveled a little farther down the corridor, stopping only at another set of doors. Two elves stood guard, each dressed in white cloaks with hoods pulled low over their faces. As we waited, the soldiers who captured us moved to the side, away from us.

Without delay, the air around us fluctuated. The white camouflage gear transformed into the same black uniforms as the others. Surprisingly, the leader was female. The elves stared at us defiantly, their eyes black as a starless night for a moment, then they instantly changed— the black membrane receded, revealing the true white and black of their eyes.

The elf leader moved forward.

"Take off your gear," she demanded.

She watched Elric as he shed his parka, hat, and finally his scarf, revealing his face. Although I knew the elf leader recognized Elric despite his cold gear, her shock still surprised me. Because something else flickered behind her eyes—joy and affection. Jealousy washed over me. Was she someone special to

Elric?

I kept watching her. Her emotions swiftly shifted from anxiety to fear. She knew what the judgment would be when he was brought before the king.

We removed our gear while the soldiers stayed stoic, inspecting us. Some looked curious about Elric, while others gazed with contempt.

When the elf leader turned to me, her expression was tough but emotionless. Until she saw the mark on my face. Hatred radiated from her even more, if that was possible.

Elric noticed her changing emotions and moved closer to me. His words were abrupt. Her focus quickly returned to him. She showed her teeth with malice, causing Ragnhild and Halvard to step closer to me. Their faces were just as menacing.

The soldiers surrounded us, guns raised. Everyone stared and growled, waiting for someone to make a deadly move.

My attention was on Elric; his expression worried me. His fists clenched in anger at his sides. I laid my hand on his arm, hoping to calm him with my energy. He reluctantly tore his eyes away from the others and looked down at me. His eyes closed, trying to ease the fury raging inside him.

When his body relaxed, he opened his eyes, silently thanking me. The elf leader growled in discontent and pushed us forward, barking orders at the other soldiers.

The cloaked guards opened the doors, revealing a long, dark tunnel. Torches flickered around us. More symbols lined the walls—each phrase flowed into intricate scrollwork and symbolic decorations. Without hesitation, my finger lightly traced a few of the carvings and then pulled back. My curiosity couldn't be helped—or the feeling of connection to the writings.

We continued further into the heart of the mountain. An ornate archway guided us into an open cavern. A wooden bridge crossed another deep chasm, connecting to a solitary pillar of rock. Two cloaked guards stood in front of the bridge's entrance and moved aside.

The bridge wobbled and swayed beneath our weight. My heart fluttered with anxiety. I forced my eyes forward, avoiding the dark abyss below. When we finally reached the other side, obsidian statues of elven warriors loomed over us. Their narrowed eyes and terrifying expressions made my steps hesitate—I thought the Vardian statues guarding the forest were fierce, but there was no comparison to the ruthlessness of Wynfalle.

My eyes locked on the figure lounging on a single throne.

King Torvald.

My heart thumped wildly. My hands itched to release their energy. My eyes instantly sought Elric, but he continued to stare at the king as we approached the dais.

But the king didn't rise when we approached.

The elf leader raised her hands to signal them to stop. She and the scarred elf continued walking toward the king. They knelt before him and carefully placed their swords at their sides. When he raised his hand for them to stand, the scarred elf grabbed his sword, sheathed it, and quickly approached him. He bowed his head and whispered.

The king immediately sat up straight and looked at our

group. The silver streaks in his pitch-black hair stood out in the torchlight surrounding the dais.

The elf leader turned to us and signaled for the guards to bring us forward. The king stayed silent, his eyes narrowing as they fell on Elric. The elf leader kept a sharp watch on me, while the scarred elf gave Elric a satisfied sneer.

Elric immediately knelt, crossing his arms over his chest. We followed his lead.

"King Torvald, please accept our sincere apologies for arriving in the Kingdom of Wynfalle without prior notice, but it is important that we speak with you about urgent news from Vardia," Elric said, still bowing his head.

We waited for a response, but the king stayed silent. I glanced sideways at Elric—the elf behind me grabbed my neck to turn my head back down.

"Your Majesty, please, if I may beg you to listen to Ambassador Ragnhild regarding an urgent message from our kingdom and the imminent danger to Wynfalle," Elric stated more forcefully.

Still no answer. The king paced slowly in front of us, his dark boots clicking on the rocky floor.

"Stand," the king murmured.

The elf warriors seized our arms and dragged us to our feet. King Torvald kept pacing back and forth, lost in thought. Finally, he stopped in front of Elric, looking him straight in the eyes.

"I do not care to speak to your ambassador at this moment," he declared, speaking slowly and with irritation. "My deepest concern—my only concern—is to inquire how the elf standing before me dares to speak to the king and then have the audacity to request an audience in the name of Vardia."

Elric kept staring over the king's shoulder, his jaw twitching. King Torvald's eyes flicked to each of us, a faint smile forming at the corner of his mouth.

With a flick of his finger, the elf soldiers grabbed our arms and pulled us back from Elric, who continued to stand quietly.

Suddenly, a lone elf approached the king, whispering urgently. Elric recognized the elf, and a brief smile slipped across his face.

The king immediately and harshly murmured in response, causing the elf to step back while bowing his head in remorse.

The elf leader stepped up to the king and muttered something under her breath, but it was to no avail. He quickly raised his hand to silence her. She backed away but briefly glanced at Elric, visibly upset.

I needed to do something.

"Please, King Torvald, let me explain our mission to Wynfalle and why it was important for Elric to come with us to your kingdom," I yelled out.

"Anwen, silence," Elric whispered in Skovmal. "Do not speak."

I glared at Elric, furious that he still refused my help. I felt Ragnhild's hand grasp mine, squeezing it firmly. She gave me a short shake of her head—showing agreement with Elric that I shouldn't interfere anymore.

I looked away from her and defied the king with my gaze,

but he only gave me a contemptuous smile as he focused back on Elric.

A long line of soldiers marched across the bridge and gathered around the king and Elric. The soldiers' strange black armor and helmets reminded me of a science fiction movie back home—and not the hero kind. Everything about them screamed villainy.

My stomach turned. The anticipation of what was about to happen to Elric scared me. The promise of not interfering hung over me—I wasn't sure I could keep it.

What if I couldn't prevent myself from interfering? My powers might take over regardless of what I commanded them to do.

Even worse was the sense of unease and fear coming from both Halvard and Ragnhild; their energy was bursting from their bodies.

"Banishment from our kingdom, Elric, son of Brynjar, is not to be taken lightly. You shall face the consequences for returning to Wynfalle—you must know this and accept your punishment," the king said. "If you survive, I will consider the request for an audience with your ambassador. But that does not mean you are welcome within our kingdom. Your banishment will stand as law."

The king leaned closer to Elric. "And if you use your powers, I will not hesitate to kill you *and* your companions."

The king's words echoed inside me. I moved forward, but Halvard grabbed my arm.

"No, Anwen," he whispered.

I was torn, uncertain how to help without making things worse, if that was even possible. The king's speech frightened me. A sick feeling punched through me.

Suddenly, King Torvald stepped back from the group. The scarred elf moved forward, holding a club in his hand. Without hesitation, he swung the deadly-looking weapon at Elric's head, delivering a loud crack to his temple.

FOURTEEN

"NO!" I screamed, trying to pull away from my captor's hold.

Blood trickled down Elric's temple. He remained standing, but when another elf stepped up and struck his side, Elric fell to his knee. He stumbled back to his feet. One by one, the elves stepped forward, delivering bone-crushing blows to Elric's body. Still, he stood silently, without a cry of pain, as each hit struck true.

Standing next to the king, the elf leader and the young elf flinched with each hit. Their faces twisted with anger.

My energy started to surge—my fingers twitched with heat. My anger triggered a quick, intense glow that gradually spread up my arms.

Feeling my energy surge, Elric looked up. Blood blurred his vision, but he knew where I was. He understood what was about to happen. He quickly reached out his hand, muttering a spell to stop me.

My entire body tensed up, stiff and powerless. His dark

spell prevented me from transforming.

"NO," he managed to say, spluttering blood. "ANWEN STOP."

Elric looked up at the king. "Take them away."

King Torvald stayed frozen, but then signaled to the warriors holding us. They dragged us toward the bridge, away from the scene.

"NO, please, stop," I managed to shout at the attackers.

Freyja, help him. Please, I beg you.

A faint voice echoed in my mind, a blend of Freyja's voice and another, more powerful voice. One I did not recognize.

"No, Anwen, he must face his punishment. He needs to prove himself to his people. Let him be," the voice echoed in my mind.

"Please," I begged the king once more, hoping he would halt the beating. But he appeared determined to see it through.

I fought back tears as the ambassador embraced me.

Elric managed to stand but trembled on his feet. His bloodied shirt was in shreds, revealing his dark tattoos. A wave of silver rippled across his body—Elric was trying to contain his energy.

Several warriors hesitated when they saw the markings of their Volun.

"Continue. NOW," the king shouted.

"Elric," I shouted, trying to get his attention, but the warriors kept pulling us across the bridge.

Still standing, but just barely, he turned around and raised his hand to me.

Suddenly, a flash of a dagger caught my attention.

And with unyielding force, the elf swung down toward Elric's side.

A low, deep cry escaped as the dagger hit its target. My energy struggled against Elric's spell, but I couldn't break through the dark magic. A wild sob rumbled from my throat and tore from my lips.

Halvard grabbed my hand and pulled me toward him, holding me tightly against his chest. I tried to turn my head so I could see Elric again, but Halvard kept me close. The brutal scene faded as the soldiers dragged us down the tunnel. I cried into Halvard's shoulder, knowing Elric couldn't have survived the brutality of the punishment.

The soldiers marched us through several more corridors. Everything around me blurred. Darkness wrapped around us. My cries echoed in the silence. Halvard held me tightly, my head resting in the curve of his shoulder.

Finally, we stopped. Several doors appeared on each side of the corridor. They opened the first door and gestured for the ambassador to go inside. A soldier grabbed Halvard, pulling him from my arms, and roughly pushed him through a separate door. A guard stood by each door.

Meanwhile, another soldier shoved me into a different room. I fell to the floor as they closed the door behind me. Pushing up on my elbows, I looked around, expecting to see a prison cell, but instead, I found myself in a beautifully decorated room.

Dark blue tapestries covered the room, each depicting a different mountain scene. The bed dominated the space, featuring a headboard and footboard made of dark wood, intricately carved with twisting, coiling designs. A tall armoire next to the bed completed the suite.

Several long tables lined the opposite wall; one was a writing desk with various drawers, a full bottle of ink, and papers skewed on top, while the other was a dresser with an oval mirror, brushes, and different bottles sitting on a delicate-looking silver tray.

A large fireplace covered the third wall, with a long wooden mantel lined with various glass trinkets. Numbly, I stumbled over to the hearth where a fire crackled, bringing much-needed warmth to the chilly room.

Slowly, I sank to the stone floor. Tears fell uncontrollably as my thoughts shifted to Elric. My mind replayed the image of the black dagger looming above him and striking his side—his expression etched in my memory, one of surprise and pain.

I buried my face in my hands and then curled up into a ball, not caring anymore about the mission.

***

Loud clattering noises in the hallway woke me from my sleep. I jolted upright and looked around in confusion.

"Elric?" I called softly.

I hurried to the door and opened it, not caring what might happen. The guard at my door quickly pushed me back inside, but not before I saw several soldiers dragging Elric's body into the room across from mine.

I couldn't believe it. Was he still alive?

I pushed the guard away, trying to break free, but his strong arms held me tightly against him.

"Please, let me see him," I pleaded. "Let me help him, please, I beg you."

He stopped fighting and looked at me, considering my request. Giving in to my pleas, the elf let go of my arms and moved aside.

"Go," he said. "Help him."

Surprised but not hesitant, I ran across the hall. I paused briefly in front of the door, preparing for what I might face.

As I slowly opened the heavy door, I called out, "Elric?"

My eyes adjusted to the dark room. A shape of a body appeared on the floor. I hurried to the hearth, thanking the gods when I found wood stacked on the grate. I raised my hands, lighting the fire.

Rushing back to Elric, pools of blood surround his body.

I carefully flipped him over—blood covered his face, making him almost unrecognizable.

"Elric," I whispered. "Can you hear me?"

I choked back tears as the room became brighter, showing the full extent of his injuries.

"Anwen?" Elric murmured.

I leaned in closer and kissed his bloodied lips.

"Yes, yes, my love," I sobbed. "Hold on, I will heal you."

His hands lifted and pushed me away. He rolled to the side and tried to stand, but his unsteady legs gave out. He collapsed to the floor. I knelt beside him.

"No," he spat. "Help me to the bed. Nothing more."

I grabbed his arm and tried to lift him up. He clung to the bed covers and dragged his body to the side. When he was close to the bed, he collapsed again. I grabbed him instinctively, feeling blood trickling down my arm.

“Elric, let me help you. Please,” I demanded. “You are losing too much blood.”

"No . . . let me be,” he said, pushing my hands away.

I stood watching him struggle, frustrated that he wouldn’t let me help. My eyes searched the room, hoping to find something to clean his wounds or at least stop the bleeding. Right away, I spotted a roll of cloth and several bottles of liquids on the dresser.

I quickly grabbed them and examined the contents. As I opened one of the bottles, green liquid spilled out from the top. The smell of antiseptic hit my nose. I grimaced at the thought of the king leaving the medicines in Elric’s room—just in case he survived the brutality of his beating and needed treatment. His sadistic afterthought angered me.

Grabbing the entire container, I quickly returned to Elric and started cleaning the blood from his multiple injuries. As I searched his side for the knife wound, I held a cloth to it—pulling it away immediately when it became blood-soaked.

“Elric, I need to heal your wound,” I pleaded again. “You are losing too much blood. I need to stop it.”

He shook his head, his voice thick and sluggish. “No, this is my burden—my judgment. I cannot be healed.”

I clicked my tongue at his stubbornness, irritation simmering inside me. I grabbed more bandages, pressed them against his side, and started to clean his face. His shirt was in tatters, so I cut away what was left and tossed it aside—his dark tattoos stark against the white sheets. A flash of silver shone through the black. Elric clenched his teeth, trying to keep his magic from healing his injuries. My lips tightened in anger.

After I finished cleaning his wounds, I covered him with a blanket and sat beside him, keeping my eyes on him and just thanking the gods that he was still alive.

Blood started to drip from his bandage, so I grabbed another and replaced it. He needed more medical help, or he would bleed to death.

I walked over to a chair and dropped down, my head falling into my hands. The voices of the Okri started their nightly whispers. After everything that had happened, the voices were restless and anxious about my energy surges and emotions. I tried to talk to them, to soothe them, but it only made things worse. My eyes welled up from the pain. I fought to quiet the voices.

"Anwen?"

I looked up to see Elric struggling to sit up. I instantly rose and halted his attempt.

"You need to rest," I whined. "I'm fine."

Elric knew I was lying. He sensed my energy struggling against the pain.

"Lie down beside me," he whispered. "I'll try to help you."

"No, you are too weak," I murmured. "I am fine. I just need time to calm them, but I just can't seem to do that right now."

I smiled faintly, knowing I was too worried about him to

fully deal with my problem. Excruciating pain blossomed behind my eyes.

A small smile appeared on his bruised and swollen lips. Even though he could barely see out of his swollen eyes, he lifted his hand to my face, cupping my cheek, then trailed down my neck.

"Lie down," he whispered softly. "Please."

I snuggled beside him. He stroked my face and gently moved his hands down my arms. I felt his energy flow into me—a sigh of relief escaped both of our lips when our magic connected.

I opened my eyes slightly to look at his face. My energy eased some of his wounds—his cuts healing and his bruises fading. A grateful thought crossed my mind. The pain of the Okri was welcomed tonight, if only to help Elric.

After that last revelation, we both drifted into a deep sleep.

FIFTEEN

A knock at the door woke me from my sleep. I pushed up onto my elbows, and panic set in. A louder knock echoed through the room. I quickly rolled out of bed and glanced over my shoulder at Elric's sleeping form.

I opened the door slightly, peering out into the hall. The regular guard stepped back from the door, revealing the female elf from yesterday. She was surprised to find that I was the one who opened the door.

"Where is Volun Elric?" she demanded.

I opened the door, revealing Elric on the bed. Relief washed over her face, but it quickly shifted to anger, and to my amusement, maybe a touch of jealousy. Her brow furrowed even more.

"King Torvald has requested to see you now," she stated. "You have five minutes to get yourselves together."

She spun around and dismissed me.

Shutting the door, I leaned against it, focusing on Elric's

injured body. He was in no shape to see the king, but I knew he would need to endure the pain.

I sat down beside him, gently placing my hand on his cheek. His face was still black and blue, though it looked slightly better thanks to my magic. I knew he would be angry if I healed him completely.

"Elric?" I whispered. "Elric, the king has requested an audience."

He didn't respond. Concerned, I softly shook his shoulder.

"Elric, please wake up," I said.

His eyes fluttered open. He clumsily lifted his hand to his face, trying to rub away the weariness, but instantly winced in pain from the simple movement.

"Elric, we have to go," I said. "The female elf is outside, ready to take us to the king."

"Sigrún," he muttered.

"What?"

Elric slowly sat up, grimacing in pain. "Her name is Sigrún, Commander Sigrún, and she is the king's daughter."

He swung his legs over the side of the bed, frowning as he clutched his side. I pulled his hand away and ran my fingers over the wound. It had stopped bleeding, but still looked like it could open up at any moment.

Elric clicked his tongue.

"Anwen, you should not have tried to heal me," he said with a slight edge in his voice.

I shook my head in protest.

"I did not mean to heal you, although it looks like I didn't do such a great job anyway." My hand gently caressed his cheek. "Please don't be angry with me; we were both in pain last night. You used your energy to help me." I shrugged my shoulders. "And I guess our combined energies helped with some of your wounds. Not all, though," as my finger gently traced his upper lip. The open cuts revealed fresh blood. At least he could see now—his eyes still black and purple, but the puffiness was lessening.

He placed his hand on mine.

"I apologize for my harshness," he whispered, bringing my hand to his lips. "Thank you for helping me last night. I am not sure I would have survived without your determination."

I smiled and kissed him softly on the mouth, careful not to hurt him. But his hand reached around my neck to pull me closer and deepen the kiss. I tightened my grip on his shoulders but stopped when he suddenly winced.

"Alas," he whispered against my lips. "I am still not well."

Stepping back from him, he tried to stand on his own. He immediately swayed backward onto the bed again. He could barely stand, let alone walk to meet the king. His eyes were unfocused, possibly indicating a slight concussion.

"Elric?" I asked. "You have to let me help you now."

He shook his head.

"No, I heal faster than most, but it will take a little time," he said, closing his eyes briefly but then opening them again, focusing on my face. He took my hand in his. "You must understand, Anwen. My wounds must stay with me, or this is all for nothing. My people need to see my sacrifice to be accepted again. As one of them." He paused. "Please, do you understand? I need you to agree with me, Anwen."

A loud knock interrupted us. The guard shouted for us to hurry.

Elric shrugged into a new linen shirt, panting from the effort of the small movement. He leaned against the bed, eyes closed, and his breath faltered.

I watched him silently, feeling worried. I smiled anyway when he looked up at me.

"Yes, I understand what you need to do to earn your people's trust, but please, don't make me go through something like that again," I said, my voice trembling. "I won't let anyone hurt you again."

My hand reached out to him. He took it, grimacing as he stood—still wobbly but a bit steadier.

"Thank you, Anwen," he whispered. We slowly moved across the room.

I opened the door to see Sigrún's hand raised, about to knock again. Halvard and Ambassador Ragnhild stood behind her.

Sigrún's expression remained impassive as we followed behind her. The darkly lit corridor curved several times, a detail I didn't remember when the guards first brought us here.

Elric stumbled beside me. I slipped my arm around his waist, hoping to steady his steps, but he was too heavy. Halvard immediately took Elric's arm from me. I smiled in appreciation.

I glanced down at Elric's side and saw a spot of blood seeping through his clean shirt. My mouth opened, ready to criticize the meeting with the king until he was better, but the intense look he gave me made me shut it without question. We kept walking in silence. He knew what he was doing and would tell me if he needed help—I hoped.

Sigrún and the guards quickly led us to another room. Several soldiers sat at a table, eating and talking, but they didn't acknowledge us as we passed by. I wondered where the rest of the elves—the non-warriors and regular citizens—lived inside the mountain. Where were the children?

Sigrún guided us to the back of the room and found the king dining. The scarred elf sat beside him, his head leaning towards the king, deep in conversation. He saw us enter the area and quickly stood and moved behind the king. A smile curled his lips when he saw Elric.

Sigrún lowered her head before taking her place beside the king. Her expression reflected the scarred elf, but was aimed at me.

We stood there waiting to be acknowledged, but the king kept eating. After a few minutes, he finally looked up and motioned toward the chairs across from him.

"I imagine you are famished from your long journey?" he asked.

"Thank you, King Torvald," Ambassador Ragnhild was the first to respond. "Yes, we thank you for your kind offer."

I held back a not-so-nice response as servants brought us plates of fruit, vegetables, and unidentifiable meat. Elric could barely lift his arm to eat, so he just sat watching everyone else. I noticed his eyes drooping slightly and flinching in pain as spasms shook his body.

The King observed Elric's distress and chuckled softly.

"I imagine you might need some help feeding yourself, Elric, son of Brynjar," he teased.

I quickly turned on the king and, without hesitation, I answered for him.

"Yes, as it would be impossible to feed oneself after being unjustly beaten to an inch of one's life," I murmured—eyes fixed intently on the king.

I noticed Elric stiffen and saw the others stop eating.

But I refused to back down, still glaring at the king.

"But, all in the name of the kingdom, right, King Torvald?" I said with contempt.

Sigrún looked as if she would rather jump across the table to strangle me. Scar elf made a move toward me, but the king quickly raised his hand, stopping him.

Everyone waited for the king's response.

Surprising everyone, including me, he started to laugh—not quietly and creepily, but loudly and happily.

He paused briefly and then looked at me with admiration.

"Yes, Healer, you are correct—all in the *protection* of my kingdom," he said with deliberate intention. "*Always* for the protection of my people."

He pushed his plate away and folded his hands in front of him.

"Well, let us discuss the circumstances of your visit to Wynfalle, shall we?" he said, glancing pointedly at each one of us. "Why would Vardia want the help of their loathsome mountain kin? And why, in the name of Odin, should we help you?"

Ambassador Ragnhild briefly bowed her head in remorse but looked the king in the eyes with resolve.

"Lord Kenrick sent one of his spies to Vardia, and she stole the Okri from our Great Tree. Commander Elric was brave enough to return to Wynfalle to warn you that your Urora are also in danger", she paused. "We have come to seek assistance, not only from you, the great King of Wynfalle, with your mighty soldiers, but also from Seer Herja. She may hold the answers to what Kenrick is planning for both of our kingdoms."

The king frowned, his eyes drifting to his hands. Silence filled the room as he reflected on her words.

Sigrún and the scarred elf kept watching the king, waiting for a response to our declaration. Elric stayed impassive.

"Interesting," the king finally murmured. He pushed back from the table and headed toward the door. "I will consider your request, ambassador, but I have other matters to attend to right now."

My hands were splayed on the table, ready to confront the king. Elric grabbed my arm, expecting my response.

This was absurd. We didn't have time for him to think over our request. Vardia needed help immediately.

Ignoring Elric's grip on my arm, I began to stand, but Ragnhild got there first.

"King Torvald, thank you for your understanding and consideration of our kingdom's plight, but I must insist that Vardia's time is critical. So, I ask you to consider our request within a reasonable timeframe."

Ragnhild and the king stared at each other—refusing to yield. Eventually, the king nodded in agreement.

"Yes, ambassador, very well," he said. The corner of his mouth twitched in amusement.

He motioned to the scarred elf.

"I will send General Geir to your quarters once I have an answer for you."

He turned toward the door to leave, but suddenly stopped mid-stride.

"As for speaking with the Seer, that will not be possible," he said, and without another word, he marched out of the room, followed by Sigrún and General Geir.

Fuming, I turned to our group—everyone was stunned by the turn of events, especially the king's declaration concerning Herja.

"This is maddening," I grunted in protest. "We can't just sit idly by and wait for him to make a decision. We're running out of time!"

Elric grasped my hand.

"This is to be expected," he whispered softly as he leaned in slightly.

He glanced at the other soldiers across the room, making sure they were not listening to our conversation.

"Reclusiveness has been their way of life for thousands of years. Any contact with the other kingdoms is rare, and for us to suddenly show up and ask for their aid is surprising to them. If we push now, all diplomatic relations will be futile and hopeless."

Ambassador Ragnhild leaned back in her chair, contemplating Elric's words.

"Yes, Commander, I believe you are correct in your assessment. We will give him until tomorrow, but we can't let him string us along. Anwen is correct. Time is running out for Vardia."

"And what shall we do about the Seer?" Halvard asked. "She is a vital part of our reason for this journey."

Elric grimaced, placing his hands on the table and leaning further into our circle.

"Oh, we will see her," Elric glanced at me. "Even if we have to contact her without the king's knowledge."

***

After our meal, we were escorted back to our rooms. I wrapped my arms around Elric's waist. Though his pain was easing, his balance still seemed uncertain. As we turned the corner, the young, distressed elf we saw earlier was walking toward us.

Elric stopped immediately. The guards escorting us bowed to the young soldier and, unexpectedly, kept marching without us.

The elf approached our group and smiled.

"Tyr," Elric whispered emotionally.

Elric pulled away from my hold and walked toward the elf.

Tyr threw himself into Elric's arms, pulling him into a hug. Although Elric grimaced in pain, he stayed silent with his young friend.

"I thought I would never see you again," Tyr exclaimed

happily. "I couldn't believe the rumors of your return—not until I saw you with my own eyes."

Elric pulled Tyr away from him and quickly turned him toward us.

"Please, Ambassador Ragnhild, Halvard, Anwen," Elric said breathlessly. "Let me introduce Tyr, son of Sindri and Inka. My cousin."

Tyr beamed at us. He left Elric's embrace, bowed his head, and crossed both of his arms in front of him.

"It is an honor to meet Elric's new friends," he proclaimed. "Please do not think harshly of us. My people are fearful of change, wary of outsiders. Seclusion has been our companion for too long, I am afraid."

Ambassador Ragnhild lowered her head.

"Thank you for your understanding, especially during a time of great need from your woodland kin," she said. Her eyes briefly flicked to Elric.

Elric nodded to her—an understanding exchanged between them. A silent resolve to her often distant and sometimes prejudiced attitude toward him.

Elric turned back to Tyr with a bright smile. Despite his injuries, he hugged Tyr again. I couldn't help but laugh at his infectious smile. Of course, they hadn't seen each other in hundreds of years.

Both Halvard and the ambassador bowed and excused themselves to their rooms. As the doors closed, Elric took my hand and pulled me to him, loving eyes caressing my face before he turned back to his cousin.

"Tyr, please allow me to introduce Princess and Healer Anwen of the Wood Elves, daughter of Prince Garrick of Lucia and Princess and Healer Eira of the Wood Elves," Elric said proudly.

Tyr raised an eyebrow in surprise when he saw how Elric embraced me.

"I am deeply honored, Healer Anwen," he said. His shock quickly transformed into a dazzling smile. "Your beauty leaves me quite flustered. It is no surprise that Elric is enchanted by you."

A flush blossomed on my cheeks.

"Thank you, Tyr," I murmured. "You are too kind."

Elric squeezed my waist, and our eyes met. I had never seen him look so happy. I smiled affectionately up at him.

"Well, not many of our people have been lucky enough to meet a Healer," Tyr said, then leaned slightly forward. "Please don't take offense at our king's actions. He has been receiving distressing information from the neighboring kingdoms. Lucian attacks are widespread, and with the recent mistakes by the younger Rock Giants, plus learning that Vardia was under attack . . . " Tyr's voice faltered, shaking his head with disdain. "I come with important news—and a warning: our own kingdom is on the verge of chaos. Loyalties are split, and that can only lead to our downfall."

"What do you mean?" Elric asked. "What is happening, Tyr?"

Tyr glanced over his shoulder, ensuring no one was close. Indecision held him back when he turned to us. He was cautious, almost frightened.

"General Geir has been mobilizing our warriors, Elric. He is preparing for war without the king's knowledge," Tyr whispered. "King Torvald does not want to join the fight against the Lucians. He is confident that Wynfalle is safe from a Lokrum attack."

He paused. "And there is a lot of speculation that Geir is getting ready to join Kenrick."

"What? How can that be?" I whispered sharply. "Why would he join Kenrick, someone who hates elves, especially your own people?"

"Because, Healer, Geir believes that following Kenrick and the Lokrum would benefit Wynfalle. He doesn't care about our kin. We have been isolated for thousands of years. Geir, and unfortunately, many of his warriors, believe that glory will be ours again if we join the Lucian forces."

"And what of Sigrún?" Elric asked anxiously.

"She does not trust Geir and still believes in the king and his decisions for our people, but with your return and the news that your Okri has been taken, she is torn—knowing the righteousness of helping Vardia but hesitant to disagree with her father. The people are in turmoil. How do we move forward as a kingdom? How can we expose Geir's deception?"

"And what of the Seer?" Elric asked.

"She hasn't been seen or heard from in months. Many are concerned about her—questioning her absence."

"So, what does this mean?" I asked, my eyes shifting from Tyr to Elric. Uneasiness twisted my gut.

Elric crossed his arms, his head slowly shaking with anger.

"It means that General Geir is getting ready to seize the throne. He is preparing for war, not with the Lokrum but against his own people."

SIXTEEN

General Geir overthrowing the king and teaming up with Kenrick couldn't happen. Not now. Not while we were here, hoping to unite Wynfalle and Vardia.

Did we just walk into a trap? Will all of this be for nothing?

"What can we do to help, Tyr?" I asked.

Tyr shook his head, realizing our fragile situation at Wynfalle.

"King Torvald has chosen to remain isolated, ignoring the growing dissent among his people. Understand this . . . I don't agree with Geir's alliance with Kenrick, but I recognize that seclusion isn't the way forward for us anymore. I agree with many who now see why you are here. They're starting to voice their opinions. They realize Vardia needs help. Elric, we need you to be part of our kingdom again. As a leader. I know Sigrún agrees. Your return has sparked hope among the people. Isolation isn't the answer anymore. You, my blood, Elric, Son of Brynjar, caused this—you brought the idea of greatness and power back to our kingdom—because the Volun—our Volun—has come home."

The intensity—and implications—of Tyr's words shocked me. The elves have faced many hardships during their isolation, haunted by the hatred for something their ancestors did thousands of years ago.

Elric looked suspicious and worried by Tyr's declaration.

"Tyr, I did not come to Wynfalle to be an instigator or leader in your fight for restitution. However, I would not object to our people returning to society again. But I am here as a representative and Commander of the woodland army, nothing more. Vardia needs help from Wynfalle; there is no other option for me to take at this moment."

He paused to gather his words before moving on.

"Now is not the time for rebellion. Our kingdom must reconnect with the rest of the world. It is time to unite, not divide. Kenrick's evil continues to grow and spread across Emberval. He needs to be stopped," Elric glanced at me. "And I realize that Geir needs to be stopped. He cannot ally with Lucia—that will only lead to devastation and destruction for our people. I cannot stand by and let Geir destroy Wynfalle. So, while here, you can count on my full support for what is best for Wynfalle's future, for King Torvald and Commander Sigrún."

A mixture of relief and disappointment marked Tyr's face.

"I understand, my cousin, because you have a mission in the name of Vardia, but be warned that it won't be long before our people come to you with their own concerns, not for Vardia, not for the other kingdoms, but for the problems that threaten our own home," he muttered. "Even when you've returned to Vardia, Wynfalle may ask for your allegiance."

Tyr smiled and placed his hand over his heart. "Our people are pleased that you have returned, and I am ready to fight Kenrick and stand beside my kin, the Vardians."

Tyr stepped back, bowed, and left.

"What should we do?" I asked Elric.

He exhaled a troubled sigh, but when he looked down at me, there was a glint in his eyes—a new hope for his people. A sense of belonging and discovering his purpose, his true calling, as a Volun.

Despite the circumstances, I should be happy for him. But I felt something change—and it worried me. Deep in my stomach, knots of dread tightened their grip. The vision from Arcadia surfaced in my mind. Feelings of loss overwhelmed me. Should I tell him about my vision? Would that alter his path to finally be with his people? Fear twisted inside me—knots continued to strangle me.

Before he could respond, shuffling and a gentle cough sounded from behind.

Turning, I was surprised and slightly annoyed to find Sigrún.

"Sigrún?" Elric whispered.

She approached us cautiously, something that was very unlike her. She didn't even look in my direction—her eyes stayed fixed on Elric.

"Yes, I was hoping to speak with you, Volun Elric," she said breathlessly, still not acknowledging my existence. I glanced at Elric, and jealousy flooded through me. He was completely captivated.

Well, this wasn't going to happen, not when I was standing right next to him. I cleared my throat to break the moment.

"Commander Sigrún, what can we do for you?" I asked sarcastically. "Are you here to escort us, your prisoners, back to our rooms? Are we in violation of anything else that could be beaten out of us?"

Elric turned to me, shock showing on his face at my words.

Sigrún looked furious—but I didn't back down. At least she's noticing me now.

"Anwen!" Elric whispered harshly. He glared at me, so I tore my eyes from Sigrún and snapped my glare back at him.

"Well, don't let me keep you from catching up on everything," I said briskly.

I quickly turned around and opened the door to my room, not slamming it but softly closing it behind me. I leaned against the door, trying to keep the talons of anger and jealousy from sinking in. But they had already pierced my heart.

***

What was her deal?

I stomped to the middle of my room, fighting the urge to rip the door off its hinges.

But I fought it—just barely.

Whatever they had in the past, it was definitely over.

Elric would have spoken to me by now.

Or would he?

More than two hundred years had gone by, which felt like a

very long time to me. However, to the people of this world—where elves live for thousands of years—it might mean nothing. It's as simple as moving away for a couple of years and then suddenly showing up at your relatives' door, ready to come back home.

Were they together before he was banished?

She was a king's daughter, and Elric was a prestigious Volun. Were they ever in love?

I shook my head at my irrational thoughts. I needed to stop my wild insecurities from taking over. I trusted Elric. I should have faith in him—in us. I shouldn't question anything about his past—especially family and friends from his life here. A life I didn't know anything about.

But something nagged inside my head, telling me there was much more to their relationship. Jealousy reared its ugly head again.

I walked to the bed, already tired from the day's endless revelations. But my steps faltered when something caught my eye—a small glass bottle sitting in the center of the bed.

I picked it up carefully, turning it gently in my hands. The glass was plain and looked empty. But if it was empty, why was the cork sealed with silver wax? I turned the bottle over and saw a symbol stamped in the wax—three interconnected triangles.

I tilted my head, trying to recall where I had seen the symbol before.

The bottle wasn't supposed to be opened, but curiosity got the better of me. My hands trembled slightly as I broke the seal and removed the cork. A faint wisp of black mist slowly escaped from the top—its tendrils rising and curling into the air. The movement was hypnotic. A hint of cinnamon filled my senses, drawing me into the smoky haze.

Within seconds, my body responded—my muscles clenched and stiffened. The bottle fell to the floor, shattering into thousands of tiny shards.

Though my mind remained unaffected by the mysterious spell, my arms and legs felt as if they were being controlled by someone else—like a marionette guided by a puppeteer—and began walking toward the door.

My legs carried me out of my room and down the dark, empty hallway.

I desperately tried to scream, but my mouth stayed shut. Now speechless and with Elric nowhere in sight, I was alone in this strange and potentially dangerous quest.

My legs moved forward through the eerily quiet obsidian tunnels—parts of the mountain that seemed even more isolated, if that was possible. Hidden doorways and long passages revealed themselves as my legs continued to carry me to my unknown destination.

Where was everyone?

Without pause, I prayed that a soldier, even General Geir, would turn the corner and send me back to my room, punishment be damned. My heart pounded wildly; terror churned inside of me.

Where were my legs taking me? Who was pulling the strings?

I tried to command my magic to stop the unknown

kidnapper's plan, but nothing happened. Frustrated, I called out to Freyja, but no one responded—only the deep silence answered my pleas.

My body paused in front of a circular doorway. Black, hazy tendrils gently waved but obscured the passage beyond.

My body felt like a statue, waiting. But for what?

The tendrils swayed to the side as if an invisible hand suddenly swept them aside, revealing another long, dark tunnel. A blue light flickered at the end of the passage, calling me toward its eerie glow. Soft whispers pressed against my mind. A slight tug in my stomach drew me forward.

Sweat dripped down my face. Dread overwhelmed my senses. The hypnotic whispers kept echoing in my mind.

Whatever spell I was under, it was incredibly strong.

A movement in the distant darkness caught my eye. Shadows flickered across the floor. Someone was waiting for me.

Will they attack me?

Once again, I called on my powers—screaming for someone to help me, to protect me from my unknown tormentor.

I needed control of my body again—I feared death was imminent. But as these thoughts echoed in the back of my mind, I heard a soft laugh. The whispers stopped—before, their startling murmurs rattled me; now, their sudden silence left me feeling empty. Lonely. Saddened.

"My child, do not fear, for death is not in the bones today," a soft but commanding voice resonated around me.

A small room, illuminated only by a flickering blue fire,

greeted me. As my eyes adjusted to the dim space, movement caught my attention. A figure stood by the hearth; shadows hid their features.

"Healer, I am honored," she whispered, bowing her head slightly. "Welcome. I am Herja, and I have been waiting for you."

SEVENTEEN

My body pushed forward as I finally regained control. I shook my head, clearing the lingering spell from my mind. Civil words wouldn't come out—both surprised and annoyed by her tactics to summon me.

"Why?" I whispered in disbelief. "Why did you put me under a spell? I would have come to you if called. You are the reason I am here . . . Seer Herja."

Herja's ability to cast a spell that effortlessly made me vulnerable and rendered my powers useless gave me pause. Anger quickly followed. How dare she!

She laughed again, to my dismay, and kept standing in the shadows.

"Yes, my child, I imagine you are not pleased right now," she said as if reading my thoughts.

My chin jutted out in defiance.

"You have a strange way of welcoming me into your kingdom," I said sharply. "Was it necessary to beckon me like a helpless pawn? To use me this way—frightening and humbling me."

Herja's eyebrow raised in surprise—my candor caught her off guard—but she soon snickered with satisfaction.

"Yes, I do believe Hrafn had his hands full with you, my dear." Her voice softened as she remembered my former teacher.

Herja stepped out of the shadow.

"You are very much like your mother, as I am sure you have been told many times."

It was my turn to mimic her surprised expression.

Herja smiled faintly and shrugged regretfully.

"Yes, Anwen, I knew your mother. Why does that surprise you?" she asked, tilting her head.

My shock wasn't because of her words. My eyes widened because of the person in front of me—the oldest of the elves.

Skin as white and translucent as newly fallen snow, delicate wrinkles covered her face, but that did not diminish her beauty. The brilliance of her complexion was not her most striking feature, though. Silver hair flowed loosely around her shoulders. Shimmering blue light from the fire danced along the pale canvas of her hair.

But what caught my attention and took my breath away were her eyes. Bright and glittery, the silver orbs consumed me, making me feel like she could see into my soul and uncover all my secrets, despite my mental block.

Regaining my composure, I smiled and threw a question at her instead of answering.

"You knew Hrafn? How?" I asked, turning away and walking to the library of books that lined an entire wall.

Those eyes were overwhelming—mesmerizing, beautiful, and terrifying. They showed so many emotions so openly. Perhaps the eyes really are the window to a person's soul.

"I thought both Vardia and Wynfalle didn't contact each other?" I asked while scanning the spines of the books. Now that I was in the presence of the great Seer, I should take advantage of my mission—Freyja's plea to learn the ancient knowledge. Surely there would be a history book—something that could help Vardia. Something that could help Jack.

I turned around when she didn't answer me, meeting her striking and now suspicious eyes. A shudder ran down my spine. Something prickled my mind—so quickly that if I hadn't been skilled at blocking, I wouldn't have noticed. Herja was trying to breach my thoughts.

When her attempt failed, she lightly shook her head in frustration but quickly regained her composure.

"Your teacher had many secrets that he didn't reveal to his king and queen, my dear," she murmured, slowly moving toward me. Another attempt jabbed at my mind block.

I frowned—still ignoring her pointless attempts to read my thoughts.

"That does not sound like Hrafn." My spoke harshly.

"Oh my, do not fret, my child. Hrafn was devoted to your grandparents—almost to a fault. Do not think otherwise," she stated tenderly. "We fought side by side, together as allies, a very long time ago before the many . . . disagreements . . . that erupted between our people." She hesitated. "Hrafn—unbeknownst to my kingdom and to Vardia—helped me in a time of great need. He offered asylum to someone I cared for deeply, and for that, I will always hold him in high regard."

My curiosity was piqued by this new information about Hrafn. But before I could ask her to elaborate, Herja tried to shatter my mental block again. This time, the slight irritation turned into a sharp stabbing pain. I winced at her efforts and shot her an annoyed glare.

What was she looking for? And why was she so aggressive?

"Oh, my child, I am the Seer. Reading thoughts is what I do," she said, briefly waving her fragile hands in the air.

Surprise flashed across my face.

Did she succeed in opening my mind? Did she read my thoughts?

I quickly attempted to block them again.

"No, my child, I did not filter through your barrier," she said softly. "Your expressions are like an open book, and that is all that I am taking from you. Although you are stronger than I thought. Hrafn has taught you well. Or was it our Volun who taught you how to protect your thoughts, my dear?"

Giggling, she busied herself by arranging several books on the table back onto the shelf. One in particular caught my eye—the patterns carved into the cover reminded me of Elric's markings. And my brooch. I couldn't tear my eyes away from the mysterious book.

Suddenly, a distant voice intruded on my thoughts. My legs grew weak. My hand gripped the edge of a shelf to steady myself.

The incoherent words slipped through my mental barrier with ease, crawling under my skin and pushing through my blood. A deep, violent tremor shook my body before the soft murmurs faded into silence. The episode happened so quickly that Herja didn't seem to notice the falter in my steps or the heavy breathing.

"But, nonetheless, I am pleased that Vardia and Wynfalle are together again, no matter how briefly," she stated sadly, a soft cough escaping her lips. She turned toward the fire, making her way to a ragged but plush chair that looked as old as she was. She drew her knitted shawl tightly around her shoulders and then picked up a delicate-looking teacup from the table beside her. Her bright eyes reflected the flames of the fire, flickering and dancing as they scrutinized me.

I walked over to a similar chair by the fire and sat down, thankful to rest my still trembling legs.

Herja didn't comment on my lack of conversation but sat quietly, watching the glow of the pulsing embers.

I casually looked around the small room and noticed it was mostly undecorated and simple, unlike the training room in Vardia.

Nothing truly revealed the true nature of the occupant—no cauldrons or bottles of herbs and medicines. Even as I looked over the books on the shelf, nothing stood out as a spell book or anything related to what a Seer would have in her room. This couldn't be the only room, the only materials of the eldest elf. She must have gathered more books over her long life.

I closed my eyes, knowing I needed to control my thoughts

around her. I wasn't ready to reveal my mission.

Herja quietly exhaled a troubled breath, prompting me to open my eyes and find her studying me.

Her piercing eyes bore into mine—confused and curious.

"Is something wrong?" I asked, feeling now uncomfortable under her scrutiny.

Can you hear me, Herja?

She quickly turned her head back to the fire, sipping her tea. Frustration was clear, but there was something else, too.

Was she impressed by how much I could control my thoughts?

I smiled at that idea.

"You are . . . puzzling to me, dear one," she said with soft bewilderment.

My mind block was still intact, but I felt her prying without shame. As if she didn't care whether she succeeded in her efforts, the probing felt like a challenge. A foolish game. But her repeated attempts became almost unbearable. Like a hammer hitting a nail—over and over, trying to pierce the surface but never succeeding.

She set her cup back on the table and stared me directly in the eye.

"King Torvald has forbidden your group from contacting me," she declared with irritation. "Although isolation from other kingdoms was accepted many years ago, discontent with this policy is now growing within our community. Tyr has revealed as much to both you and our Volun."

"Yes, he seems to think that Elric can help Wynfalle

against," I hesitated. Did she know about General Geir's intentions? Should I reveal his deceitful plan?

Herja frowned when I paused.

"Elric clarified his—we, I mean—our intentions for being in Wynfalle. Our first priority is with Vardia."

Herja cut me off.

"Many moons ago, King Torvald valued the guidance I offered him. He listened to my opinions on Wynfalle's affairs and policies—especially regarding how to help our people during the early years of seclusion. But now, the king ignores my advice—ignores my purpose, my gifts given to me by the gods." Herja stared into the fire. Anger darkened her features. "He has become steadfast, which makes him blind to the mutiny threatening Wynfalle. I can hear the less controlled thoughts of my people—I know the relentless drive of Geir and his mission to gather enough followers to join Lord Kenrick—Geir believes this will restore greatness and power to Wynfalle." Herja's gaze dropped to her hands, folded neatly in her lap. "I will not let that happen. The path he follows will lead our people to continued isolation and ultimately, our death."

My mind raced with her declaration. Does she mean to help Vardia against Lucia? Without the king's permission? The nagging feeling returned, but my mental block stayed strong. I raised an eyebrow as she continued her assault.

Herja laughed. "Although I am considered an elder, it does not mean I am feeble. Mind blocks do not usually work on me . . . but you, my young Healer, are quite impressive."

"Regarding Vardia's struggle . . . yes, Anwen, I know about

the Okri, my dear—and I am aware of your special bond with them. It is truly extraordinary. I sense your energy, Healer, stronger than I imagined— even Hrafn's power flowing through you cannot compare to the power bestowed upon you by your goddess. It feels familiar yet different in so many ways, constant yet always shifting into something beyond understanding, protecting you but also . . ." she paused briefly as she considered her next words. "Guiding you carefully."

She watched me with wonder—as if she had uncovered a long-lost secret. Her reverent silence pressed down on me, her eyes scanning my face, trying to find the source of my seemingly extraordinary powers. I sighed impatiently—my magic wasn't the topic right now. Herja needed to concentrate on Vardia, not me.

"Herja, there is more to the situation with the Okri. Something—or rather someone—recently discovered. The Okri were kidnapped by a ---"

"Lirrean," Herja interrupted sharply. "Yes, I know, Anwen, a Lirrean stole your Okri." She pushed herself out of the chair and moved toward the stone mantel—her eyes clouded, as if recalling another place, another time. Her fingers brushed the smooth stone until they settled on an oddly-shaped silver trinket.

"Yes, Anwen, it is truly remarkable that she is still alive after all these years," her words tinged with sadness.

"You know of her?" I asked surprisedly.

"Yes, my dear, I know her," she murmured. "Her name is Anu."

I jumped up.

"So, you know she is working with Kenrick? They are planning something terrible, and we need to come up with a plan to rescue the Okri as soon as possible." I watched her tormented expression with reservation. "And I think you have the answers on how we can do that!"

Herja didn't respond, still tracing the object in a trance-like state and ignoring my statement.

"Herja, listen to me! Our Great Tree is dying—our people will be lost without the Okri. We have information that the Urora and the Aura will be next. We have a group of dignitaries and warriors heading to Sorayn right now. Kenrick must be defeated—the Lirrean destroyed—before it's too late for all the kingdoms of Emberval!"

Her eyes eventually locked onto mine.

I was shocked by what I saw—desperation and vulnerability.

"I know, my child," she whispered. "But, you see, it'll be difficult for me to help you—help you destroy the Lirrean as you so casually put it."

"Why? She's vindictive and hates the elves. She wants nothing more than to kill all of our people! She's working with the man who killed my family!"

My anger grew—energy started to build inside me. My hands clenched at my sides. I tried to keep my feelings in check.

"Why won't you help us?"

Herja calmly shook her head.

"Because, young Healer, the Lirrean is my daughter."

EIGHTEEN

Nothing could have prepared me for her revelation.

Daughter? How was that possible?

Turning away from her, I tried to calm my thoughts, but my energy kept building. I swallowed against the sudden tightness in my chest. Whispers twisted inside my head.

I walked to the mantel, shaking my head in denial. I grasped the edge with my hands to keep them busy.

Herja didn't move or make a sound.

"How can that be possible?" I mumbled. "You are thousands of years old! Why does no one know about this?"

I turned back to her, anger boiling inside me. "Did she help Kenrick kill my family?"

And then it hit me. Dread took the place of anger.

"Did Hrafn know about her?"

Herja turned away from me, her shoulders sagging even more. She walked across the room to a stool in the far corner—almost as if she needed to put distance between us.

"Anwen, you need to control your energy," Herja said softly.

My hands pulsed with fiery gold, but luckily, my markings didn't show up.

I closed my eyes, trying to steady my rapid breathing, calm my pounding heart, and listen calmly as a faint but clear, feminine presence was felt within my thoughts.

Freyja, did you know about Anu?

Minutes passed by until I finally opened my eyes and saw Herja in front of me.

"Yes, Hrafn knew about Anu because he is the one who protected her when I could not." Her pain was clear, even after many years. "Anu's father was killed during the Lirrean civil war, and I was left with a halfling whom no one knew about, a secret to all." Herja paused. "And because of my Shadow Magic, the gods were unable to detect her."

She continued, crossing her arms in front of her as if a ghostly chill touched her skin. "Young, new to my position as the Seer, I thought all was lost. I felt so alone. If anyone found out, Anu would be in danger. I couldn't lose her, too. So, Hrafn graciously offered to take her to Vardia, where the Wood Fairies would help raise her. Away from my people, away from the civil war, away from the judgment of Wynfalle. He would be near her and guide her as she grew. I watched her with my scykra, wishing I could be with her. I felt all of her emotions, from the wonder of new discoveries to her never-ending loneliness and seclusion from the rest of the world," Herja shook her head. "But Hrafn could not control her darker side—they could not ease her anger as she became older. Resentment grew toward me and eventually spread to Hrafn. Her hatred extended to our fairy kin, with the elves bearing the brunt of her bitterness. Her Lirrean traits couldn't be denied."

Herja's eyes drifted to the fire. She moved toward the mantel, her hand wrapping around the mysterious silver trinket once more.

"And then one day, she disappeared. Never to be seen or heard from again," her voice so soft that I could barely make out her last words. "I couldn't feel her presence anymore."

She absentmindedly lifted the object and brought it to her chest.

I moved toward her and gently took her hands, easing them open—noticing for the first time the black runic inscriptions and intricate woven patterns on the backs of her hands, disappearing into her tunic sleeve.

The silver object rested in her hand, flickering in the blue firelight.

I knew this strange contraption.

I lifted my tunic to the side, revealing a small bag at my belt. I opened it and rustled through the contents, finally finding what I was looking for—lifting it so Herja could see.

The timepiece that Hrafn always carried with him—an object that seemed more significant than it appeared.

Herja smiled hauntingly. "Yes, dear one, Hrafn and I communicated with the scykra. I gave it to him so we could communicate. Our scrying sessions were the only link I had with Anu."

The sudden surge of energy from Herja overwhelmed my senses. Sadness. Pain. Regret.

My chest clenched with the intensity of her pain.

Guilt haunted her memories. She lost someone important—like me. I couldn't imagine losing a child—not knowing what had happened to her must have been agonizing.

But still, she was very much alive and wreaking havoc on the people of this world, especially the elves.

What are the plans for all the sacred orbs?

I gently placed my hand on her shoulder and turned her around to face me.

"I am sorry for what you have been through, Herja," I said sympathetically. "I know the memory you have of Anu is of an innocent girl—a daughter you tried to keep safe, a daughter you sheltered from the hatred that she surely would have encountered because of her parentage, but you need to understand that Anu is no longer that innocent child you remember. She is gone—her hatred for those she thought wronged her has taken hold. Vengeance has consumed her. Kenrick's soldiers will arrive in Wynfalle today, tomorrow, or next month. The war is coming to the Disappearing Mountain, and we need to prepare. Vardia is in a dire situation and needs Wynfalle's aid. Please, Herja—for Hrafn, for the many sacrifices he made for your people and mine."

Herja's eyes gradually dropped to the scykra in her hand.

"Was it not a sacrifice for me to give my daughter to Hrafn? To protect the most precious part of my soul, keeping her safe from our vengeful kin?" she said softly. "My thoughts are inundated every waking minute by my Anu and what she must have gone through to reach the point of hating everyone around her, even her mother. What else can I do but hope she will see the good in something in her life? Hope and love. Isn't it a mother's wish for her daughter to have love and be loved?"

Her eyes shimmered with unshed tears as she gently rested a cold hand on my cheek.

I couldn't find the words as my throat constricted with grief. Thoughts of my mother came to mind.

Instantly, the Okri became alarmed by my emotions and cried out. Shaking my head, I wiped the wetness from my eyes and stepped back from Herja.

"I have to go," I whispered, trying to hide the pain on my face.

She pulled back from me as well, clarity replacing the fog of sadness in her eyes. A small smile touched her lips. She walked slowly to the hearth, gently restoring the scykra to the mantel.

"Yes, Healer, you should go, for the king has summoned your ambassador," she said more boldly. "I shall call for you again, Anwen. Soon."

I quickly turned toward the door but paused.

"How shall I get back?" I asked with concern. Thoughts of the soldiers finding me rambling through the halls did not seem like a good idea at this point.

Herja genuinely smiled, showing she understood my dilemma.

She flicked her hands toward the corner of the room. A large piece of cloth suddenly lifted, revealing a small cage.

The door swung open, and a strange-looking creature shot out. Dark as coal and as big as a barn owl, it fluttered around my head. Its small beak seemed harmless, but its sharp talons could rip flesh from bone swiftly and effortlessly.

"Follow Tarek, and he will show you the way back to your room. You shall not meet anyone on your travels. All will be clear," she turned back around to the fire, dismissing me.

As I began to leave, I paused again.

I wasn't sure whether I should share my next words, but something compelled me to say them.

"When I was with Anu in Vardia, I sensed something unusual in her thoughts. Her mind was mostly guarded, but I glimpsed a desire for happiness and connection."

I quickly turned and walked through the door, not waiting to see Herja's reaction to what I could only consider my one offer of hope.

***

Finally standing in front of my door, calmness washed over me. I looked up and saw Tarek flutter down the dark corridor. His shadowy shape blended into the surroundings.

I cast a quick glance at Elric's door, wiping stray hairs from my eyes as I silently hoped he'd come out.

And then what?

That he would hear my arrival, pull the door open, almost tearing it from its hinges, and rush to me, pulling me into his arms?

Proclaiming his everlasting love for me and not Sigrún?

But how could I compete with a love that began over two hundred years ago? Why would he choose me when it all comes down to it?

Tears started to blur my sight—either from the sudden ache of the Okri or the loss of Elric's love.

Sniffling, I pushed my door open and, without looking up, I shut it again, leaning my forehead against the cold surface. I needed to sleep but knew it wouldn't come—not without Elric's help. The Okri were extremely agitated tonight.

I slowly turned around with my eyes closed because of the pain.

I instantly felt a presence in the room.

Elric stood in the center, arms crossed over his chest. A moment of relief flickered across his face, but was quickly replaced by anger.

"Where have you been?" he roared. "I was gone just for a few minutes—where were you? Roaming the corridors without an escort and without me was a risk that should not have been taken. The king has summoned the ambassador, and you could have jeopardized everything we are here to accomplish."

His words only intensified my growing anger as I pressed an accusing finger into his chest.

"Whoa! Wait a minute! I left you because of Sigrún, remember? What did you talk about with her? Did she want to reminisce about old times? You have no right to question my actions. You have no idea what I just went through."

My words sounded sharp with jealousy, and I hated it. But he should have been here when Herja cast a spell on me.

I stepped back from him, suddenly needing space. But defiance still shone through me. Our energies sparked—an eerie glow surrounded us, silver and gold.

The Okri's worried cries echoed in my mind and shook my body. My anger pulsed along with the cries.

Elric turned his back to me, trying to soothe his uncontrollable emotions. He took deep breaths to calm his frantic heartbeat. That's probably something I should do too, but with everything that had happened in the last hour or so, I just couldn't.

Not yet.

Okri cried out again. My energy began to fade, but only because of sheer exhaustion. The past few weeks were taking their toll. A soft, desperate sob escaped.

Elric whirled around, his expression tense with concern and guilt. Legs moving quickly to close the distance, he pulled me into his arms, kissing the top of my head. "Forgive me. I am so sorry I shouted. I didn't mean to be harsh. I couldn't find you, and if something had happened to you . . ." he muttered, his voice full of anguish. "Please forgive me, Anwen."

He gently pushed himself away from me, keeping me at arm's length. His eyes surveyed my face and then traveled down my body.

"Did someone hurt you?" he asked, anger starting to build again, but this time not directed at me.

My legs gave out, but he caught me and lifted me into his arms. More tears fell.

Alarm and concern now tempered his features. His

expression brought even more tears to fall. I buried my face in his shoulder. He carried me to the bed, trying to lay me down. But I refused to let go of him.

"Please, don't leave. Stay with me for a while," I begged, turning woeful eyes up to his concerned face.

Tenderly, he wiped away a tear with his thumb and lay beside me. My body curled up at his side.

Elric didn't say anything, allowing me to cry—all the feelings rushing to the surface. I wasn't sure if I could keep going. Healers are supposed to be strong.

Compassionate.

A fighter.

A leader.

I was none of those. And right now, I was a crying girl who could barely handle the pain in my head or keep my emotional breakdowns in check because of jealousy.

Elric realized that the pain from the Okri might be contributing to my distress, so he released his energy. I burrowed deeper into his side, savoring the relief, no matter how brief.

My worries eased—at least for a little while.

Sighing deeply, sleep finally settled over me.

NINETEEN

A slow, gentle caress zigzagged up and down my arm, bringing a lazy smile to my lips. I opened my eyes—my body and mind now at peace.

"How long have I been asleep?" I mumbled into Elric's tunic. I lifted my head to look into his eyes.

"Several hours," he said, guilt written all over his face. "I didn't realize you were so exhausted, Anwen."

I reached up and gently traced my finger down his cheek, reassuring him that there was no need for his remorse.

"Thank you, I needed the sleep," I whispered. "I feel better."

But knowing our time was almost up, I pushed myself up and out of his embrace.

He caught my arm and pulled me back toward him.

"Ambassador Ragnhild and Halvard are exhausted and asleep as well. They will return within the hour, and we will discuss their meeting with the king."

I leaned my head against his chest.

His shirt was open enough for me to see the dark markings.

Boldly, I slipped my hand inside his tunic and started tracing them with my fingers.

A quick intake of his breath halted my movement, but when he didn't stop me, I continued my slow exploration of the intricate scrollwork. My finger lightly brushed the beautiful and mysterious symbols along his collarbones. I widened his shirt and noticed that the scrollwork now seemed to have spread lower on his chest, stretching to the top of his stomach. My palm moved even lower, surprised by the apparent evolution of his markings.

My hand moved back to his chest. Any doubt I had about his feelings for me disappeared—the quick, heavy beat of his heart was felt beneath my hand. Gold flowed through my fingers. The gentle touch of my hand traced the beautiful patterns across his chest—stirring something in him as the dark markings slowly shimmered into silver.

Elric put his hand on mine, halting the movement.

Our eyes met, and I was pulled into their sparkling depths. I couldn't breathe as his energy pulsed through my hand. Gold and silver gleamed brightly where our hands touched.

With a soft groan, he drew me closer, bringing my lips to his. Gentle at first, but when my tongue caressed his, a rush and wild need overtook us. Straddling him, I pressed my weight down while his hands tangled in my hair, deepening our kiss. My hand reached for his side, clutching a handful of his tunic, but I must have been too rough because his body tensed and a sharp breath escaped. He gently pushed me away. The purple and green bruises, though nearly healed, starkly contrasted with the sudden paleness of his face.

Embarrassment and guilt overwhelmed me. Elric was in no shape to do anything right now, especially dealing with my aggressive and lustful behavior. I began to climb off of him, but he pulled me closer into his arms, holding my head against his chest. His silver markings pulsed intensely beneath me. His breathing was labored, revealing the effect of our kiss. Whether injured or not, we both were on the verge of something more in our relationship—that was obvious with each maddening encounter.

A few minutes went by before we could speak. My thoughts twisted and turned with the realization that next time, in a less stressful and dangerous situation, we might not be able to stop with just a kiss. A smile spread across my face at the exciting thought.

"I feel like I should apologize," I muttered, still trying to quieten my racing heart.

Elric's voice rumbled in my ear. "And why should you do that?"

Leaning on my elbow, I was still often surprised by the depth of his feelings for me, his eyes still shimmering from our passionate kiss.

I smiled.

"Because I had only a few, just a few, I should point out, wicked thoughts when you left with Sigrún," I whispered.

Elric let out a slow breath. He sat up and leaned against the headboard, but he didn't let go of me, pulling me back into his arms. My head rested in the curve of his neck.

"No, my love, it is I who should apologize to you for not realizing that my actions would hurt your feelings," he confessed. Sadness brushed across his features, and as he slowly exhaled, a wave of guilt clouded his eyes.

As the worst images played again in my mind, I moved away from him.

Hurt was clear in my actions. Anticipating what he was about to say, I shook my head and raised my hand.

"Stop, please," I said, holding back the tears threatening to fall. "I noticed how she steals glances at you, hoping just for one look in her direction—a look that matches her need for you. I see in her eyes that there is something from the past that you shared with her. Something special."

Silently, I lowered my legs to the floor to create some distance between us.

He grabbed my arm.

"Don't run away from me, Anwen. Please let me explain."

I turned and just crawled to the end of the bed, tucking my feet underneath me. Careful not to touch him, waiting for him to tell me he was still in love with Sigrún.

He looked at me with concern. "No, Anwen, I am not in love with her."

Rats.

My face crinkled at my clumsiness in letting my mind block waver. Before I said anything more, Elric held his hand up, silencing my words.

"What Sigrún and I had a long time ago is no more, I can assure you of that," he said as he gently took my hand in his, laying it across his leg. "My banishment changed everything—how I regarded my people, about our way of life in Wynfalle. And even how I felt about Sigrún, who played a large part in my removal from the kingdom. Leaving Wynfalle changed me in ways I never thought possible—change for the better. But my life in Vardia never felt complete, never felt whole—until you came into my life. Something changed inside me—a calling, a connection. The link that I have been missing."

Do I dare look up into his eyes?

What would I find?

Excuses?

Guilt?

I took a chance and slowly raised my eyes to his.

Love.

I found love—so deep, pure, and powerful.

Love that overcomes hate and evil—and silences the doubters of our union.

A single tear escaped.

Elric leaned over and softly brushed it away with his thumb.

"There was a time when Sigrún and I were supposed to unite, but in an instant, my world was turned upside down. My people disowned me. My family turned against me. I found another family with Ansgar and Eydis. And Hrafn," he leaned over and kissed me softly, "but nothing could have prepared me for you. I love you, Anwen. My heart is entirely yours. Don't worry that because I am here with my people again, with Sigrún, my thoughts, no, my love for you, will ever stray."

I now felt ashamed of my jealous and wayward thoughts. He kissed me again.

"I have never felt this way about anyone, Elric. Trust and such unconditional love were never part of my life before I came to this world. Until I found you," I looked down at our hands, still clasped tightly against our legs. "I love you so much, and when I saw how you looked at Sigrún and the way she looked at you . . . I let jealousy take over."

He smiled, shaking his head. "What you saw in my eyes was just a glimpse of what my past was like with Sigrún. She is a good person, Anwen." He laughed when my nose wrinkled with disgust. "Though she may still hold love in her heart for me, she knows that my heart completely and unequivocally belongs to you."

I looked up at him, feeling giddy from his reassurance.

"You are my life, Anwen. Never doubt my love and loyalty for you—you are my world, no matter the circumstances we face," he whispered. "Especially now, in these desperate times. The decline of Wynfalle and the loss of faith in King Torvald worry me—our time here is perilous at best. When speaking with Sigrún, she worries about her father. She loves him deeply, but she fears that continued isolation from the outside world will be their downfall—their extinction. She's also afraid of what General Geir is proposing and instigating. A full rebellion is brewing. There has to be a middle ground. If only we could talk to Herja."

With his final words, I squeezed his hands so tightly they

turned white.

"Anwen," he looked down and laughed. "What is wrong?"

"Herja! I spoke to her!" I exclaimed, temporarily forgetting the strange encounter.

"What? How?" Elric asked, pulling me closer, surprised.

I quickly told him how I found the bottle in my room and the strange, terrifying trek to her room.

Of course, he was furious that she resorted to those drastic measures, but he soon calmed down when I told him about Anu.

Although I felt a hint of guilt telling Elric she was Herja's daughter, and even more about Hrafn secretly hiding her, I knew I couldn't hold anything back from Elric now.

He stood up and started pacing the room, muttering about this new revelation, but also fuming over Herja's dark tactics to get my attention.

"We need Ambassador Ragnhild and Halvard with us. Having Herja vocalize the need to help Vardia will help us persuade the king, but it could also incite the general into action. We need to proceed with caution," Elric stopped pacing and knelt beside me. "But the Lirrean, Anu, we cannot tell anyone about her parentage yet, Anwen."

He took my hands and squeezed them softly.

"Herja's secret and the identity of Anu must remain hidden a little longer. We must not betray Herja, as this could have devastating effects on both her and Vardia."

"What do you mean? Would they hold Vardia responsible?" I didn't understand why we couldn't reveal that Anu was a Lirrean or what she did to Vardia . . . to our Great Tree.

"Because blame would be placed on Hrafn and discord would spread throughout Wynfalle regarding the trust of Vardians, especially you, Anwen, as the Healer," he said.

I scoffed at his statement. "Me? I didn't do anything! And neither did Hrafn. Our kingdoms were friends back then, and what he did was to help another of his kin in a terrible situation. If anything, Wynfalle should be grateful."

"But look at how they treated me! I was banished for some unknown reason, Anwen. For something that is still unspoken—still lingering throughout Wynfalle. I see how many still look upon me. Distrust. Hate. Even fear. How would they feel about knowing our great Seer and Vardia's Healer hid something from them? You are an extension of Vardia, a student of Hrafn. They would see you as a deceiver."

"Then what should we do? If Kenrick's army comes to Wynfalle, this could be crucial information for defeating them."

"Aye, I know," Elric said, standing with his fingers caressing his temple as if working out a plan. "We need to see Herja now. We need to gather Sigrún and Tyr. Let them know about Herja's discontent with the king as well. If we solve this without Geir . . . if the majority of my people voice their grievances to the king . . . we may have a chance to defeat Kenrick." Elric walked to the door.

"Let us gather the ambassador and Halvard," he said, turning around to face me. "Because it is not a matter of if Kenrick's army will attack, but when they will attack. And it will be soon, Anwen. I feel a strange coldness coming to Wynfalle."

TWENTY

Our news left Ambassador Ragnhild and Halvard nearly at the point of anger. The ambassador paced back and forth in her room, clearly frustrated as she thought about her earlier conversation with King Torvald.

"The fool," she seethed. "The king has no idea of the discontent among his people, especially with his daughter! His arrogance will be his downfall—he is blind to his people's treachery. And General Geir . . . joining Kenrick? How absurd!"

"I agree with Ambassador Ragnhild's observations—King Torvald was clearly complacent with his people's judgments. General Geir's mutiny will surely shock the king, and then who knows what he will do," Halvard said. "The small and fragile thread of faith he has in us will be entirely broken, and any chance of forming an alliance with Wynfalle will be lost."

"We are running out of time, Commander," Ragnhild whispered. "We need to find another route to secure Wynfalle's alliance."

The ambassador ceased pacing and turned to face our group.

“We need to contact Herja now. Anwen,” she said, looking directly at me, "can you send her a mind message?”

Elric cautiously shook his head.

“I don't believe that would be wise, ambassador. The king will know if Anwen contacts one of his people, especially Herja.”

“Commander, I understand the risks, but we need to act now. Besides, our group has been slipping in their mental blocks anyway, and the king has yet to send his soldiers to punish us.”

Ragnhild proudly lifted her chin in the air.

“Anwen knows the risks. Herja is the one who contacted her first; she will already be aware of the breach, and hopefully, she will provide a mind shelter for her before the king realizes the deception.”

Elric approached me and placed his hands on my shoulder, giving them a gentle squeeze. Worry flickered in his eyes.

“Anwen, I can't deny the truth in what the ambassador said, but you need to act quickly and hide your thoughts as soon as you send them Herja’s way,” he lowered his voice. "Just think of one word—a word that only you and Herja know. Something only revealed to you. She will recognize it and call on you soon.”

I nodded, understanding what he was telling me without letting others know.

I closed my eyes, thinking for a second as I let the mental block fall away.

Anu.

Quickly, the block was replaced. I opened my eyes to see

the group staring at me expectantly.

"It is done," I whispered. "Now we wait."

***

It didn't take long for an answer to appear. Both Elric and I sensed the disturbance in the air as soon as my mind block started again.

A strange thump echoed at the door, startling everyone.

Halvard headed for the door. Elric signaled him to stay.

"Let Anwen answer it."

My heart thumped wildly as I walked to the door. The strange whacking sound made me jump.

I carefully opened it, peering around the edge of the door.

Suddenly, the strange owl-like creature swooped in through the entrance, flapping to a stop in front of me and blinking with recognition. Interestingly, it moved toward the others, flitting and weaving until it finally landed on the bed.

Making my way to the creature, I looked down and smiled. Silver runic markings lined the wings.

"What is this—thing?" Ambassador Ragnhild muttered in surprise.

The creature started to shimmer and flicker—a black wisp tornado funneled upward until a sparkling vision appeared inside.

Herja appeared before us, arms and legs crossed, sitting on the bed. A Cheshire-like smile spread across her face.

"Good," she said with pleasure. "I was wondering when you would call on me! By Odin's patience, took your time, didn't you?"

She stretched her limbs and leaped out of bed, laughing softly. Her swift movements and agility belied her age.

"What adventure awaits us, my Vardian friends?" Herja exclaimed, clapping her hands in anticipation.

The ambassador and Halvard stared at Herja in stunned silence. Elric quickly and smoothly knelt, bowing his head.

"Seer Herja, it is a great honor to see you again," he said with reverence.

She placed a hand on his head. "Volun, it is I, standing before you now, humbled and honored. You have come home to your people—I know the great price you paid in doing so."

Her hand lifted his chin and helped him stand.

"But enough, we have much to do," she said as she looked at Ragnhild and Halvard. "I know your discussions with our king have been wearisome to say the least, but he is a good man—his intentions are what he believes to be right for Wynfalle. However, he needs his eyes opened to the mutinous General Geir and also needs reassurance that Vardia will be there to help if Geir succeeds in usurping his power."

Ambassador Ragnhild shook her head in frustration.

"King Torvald refuses to listen to his people—so why should he listen to us? Hurt, betrayal, and suspicion run deep in both our kingdoms. Our need to rebuild our relationship stems from desperation for survival, but what drives him? Civil war? Keeping his people more isolated? I fear our needs are minor compared to the chaos inside his own land," she paused, "but still, if he at least listens to us instead of acting bored and aloof, that would be a step toward securing an alliance."

"I agree with your observations, ambassador—aye, your frustration with our way of life—but that is in the past," Herja stated. She glanced in our direction. "We will need the strength of both our kingdoms to extinguish the growing insurgency within Wynfalle and the forces of Kenrick, who, as we speak, may be marching upon our kingdom."

"What shall we do, Seer?" Elric murmured. "We cannot fail, for it will be the downfall of both our kingdoms. For all the kingdoms of Emberval."

"Well, my Volun, I need to take Anwen to our Urora and the Sacred Spring," she peered up at me and took my hand. "We need to speak to our All-Father, the great Odin."

***

Herja held my hand firmly. We ventured deeper into the mountain—maze-like tunnels crisscrossed before us. Obsidian walls shimmered with gold and white crystals, sparkling like distant stars in the midnight sky.

Elric followed behind us, looking cautiously around, aware of the danger if we were discovered.

He was opposed to visiting the Sacred Spring—worried that if we were caught inside the holy area, punishment would be quick and severe.

Herja, of course, thought he was too protective and said so, which made him even more defiant because of her lack of security, especially around me.

But for some reason, I trusted Herja's decision—my

thoughts shifted to Hrafn and his faith in her. I trusted Freyja more now—Herja was the only one who could save Vardia. And when we defeated Kenrick, maybe, just maybe, Herja could help save someone I loved—someone who needed protection—Jack.

I desperately grabbed Herja's hand as she led us to their sacred place of devotion, hoping that Odin would guide us.

Suddenly, the steady rhythm of heavy boots and the deep rumble of voices echoed through the tunnel, making it difficult to determine their direction.

Elric pulled my hand back, stopping both Herja and me from moving. He held up his finger to his lips, silencing the question on the tip of my tongue.

Where should we hide?

Panic took over. I glanced at Herja, expecting she might have an answer.

She placed her arm over our chests, pushing us against the tunnel wall. She gave us a brief smile before closing her eyes.

Instantly, I felt a cold sensation spread from her arm into my chest and then throughout my body. I looked down and saw my body darkening—flickering as a black void opened and swallowed us.

We were disappearing.

Feeling like I was submerged in ice water, my eyes focused on the empty space where Elric once was. But even though I couldn't see him, I felt his cold fingers grabbing my hand.

A group of warriors rounded the corner and marched past us without noticing anything unusual. When they finally passed, Herja let go of her grip. Warmth surged through my body. The sudden heat made me bend over, the painful feeling spreading into all my limbs.

"How did you do that?" I asked breathlessly. The prickles of awakening nerves raced through me.

I definitely needed to learn that trick.

Herja smiled and laughed softly. "Ah . . . that's just minor magic, my dear, you haven't seen the best yet!"

Elric shook his head and laughed softly.

"Thank you, Herja, but next time a little warning would be helpful, especially with Anwen, since she hasn't experienced the Shadow so intensely," he said, shaking his head. "Aye, even for me, it's been a long time." Though Elric was smiling, I could tell he was just as shaken.

"As you wish, my dear Volun, as you wish," she said, taking my hand again and leading us down the tunnel. "Maybe it's time for you to use your Shadow more often. I can feel the restlessness inside you. It's been asleep for too long."

Surprise flickered across my face. So that was Herja's Shadow Magic. How different it felt from my own magic—and how easily it connected to it. Elric's power left me breathless, but with Herja, it was on a completely different level. The tingling sensation persisted, teasing prickles of awareness that danced across my blood and sank into my bones. Its presence still lingered deep within my body. But I didn't push it away—I wanted it to stay.

We walked a short distance until we reached a dead end.

Did we take a wrong turn?

"Now what, Herja?" I asked, turning around and thinking

we needed to double back.

Herja released my hand and leaned against the wall—her hands finding two shallow cracks. With wide eyes, I watched as her hands vanished into the wall, the dark stone wrapping around her pale hands. She pressed her forehead to the stone, a low droning chant escaping her lips.

A shimmering silver line slithered up the wall, outlining a square doorway. Herja pushed on the door, but her hands connected with air. The wall disappeared, revealing a room. The lantern's light, fixed upon the wall of the corridor, cast an ominous glow that only reached a few feet into the cavern. All was quiet except for the occasional hiccup of bubbling water.

"Let us hurry," Herja whispered as she entered the shadowy chamber.

Turning back to Elric, not sure if we should enter, I noticed he had shifted around me, walking slowly after Herja. His expression made me pause—deep and absolute devotion shadowed his features. The chamber was heavy with magic—an unnatural fog crawled along the ground and wrapped around my feet. A gentle breeze brushed my face and traveled down my arm. Pressure pressed against my palm.

Feeling the phantom fingers of the magic pulling me into the room, I crossed the threshold. Before I had a chance to change my mind, the wall closed behind me—the dim glow of the tunnel lantern disappeared, leaving the room suddenly in total darkness.

Panicking, I turned around with my arms outstretched, hoping to find Elric nearby.

"Elric?" I asked nervously. "Herja? I can't see! Where are you?"

A small pulsing light appeared beside me. Several more spots of light moved intermittently around—one light brightened as another dimmed. No larger than my little finger, the lights fluttered—tiny wings brushing against my ear. A smile crept to my lips.

My eyes darted around the synchronized dance of the fairies and noticed Herja standing near a pool of water, Elric several feet behind her. Both elves dropped to their knees, crossed their arms over their chests, and bowed their heads.

The dancing fairies fluttered around the chamber, their lightning flashes reflecting on the walls. Tiny crystals embedded in the rock shimmered as the fairy lights grew brighter. Stalactites and stalagmites met, forming thick and thin columns that encased the spring pool. I gasped at the surreal beauty unfolding all around me.

I moved closer to the shimmering, pale-blue water, mesmerized once again by a cluster of lights gathering at the bottom of the pool. The silver-white orbs of the Urora slowly rose to the surface of the water, only to sink back down again—each motion reminding me of the gelatinous globes of a lava lamp.

Herja suddenly leaned forward and dipped her hand in the water. Knowing that touching the water in the well of the Great Tree could have serious consequences, I automatically moved forward to warn Herja.

Elric surprised me when he touched my arm.

"No, Anwen," he said gently. "It is allowed."

I turned back to Herja. She began to sway back and forth, softly chanting, her words jumbling together. Her movements and incantations started to quicken. I felt the magic intensify around her. Disembodied voices echoed within me—familiar ones mingled with unfamiliar ones. A shiver crawled down my spine.

I glanced at Elric, ready to ask him what was happening, but his eyes were closed. He dropped to his knees again, now infused with the magic that held Herja, his incantations mimicking hers.

Ignoring caution, I slowly approached the water's edge.

Immediately, the Okri started to chant in my mind, making my steps stumble. Their high-pitched cries called out to me, but I couldn't understand them.

I closed my eyes, hoping the voices would quiet down. A violent tremor shot down my spine. I dropped to my knees and grabbed my head, the weight of the pain growing stronger. My mouth opened. An agonizing scream built in my throat. Suddenly, the chanting changed—although the noise grew louder, the sound, not the words, started to make sense, forming in my mind and bursting into vivid colors. The movement moved through my body, easing my pain. Instead of a scream, I let out a faint sigh.

The sensation of cold water between my fingers snapped me out of my trance. I was immersed in the sacred water.

Fear of the consequences overwhelmed me. I tried to pull my hands away, but I couldn't move them. It was as if someone was holding them underwater.

A prickling behind my eyes, followed by a tingling sensation spreading across my forehead. I sensed another presence, another voice inside my head, calling softly at first but growing louder with each pulse of the orbs in the water.

"Great Odin, hear my call." I didn't understand why I said those words, but I knew it was the right thing to do. "Your guidance is needed."

Everything around me froze—from the voices and lights to the chanting drone of Herja and Elric. But I stayed focused on the water. Waiting. But for what?

Freyja? What are you doing? Why couldn't I move?

"Anwen?" Elric murmured. He knelt down beside me. "Can you hear me?"

A deafening ringing burst in my head—so loud that my eyes bulged and tears streamed down. My hands broke free from their watery prison—my body regained control. But the painful blast of noise persisted. I covered my ears and screamed.

"Stop it, now," I begged the source of the noise.

My eyes struggled open, and I saw Elric still kneeling by the pool, lost in a trance with his eyes closed.

Ignoring the stabbing pain, I quickly got up and knelt beside him, discovering Herja in the same condition. Was I just hallucinating?

A sudden burst from the center of the pool startled me. Sconces along the wall suddenly erupted with green fire. The embedded crystals blinked like millions of eyes, as if accusing me of desecrating their sacred water.

Sloshing and gurgling echoed behind me. I spun around

toward the pool just in time to see a bright glow in the center. As it faded, a formidable figure appeared.

"Greetings, Healer," he bellowed loudly in a deep baritone. His long, blond hair and heavily curled beard swayed back and forth as he spoke. "How may I assist thee? Is it a call to battle that I desperately desire?"

Stunned and completely captivated by his pure light and overwhelming aura, I couldn't find my voice.

To my surprise, a small laugh burst inside my head.

A familiar laugh echoed as I closed my eyes.

Freyja?

Silence. No response, but I heard the laugh again—this time not inside my head, but beside me.

I slowly opened my eyes.

"Anwen," Freyja whispered from my side. "Please, greet the All-Father, the Great Odin."

TWENTY-ONE

The blond-haired god stood silently and indifferently. He was stunningly beautiful, with features perfect in every way except for the strange sunken void of his right eye. However, having only one eye certainly wasn't a barrier to the overwhelming power and authority radiating from him. His gaze swept over the group that summoned him, finally resting on me. A frown appeared and deepened as he quietly considered the situation. His golden armor seemed to shine from within, while a phantom breeze lifted his light blue cloak around him. The hilt of a large sword swung precariously at his side.

Freyja moved away from my side and lowered her head.

"Great Odin, I apologize for calling upon you in the presence of the elves, but warring men are marching to the mountain as we speak," she said urgently. "There is great peril within the kingdoms, for they are aided by---"

Odin raised his hand to silence Freyja.

"And why should I help them, my dearest Freyja?" Odin

boomed, anger flaring. "Other than watching the violence that is sure to prevail, I do not care and will not intervene in the lives of this world."

Freyja bristled, a defiant glint flashing in her eyes.

"I shall not be interrupted, dearest Odin, for I was about to proclaim that these men are being aided by none other than our brother Loki," she proclaimed. "He is meddling in the affairs of men and inciting war. This is not acceptable, even for you, mighty one, as I know you take pride in the violence that erupts in this world—especially when it is caused by your own magic of persuasion. But not now . . . the troubles of these beings are caused by our brother, whose only intent in the end is to bring us—the gods—harm."

My mind froze at the realization of what Freyja proclaimed.

Loki?

I swallowed against the sudden tightness in my throat. How did Kenrick and his Mage align with the trickster god?

Pushing the rising questions to the back of my mind, I couldn't just stand by and let Freyja bear the brunt of Odin's anger.

"Please, Odin, help us defeat Kenrick and his men. Help us defeat Loki," I said, trying to quell the uncertainty in my voice.

Slowly, Odin's eyes drifted over me, squinting and considering as if trying to choose my punishment for speaking out.

My breath caught in my throat.

"Healer, though I understand the importance of your role in this effort."

"But what is my role?" I interrupted Odin. "I don't understand because no one will tell me."

Odin looked at Freya, surprise lighting up his single eye.

"She does not know, dear Freyja?" he asked warily.

Freyja slowly shook her head. "No, I did not know the reason for Loki's alliance with the humans, dear one. But now, his threat has been revealed. He has found out about her, Odin, and he will stop at nothing to take her and use her against us."

I looked back and forth between Freyja and Odin. "I don't understand. Why does Loki need me? Will someone please tell me why I am so important to him?"

My legs trembled, my body shuddered, my throat tightened—silencing any other questions that formed on my lips. Odin entered my thoughts, reaching into my soul—searching for something. The probing ended abruptly, leaving me breathless. My eyes met his, and I faltered at the emotions pouring from within.

Regret and pity.

Suddenly overcome with fear, I called out to Freyja.

"Tell me why Loki is after me. Why is he helping Kenrick?" I pleaded, afraid to know the reasoning behind the great Odin's reaction to my situation.

Freyja sighed unhappily and rested her hand on my shoulder.

My body started to glow, and markings appeared along my skin. The sudden rush of magic stole my breath as disembodied whispers hummed inside me. Odin and Freyja exchanged looks that were deeply expressive. Dread seized my heart, causing me to exhale even more air.

Freya's hand dropped from my shoulder, but my markings kept glowing—the irregular pulses of the symbols made them appear as if they were scrolling across my skin. Freyja moved to Odin's side. A look of wonder brightened their features.

"My Freyja, I believe the Volun and the Seer must hear this tale," Odin said.

Elric and Herja snapped awake from their trance, both throwing out their hands to catch themselves from crashing to the floor.

"Anwen, what happened---" Elric said, hesitating in his question when he saw who I stood by.

Elric's eyes widened with reverence as he doubled over, bowing to the gods. Herja paused but then bowed her head slightly. A knowing smile played on her lips.

"Odin and Freyja, it is an honor to see you again."

"Please, Volun and Herja, we have awakened you so that you can hear the importance of your Healer as well as the dire circumstances that we are in," Freyja said.

Elric helped Herja to her feet as he stood. Herja's eyes widened when she saw my appearance.

"My gods, what have you done?" she asked.

"What tale I have for you exemplifies a great triumph, but also, a regrettable and devastating chapter of our godly lives," Freyja sighed with remorse. "We did not foresee the chaos that Loki would bring upon the many worlds entrusted to us. We never imagined he would succeed in the destruction of our own kingdom—try as he might, we thwarted his plans with desperate measures.

"Loki was always the instigator of mischief—many of his tricks were harmless, but in one instance, he went too far. The gods punished him, and it was severe. Not only did the gods punish Loki, but we made those he loved bear witness to his pain. However, he escaped and vowed to destroy us once and for all." Freyja looked up to Odin, who nodded, then found me. A soft smile touched her lips. "And he would have succeeded if your mother hadn't helped us—Eira was the one who gave you to the gods so we could use you as our protector, our shield."

"I don't understand," I asked, bewildered. "How am I protecting you?"

Freyja touched my arm again, gently tracing her finger over several of the ancient runes on my skin. The symbols slowly circled around my forearm.

"These markings are spells, Anwen. Magic from each of the gods. Told to our All-Father in confidence. Magic that only we should know—hidden magic of our existence—of our powers. Loki cannot destroy us. Not while part of us lives within you."

I raised my hands and examined them more carefully. The symbols circling my wrist pulsed as they spiraled and whirled up my arm. My heart fluttered with the sudden movement of the ink—the power of the spells surged through my body.

Odin moved closer to me, took my hands in his, and held them against his chest.

"Healer, you were crucial to our survival when Loki sought to destroy us for imprisoning him. It was your mother who knew Loki was secretly working with the kingdoms, inciting the men and creatures of Emberval to turn their backs on the gods. Eira was scared, not just for her people, but for you, Anwen. Those who abandoned the gods would also direct their violence toward the beloved elves."

Odin placed his hand on Freyja's shoulder. He displayed undeniable love for her.

"And with Freyja's guidance, Eira offered you as the vessel to carry our sacred secrets. Eira brought you to me, and with all the gods' spells imprinted in me, I seared them into you. But Loki and the man called Kenrick found out about our plan, and Eira cast you into another world before you were captured," Odin laid his hand on my cheek. "Your mother was very brave, Anwen, a great warrior."

Freyja moved to my side. Urgency filled her words. "But now you are here, Anwen, and Loki knows about you. He is determined to capture you and use your powers against us."

Elric took my hand and gave it a gentle squeeze to reassure me.

"How can I help—I will never let anyone harm Anwen." His words are firm and lethal. "They will have to kill me to get to her."

Freyja waved her hands in front of me. My markings vanished, and the golden light faded away.

"We cannot let him take you, Anwen, but as gods, we cannot interfere again," she glanced at Odin with resentment. "I have disturbed the balance far more than the gods should be allowed, and the All-Father has forfeited the fight, even though our existence is in peril. It is up to the creatures of this world to fight back, albeit because of our role in the beginning, but you need to take up that fight now."

"How can I do that?" I asked in desperation. "Loki is a god! You just admitted to causing this situation, so why can't you take him away? All of the gods . . . you deal with him! You did this to me—make him go away. Stop him!"

Odin suddenly reached out and laid his hand on my face. A sharp pain shot through me, from my neck to my chest, but he held on tight, and I couldn't pull away.

"We will watch over you, but we can no longer provide assistance. We weaken from the darkness within this world—Death eagerly awaits its release. Chaos thrives inside the other realms, and the gods are tired of the battles. Soon, we will lack the strength to fight."

Odin pulled his hand away, and I dropped to my knees, pulling Elric down with me. His arms wrapped around my waist as my body nearly collapsed. Despite the intense heat consuming me, chills ran down my spine, followed by sudden numbness.

"What did you do to her?" Elric asked angrily.

"What . . . what happened?" I stammered in confusion. Coldness spread across my skin.

Odin slowly entered the water, light beginning to shine around his feet. Freyja hesitated, then followed him.

"Don't go, please. Tell me what to do? How can I destroy Loki?"

Freyja quickly moved away from Odin, but he grabbed her arm and pulled her back. Desperately raising her hand, she yelled to me.

"The water, go to the Sea of Saerún," she shouted as the light engulfed her. "You have the key . . . salvation lives within Saerún. Find the monks . . . once your mark is discovered, assistance will be offered."

I covered my eyes. The lights flickered briefly before darkness swallowed the cavern. Odin and Freyja were gone. My fists clenched as I slammed them into the rocky ground in anger. A low growl escaped, turning into a cry of frustration. The gods provided some information, but never enough to solve the problem. They started the war but had no intention of finishing it.

When I finally looked up, Elric and Herja were staring at me.

"Please tell me you saw what just happened," I said desperately, hoping the appearance of Odin and Freyja was not a figment of my imagination or a dream.

"Anwen?" Elric whispered nervously.

"What?" I asked, slightly annoyed. "Why are you both staring at me like that?"

I looked down at my hands and arms, thinking my markings were showing again, but I saw nothing. Suddenly, I felt Herja's slight touch around my left ear, and I pulled back, surprised.

"What?" I asked her irritably. "What is wrong with you?"

Herja brought her hand back to her mouth, confusion visible on her face. A gasp escaped.

I quickly scrambled to the water, looking down and turning my face into the calm, mirror-like surface.

I raised my hand, tracing the new marks on the side of my

face—two more triangles overlaid my original mark.

The symbol from the bottle.

I faced Herja and Elric again, stunned by the new adornment.

"What is it? What does it mean?" I kept tracing the strange symbol with my fingers.

Herja shook her head in wonder—with reverence.

"You are blessed, child," she whispered. "You have been touched by the All-Father—you have the mark of Odin."

TWENTY-TWO

Stunned silence. Nothing could have prepared me for the overwhelming feelings—the crazy revelations and new markings. The pain from my fresh ink had now fully subsided. I gathered my feet beneath me and tried to stand, but faltered. Elric was quick to offer his support.

"Anwen," he said with concern.

"I'm fine. I don't understand?" I whispered, more to myself than to Elric and Herja. "Why would Odin do that?"

I looked up at Herja. "What does it mean—this mark of Odin?"

"It is a declaration to all that you are blessed by the All-Father—he has granted you special privileges. The mark of Freyja was a gift, Anwen, but Odin's mark . . . I know of no one who has received such blessings."

Herja paused, and with a glimmer of anger, she gave me a look powerful enough to bring the weak to their knees. I could feel the questions bubbling inside her.

"Why did you hide the markings, Healer?" Herja asked, looking from me to Elric. "Don't you trust me too, Volun?"

Hurt and sadness quickly replaced the anger in her words.

Elric was the first to speak. "Herja, with respect, please accept my humble apology for the decision to keep Anwen's peculiar markings hidden; it falls on me—my purpose was to protect Anwen, not to be malicious or disrespectful. I would do anything to protect her. Our journey to Wynfalle had many facets—with my punishment and considering Wynfalle's current state, I wasn't willing to risk Anwen's life."

"The markings—you didn't know what they meant, did you?" Herja asked.

"No, Herja, truly, their purpose and significance were mysteries. Until now," I admitted, now avoiding her piercing stare. I nervously glanced at Elric and then shifted my weight from side to side. Guilt clenched in my stomach—they needed to know the purpose of the mission. My mission. "But I haven't been completely honest with Elric either."

I cleared my throat. I felt his eyes burning right through me—hurting for keeping more secrets from him.

"During our journey to Wynfalle, while everyone was asleep, Freyja called out to me. My mother was with her. She didn't say much, but she advised me to find you, Herja, to talk and learn from you—about the ancient knowledge and the Shadow Magic. They are key to stopping Loki and Kenrick."

I risked a glance at Elric, hoping he understood why I kept this secret meeting from him.

"I was told not to tell you, Elric," I whispered. "Not yet."

Guilt surged as he looked away.

"I'm really sorry, Elric. I didn't lack trust—Freyja and my mother wanted me to keep the fact that a god was involved a secret. I didn't even realize the god was Loki. I hated hiding that from you—and hiding the reasons for seeking Herja. Not until Wynfalle could be trusted and committed to being Vardia's ally. Please, please don't be upset with me."

He stepped further back.

In desperation, I grabbed his arm. "Please, don't walk away. You must understand."

"Volun Elric, you should forgive her and move on," Herja said sharply. "We all have secrets, don't we? Some more than others, but there's usually a good reason why they're kept hidden. No matter. We have a lot to think about tonight. We need to discuss our next steps."

Elric reluctantly pressed his hand down on mine.

"Yes, Herja, you're right. We need a plan. Our time is running out," he paused, applying more pressure with his hand. "Anwen, I need you to be honest with me, no matter what, from this point forward. Our situation won't succeed if we're not truthful with each other. Our lives, and those of our loved ones, depend on it. No more lies, not now, not during our time here. Do you understand?"

I nodded—without voicing the promise out loud. I was torn between loyalties now—Freyja wouldn't have warned me if she didn't have her reasons.

"Well, enough of this. Let us gather the ambassador and Halvard," Herja interrupted. "We have much to discuss with the king."

Suddenly, a loud, thunderous laugh echoed throughout the cavern.

"Yes, Seer, it seems we have much to discuss with our king," General Geir said, crossing his arms arrogantly.

Sigrún and a dozen warriors stood behind him, armed and prepared for Geir's command.

Sigrún moved forward—her face flushed with anger.

"How dare you enter our springs," she said, directing most of her hatred at me. She quickly looked at Herja and then finally at Elric. "How could you bring her here? She doesn't belong here."

Herja tilted her head and looked at Sigrún harshly.

"She has every right to be here for our great Odin called to her—the dearest Freyja spoke to her," she proclaimed, then waved her hand impatiently.

She looked at Geir.

"Yes, yes, general," Herja said. "Take us to the king."

Geir squinted his eyes at her, with a slight curl at the corner of his lips.

"Seize them," he commanded his soldiers. "Gather the ambassador and the warrior and bring them to the king's chamber."

Rough hands grabbed us and pushed us forward. Elric tensed as Sigrún wrenched my arm behind me, but I shook my head and only offered her a slow, yet deadly smile. No one dared to touch Herja—either out of respect or fear. I leaned more toward the latter. As for Elric, Geir ruthlessly secured his hands with a lethal-looking metal restraint. He winced as it latched onto his wrists, his eyes briefly closing in anticipation of the pain sure to come. Instantly, needle-thin wires slithered out of the device and wrapped around each finger. The pain must have been excruciating, but Elric never gave Geir the satisfaction of showing it. One side of Elric's mouth curled into a smirk. Angered by Elric's defiance, Geir shoved him through the doorway and then struck his chin. Blood trickled from his mouth, but Elric's smile only grew wider, fueling Geir's rage.

"Enough," Sigrún cried out, stopping Geir from lashing out again. "The king will handle their punishments."

She guided us down the corridor toward the unknown judgment of King Torvald.

***

The narrow tunnels twisted like a maze.

Sigrún walked beside Elric, anger clouding her features.

"Why?" She asked.

Elric didn't reply. His eyes stayed fixed ahead.

"Answer me," she seethed through clenched teeth. Elric kept ignoring her, fueling her barely controlled anger. A scent of desperation hung on her body.

"Why couldn't you leave it alone?" she whispered. "I almost had my father convinced to allow you back into our family again."

His expression stayed indifferent. As the soldiers led us further into the mountain, her frustration with his silence increased.

"Answer me, Volun!" she yelled.

"All will be told soon enough, Commander," he finally said.

Her emotions surged with such intense force, but she didn't say anything more.

I, however, held back a vengeful smile.

Deep rumbling voices greeted us as we turned the corner and stepped into a dimly lit room with a long table in the middle. Scrolls and strange-shaped blocks covered the surface. The king and two other soldiers were examining one of the papers when we arrived. Their conversation immediately stopped. King Torvald's brow furrowed.

"What is this, General Geir?" he asked. "Why did you bring them here? I did not authorize this."

Geir and the soldiers halted. The king cautiously approached to stand before our group. When Geir didn't respond, the king grew wary. His head tilted in response to Geir's insolence.

The ambassador and Halvard arrived at the door, led by a larger group of soldiers.

Anger now seized the king.

"What is the meaning of this disruption?" He directed his question to Sigrún.

Sigrún was about to speak to her father when Geir suddenly stepped forward.

"My king, we found the Seer and the two Vardians by the Sacred Spring," he said. Contempt seeped from each word. "They were corrupting our sacred Urora with their presence."

Herja laughed and stepped forward.

A soldier grabbed her and pulled her back forcefully. She winced in pain.

Elric's face twisted with fury.

"How dare you treat our great Seer with disrespect? Release her now," he shouted.

Before Elric lunged forward to help her, Herja casually flicked her hand in the air—her index and middle fingers briefly crossed.

The soldier started to scream and dropped to his knees, clutching his head.

Herja carefully stepped around the writhing man, swishing her hand to the side. More soldiers lunged forward to apprehend her but instead fell to the ground. When she focused on the soldier holding me, he dropped to the ground instantly and joined the growing number of Geir's men twisting around us. Their deafening cries echoed in the room. Herja swiped her arm through the air. The screams stopped, but not the pain. Mouths continued to gape wide, pushing out their silent agony.

My stomach clenched. I wasn't sure how I felt about her cruelty.

"Now, that is better," she said with satisfaction. The soldiers immediately slumped into unconsciousness.

Both Geir and Sigrún started to move forward but then stopped, aware of what would happen if they tried to hold her back.

King Torvald stared at Herja, eyebrows raised in surprise but not anger—he actually appeared entertained by the scene unfolding before him.

"And what do I owe this interesting show before me, Seer?" the king asked with barely contained delight.

I couldn't believe it—his own soldiers were writhing in pain, and he was laughing?

Anger boiled inside me. I crossed my arms over my chest, holding my hands tightly against my body. My energy yearned to be released.

"It seems, King Torvald, there has been a misunderstanding," she said, clearly directing contempt at Geir.

Geir squinted his eyes at her again, hatred bubbling up to the surface. He began to speak, but Herja raised her hand again and flicked.

"Quiet," she whispered. Undeniable power was embedded in that single word.

Geir's hand immediately clasped his throat. His mouth moved, but no sound or words came out.

King Torvald looked suspiciously at Herja—now uncertain of her motives for the attack on a high-ranking officer.

"What is the meaning of this, Herja?" the king's voice now sharp. "Why are you attacking my soldiers?"

Herja's silver eyes glistened with determination.

"There has been a lot of talk among your soldiers, talk of sedition and rebellion."

Herja paused and only continued when the king didn't try to interrupt her.

"I am aware of the Vardians' dire situation and do believe that we should grant their request for assistance," she stated matter-of-factly.

The king scoffed. "This is what the dramatics are in regards to, Seer? Simply yielding to the Vardians' demands?"

"King Torvald," Ambassador Ragnhild bristled. "Demand seems like a harsh choice of words for what King Ansgar and Queen Eydis are asking of our kin. In no way have I demanded your commitment to assist Vardia!"

King Torvald smirked at her insolence. He turned to Elric—his look accusatory.

"And you, Volun? I imagine you have something to do with all of this," he paused and then sneered at me. "And your *mate* . . ."

Face flushed with rage, Elric lunged at the king, but Geir, recovering from Herja's spell, grabbed him and forced him to his knees, pressing a dagger to his throat.

"Your Majesty, let me end this once and for all," Geir spat out. "The Volun has placed a spell on our Seer—his words enthralled and turned her against Wynfalle—this should be no surprise, for he is his father's son."

King Torvald waved his arm toward a group of soldiers standing by Sigrún.

"Seize the Healer," he exclaimed angrily.

Without hesitation, Sigrún was the first to leap and grab my arm.

Elric continued to fight against Geir, struggling as he pushed and pulled against the vise-like hands pinning him to the ground.

"Release her, Sigrún," he yelled, fury still burning behind his eyes.

Sigrún's hands clenched and latched onto my arm, pulling me closer to the king.

My anger consumed me. My hands moved freely. Wisps of golden mist seeped from my palms. Imitating Herja, I began flicking my hands toward Geir. A hand pressed down on my shoulder. Calmness washed over me. Herja squeezed my shoulder again until my mist vanished completely.

"King Torvald, we have a problem," she chuckled cynically. "For what you believe is not the whole truth."

She bowed her head in respect as she stood before him.

"The Varidans have requested our aid, not demanded. They have arrived in our kingdom at a critical time for our people. Wynfalle is at a crossroads, and you're not listening to your subjects—discontent spreads throughout your ranks, and General Geir has been the one stirring trouble."

Geir swallowed his anger and briefly loosened his grip on Elric, who didn't hesitate to seize the chance. He twisted free from Geir's hold, spinning around with incredible speed and disarming the general using his own dagger. In seconds, the black blade was pressed against Geir's throat.

"Tell the king, Geir," Elric seethed. "Tell him that you are planning to join Kenrick in his fight against your people, against your kin."

The king frowned at the accusation. Distrust flickered in his eyes, but was quickly dismissed. He considered Elric's words longer than I had anticipated.

Sigrún's grip on my arm loosened slightly, but she still held firm.

"What is this, General Geir?" King Torvald murmured, slowly and deadly. "What heresy does the Volun declare?"

Geir tried to back away, but Elric pressed the dagger against his neck, and a drop of blood appeared.

"Tell the king about your rebellious speech against Wynfalle, hoping not only to take the throne for yourself but also to destroy all who oppose you—helping Kenrick and the Lokrum wipe out your people and the Vardia's. All for the glory of the Mountain Elves. All for the memory of the old ways of deception and betrayal." Elric whispered menacingly into Geir's ear. "TELL HIM!"

A contemptuous sneer curled Geir's lips, followed by a deep, threatening laugh.

"You are a traitor, Volun. How can you stand there, blood kin—the only son—of one of the greatest and most powerful Voluns of our time? He who brought great honor to our people, only to be betrayed by the weak and cowardly. How can you claim innocence when the stench of betrayal runs through your blood? You, of all, should revel in what I am doing in the name of our kingdom." Geir spat at Elric's feet. "Your punishment should have been execution."

He turned his hatred on the king. "And you . . . our people cower in the mountains, afraid of retribution from the outside after all these years, and you make the situation worse by continuing our isolation, bowing and reinforcing our so-called guilt. But we should be proud of our ancestors and what they accomplished. Lord Kenrick promises our rise to greatness again." Geir looked at our group, ending with me. "And those who defy our new kingdom will suffer death in the most heinous ways."

Geir's threat hung in the air. Rage overtook Elric. His hatred for Geir and the underlying threat to me pushed him over the edge. He turned Geir around, face-to-face, with the tip of the dagger pointed upward, slightly piercing his throat. A steady stream of blood ran down his pale skin.

Instead of cowering from Elric's blade, Geir laughed—a low, deadly sound that sent chills down my spine.

He called out calmly, staring at Elric with a malicious grin.

"Kill them."

What happened next was a haunted blur. Geir's men tackled the king and Sigrún. Herja swung her arm in the air but was struck on the side by a soldier and thrown to the ground. Other soldiers appeared out of nowhere, emerging from the walls and rushing forward with swords raised high, ready to deliver deadly blows.

I hurried to Elric, knowing the general would show no mercy to him. Geir threw himself away from Elric, knocking him to the ground.

Elric recovered and spun around to face him, then swiftly punched Geir in the side—nothing too hard or deadly, but enough to catch him off guard.

Geir doubled over and was about to lunge back at Elric when, suddenly, a deep rumble echoed through the mountain from somewhere in the distance.

Everyone stopped, waiting for the sound again, uncertain of what might have caused the dreaded noise.

Breaking the deathly stillness of the air, screams rang out as another thunderous explosion echoed through the cavern.

I looked for Elric and our eyes locked.

Kenrick's army had arrived.

The battle for Wynfalle had begun.

TWENTY-THREE

Geir, sensing that the time for his revolution had arrived, recovered from Elric's blow and rushed toward the king. The king's hand reached for Sigrún, unaware of Geir behind him.

Geir pulled a hidden dagger from his tunic, grabbed the king from behind, and dragged the blade across his throat. A strangled scream tore from my mouth. Elric turned at my distress. I pointed to Geir still holding the king in his arms.

"ELRIC, THE KING!"

Blood splattered on Sigrún, a stunned expression frozen on her face, not quite believing Geir's treachery. But when Geir pushed the king away from him, and his lifeless body crumbled to the ground, the reality of what the general had done finally sank in. Rage overtook her. Screaming, she charged at Geir.

Both Elric and Herja raced forward, but Elric was faster—he collided with Geir, knocking Sigrún aside.

Another explosion vibrated beneath our feet, knocking several soldiers to the ground. I grabbed the nearest support, a small stone table, but it cracked and collapsed to the floor. Small splinters of stone fell from the ceiling, hurtling toward us. A deafening roar erupted around me. The walls began to crack under the force of the blast.

Fear seized me. We were about to be buried alive.

Herja grabbed my arm.

"Anwen, the spring, I need to save the Urora."

Agreeing, I shouted our intentions to Elric, but he was too busy fighting Geir. Sigrún tried to help Elric but only continued to hinder his efforts to gain the advantage.

"Sigrún!" I shouted to her. "Gather your warriors. Help your people escape the mountain! NOW!"

She ceased her attack. A blank stare replaced her rage as if she didn't realize Wynfalle was falling all around her. Her face twisted with the realization of her father's death.

"Sigrún, gather your forces, help your people, child," Herja said with sympathy. "We will save the Urora. GO."

Without waiting for Sigrún's response, Herja grabbed my arm and pulled me into the tunnel.

"Herja . . . the king . . . Geir . . . ," I muttered in disbelief. "We need to help Elric."

Dread pierced my heart—Wynfalle would be destroyed and all would be lost in Emberval. Vardia was doomed. I tried to pull away from Herja's grip. Elric needed me. Herja held firm, clutching her fingers tighter around my arms. I called upon my powers, but nothing happened. Betrayal flooded my insides. How could Freyja and Odin leave us to die? And my powers were useless to help.

Herja shook me until I looked into her eyes.

"Anwen, listen to me carefully. You need to focus. The time to save our Great Urora and my people is upon us. The time to fight is now. The Volun can take care of himself. What we need to do is protect our ancestors from the Mage." Herja hesitated and tilted her head. Her eyes fell from mine and scanned the darkened corridor. Surprise erupted. "Anu?"

She pushed me away, and I lost my balance. She caught my arm before I fell to the ground. She dragged me down the corridor. Her behavior puzzled me.

"GO NOW, ANWEN," she screamed, dread consuming her expression.

I ran as fast as I could with the walls and ceiling crumbling around me. My mind raced with what needed to be done. I silently called to Freyja.

Can you hear me? Do you see what is happening?

Help us!

Racing through the dark tunnel and dodging falling debris, we finally turned a corner that I recognized. The archway that was hidden so well before now stood open, jagged and threatening. Panic began to surge through my body.

I hesitated before stepping inside, allowing my eyes to adjust to the dimly lit cavern. A movement caught my eye. A dark, cloaked figure emerged from the shadows, walking slowly toward the spring.

Herja brushed past me, her steps cautious but determined.

"I knew you would be back to wreak havoc on your people. Corvus," Herja proclaimed.

A violent shudder coursed down my spine. My eyes trailed to the figure, still encased in darkness. He stopped in mid-stride.

Corvus? His people?

I stepped forward, following Herja, my insides in turmoil from the memories of my kidnapping and the familiarity of this shadowed figure.

He slowly turned, gradually lifting his arms and pulling the hood off his head. The torches embedded in the walls flickered to life. A sinister laugh broke out.

"Herja," he murmured. "Time has grown long for us since our last meeting. How you have changed, my dear Seer."

"Ah, yes, and I could also say that about you, my dear Mage." Contempt edged her last word, her voice shifting into something fierce and perilous.

A rustle sounded close to the spring. My eyes probed the shadows until another small figure shifted to Corvus's side.

"Anu," Herja murmured.

Anu's face, shining with gold and black like stars in the firelight, radiated deep and immense hatred.

"Don't speak my name, Seer," she spat out, her darkened gaze sweeping Herja up and down, revulsion clear.

Her eyes trailed to me. A slow smile formed.

"And you . . . *Healer*," she screeched. "Are you ready to die?"

My eyes narrowed, mirroring her deadly smile with one of my own.

"No, Anu, are you?"

I threw up my hands. Thick golden light shot out from my palms, hitting her directly in the chest. Her body lurched upward and slammed into a stalagmite.

"No, Anwen," Herja screamed. A cloud of black mist erupted from her hands, knocking me off my feet. My energy faded away.

What was she doing?

Slow, thunderous clapping was followed by a hollow snicker. In the distance, another round of deep rumbles echoed off the walls and beneath our feet.

"Well done, Healer," Corvus sneered. "And Herja, that was truly unexpected. What pray tell possessed you to attack the Healer?"

Suddenly, Corvus was right in front of me, kneeling and just inches from my face. A slow smile spread across his face.

"You see, Anwen, you of all people should understand the basic instinct of a mother to protect her daughter," he said. His words eerily echoed throughout the cavern.

"Stand away from her," a voice rang out of the dark.

Elric stood in the archway, sword in one hand and the other raised high. Silver electrical charges pulsed from his palm. My breath caught—his eyes and skin shimmered.

Corvus suddenly stood, his eyes drifting slowly over Elric as he considered his next move. His eyes narrowed into slits. He opened his mouth to speak, but then closed it without saying a word.

Corvus turned around, signaled to Anu, and then pointed to the spring.

"Get them," he ordered.

Anu quickly pulled her feet underneath her and, in a blur of motion, she sprinted toward the spring.

Elric and I knew her mission—to steal the Urora.

She was taking them, just like the Okri.

I lunged at her, grabbing her around the neck. She spun around and ducked under my arms, landing a quick jab to my right leg.

Falling, I screamed out in pain, but kicked my left leg under her, sweeping her off her feet.

She hit the ground on her back with a sharp jolt. I felt hands roughly grab my arms and pull me away from her. Landing a few feet from Anu, I saw Herja standing above her, with her hands outstretched.

Black wisps trickled from her fingertips, wrapping around Anu's arms and tethering them to her torso, then looping around her legs, holding her in place—immobilizing her. Cursing and thrashing, Anu's body rolled away from the spring, trying to move toward Corvus.

I jumped up only to fall back down again when another explosion erupted, this time right outside the cavern.

My eyes scanned the room, spotting Corvus and Elric in a magical duel. Silver and red energies swirled around each other in a deadly fight. When Elric got close enough, he slashed his sword at Corvus, but Corvus easily dodged each well-aimed blow.

Jumping up despite the pain in my leg, I ran toward Elric, but another explosion threw me back to the ground. Debris and dust blocked my direct view of the fighting.

My name echoed around me—the familiar voice seized me

with deadly intent. Coughing and gagging on the thick cloud of dust, I searched for the source. A broad-shouldered figure, barely visible through the rubble surrounding me, emerged from the dust. Heavy boots crunched the rocks scattered on the ground and stopped in front of me. Kneeling, the masked fiend placed his blade next to my throat, preventing me from screaming.

"Hello, Anwen," he whispered in my ear. "How pleasing it is to see you again?"

As he pulled his mask away, the deep sneer of the most hated man I knew looked down at me.

Draugr.

TWENTY-FOUR

A surprised gasp escaped. He grabbed my hair and pulled me closer to his face. I tried not to wince from the pain, to give him the satisfaction.

His eyes pierced mine. I swallowed the dread rising up into my throat.

"You are mine now," he murmured. Without warning, his mouth pressed against mine, firm and unwavering. His tongue forced my mouth open. His teeth ground against mine with brutality.

Revulsion spread through my body. I tried to pull away, but his weight held me down.

I felt the energy build up in my hands. Long, silent whispers surged inside me. My hands automatically found their target. His face was shadowed in the glow of my magic. My fingers pressed into his eye sockets, sending a wave of energy through his body.

Draugr screamed in pain. He swung his dagger at me, hitting my arm. The force of the magic pushed him away. Blood dripped from a cut above my elbow. Pain shot through my body. Before I could respond, Draugr charged at me, laughing with his dagger held high.

A deep roar echoed around us. Elric appeared in front of me, crouched low and ready to pounce. He launched at Draugr—arms wrapped around arms, both fighting to grab each other's sword. I managed to pull my feet underneath me when I felt a touch on my shoulder. Recoiling, I glanced to my side and saw Herja kneeling beside me.

"Come, my child. We need to rescue the Urora," she muttered, pulling me to my feet.

We ran to the water's edge. Herja swirled the water with her hands. Her lips moved in a silent spell. Silver lights illuminated the bottom, pulsing in time with her softly spoken words. The chants grew louder and now, with desperation.

Pulsing erratically, the Urora floated to the surface. Herja reached down and lifted an orb out of the water. She held it in the air for a few seconds until the pulsing subsided and turned into a steady light. She quickly pulled a knapsack around to her front, carefully placing the orb inside. Then, she swiftly grabbed another orb, placing it inside the bag, and continued retrieving one after another.

My eyes widened with awe at how easily I caught these great beings and placed them inside a raggedy, old bag.

A flash of misty darkness flickered at the corner of my vision. Corvus was gliding through the rubble, heading toward Draugr's side.

Elric was in danger.

I instantly forgot about Herja and our mission. Ignoring my safety, I leapt up and ran toward Corvus, hands outstretched. He didn't notice my intention until it was too late. My energy knocked him off his feet and into the wall. He quickly recovered from my attack. Red bolts of energy struck around my feet, jolting my body upward and flipping me through the air.

Landing with a heavy thump on the now jagged and debris-strewn floor, I felt a shard pierce my leg. My breath escaped from my lungs. Barely conscious and my vision hazy, I looked up and saw Draugr holding Elric in a chokehold while Corvus raised his arm to deliver the kill.

"Elric," I whispered. Coughing shook my body from that single word. Pain surged through my chest.

"STOP!"

I was startled by the sudden demand from my side.

Herja glided past me, checking to see if I was okay, then kept going toward Corvus.

"Corvus . . . or should I call you by your given name?" she called out to him, walking closer to the enemy. Their eyes now focused on her, not on Elric.

I pulled myself up, grimacing as the shard pushed deeper into my leg. I reached down to remove it, blood flowing from the deep cut. Struggling, I slowly made my way to Herja. Draugr squeezed Elric tighter, his face starting to turn red from the lack of air—his struggle lessened.

Corvus pulled his hand back slightly more, prepared for his energy to consume Elric.

"You cannot do this, not to the Volun," Herja continued.

"Do you not recognize him? Has the darkness shrouded your mind so much now? Can you not see he is your own blood?"

I stopped, turning to Herja, and staggered slightly at what she was saying to the Mage.

Elric related to this . . . this evil being?

Kenrick's Mage?

"Look at him, see him," Herja paused and then barely muttered the last word—almost testing warily for his expected reaction. "Brynjar, he is Elric, your son."

My ears buzzed at the name.

It couldn't be. Herja must be playing him.

I quickly turned to Elric, who had stopped struggling completely. His expression must have mirrored mine—horror, disbelief—shocked didn't seem like the right word for this mind-blowing revelation.

Draugr, appearing just as stunned, loosened his grip on Elric a little. But enough that Elric, now recovering from the news, felt the opportunity to act.

His elbow shot forward and slammed into Draugr's ribs, knocking him back and doubling him over in pain. Elric quickly grabbed his sword and arched it over Draugr.

Corvus backed away from the fight now, his expression blank as he stared at Elric—his eyes narrowing, as if trying to recognize him or dispute what was revealed to him. But his indecision didn't last long. He threw his hands up. Shoots of thin red energy slammed into Elric's back, with each stalk coiling around his arms, legs, and chest, sending him up into the air before crashing to the ground repeatedly. Each painful blow reverberated within my soul. Elric's head is now beginning to loll to the side. Consciousness fading.

Draugr, still catching his breath from the attack, staggered over to Corvus' side, laughing as Elric kept screaming in pain.

Looking down at my hands, I saw darkened-gold light expanding around my palms until a large globe formed. I threw the ball of light toward Corvus, but when I released it, it immediately split into two, hitting both Draugr and Corvus.

Draugr was thrown against a pillar, where he stayed motionless. Corvus only hesitated, dropping to his knees, but he was quick enough to cast another spell at me.

My hands flew to my throat.

I couldn't breathe.

My fingers clawed at my neck, desperate for air, hoping the movement or anything else would help me breathe. I dropped to my knees. Darkness filled the edges of my vision.

But as quickly as the spell left me breathless, a burst of air into my lungs pushed me forward. My hands barely managed to catch my fall. Gasping like a fish out of water, I looked up to see Herja intercepting Corvus. Black and red energy collided, swirling into each other—dancing to the death with elaborate choreography. Slightly delirious from lack of air, I smiled at that macabre thought.

A large shadow loomed over me, fear coursing through my body. I slowly looked up, expecting more Lucian soldiers to enter the cavern, but instead, a big, pebbly hand gently lifted me off the ground.

"Healer, ye okay?" the familiar voice bellowed out.

"Barik!" I cried, my voice just as gravely and coarse.

Vidar stood beside him. His arms wrapped me in a warm hug.

"Anwen?" he asked.

Surprised but deeply relieved, I shook my head vigorously.

"I am so glad to see you!" I exclaimed.

Vidar quickly looked around at the chaos. "Aye, it is a good day to fight!"

He motioned toward Barik. "Help Herja. And Anwen, go to Elric." He sneered at Corvus. "For I am sending this evil back to where it belongs."

Vidar charged at Corvus, sword raised high and a deep growl erupting as the battle loomed.

Corvus, realizing he was quickly being overtaken, suddenly grabbed Herja and threw her headfirst across the room. She landed near the water, tried to stand, but fell back to the ground. Blood dripped down her temple.

Vidar kept running toward Corvus, weapon ready, but Corvus jumped into the air and landed behind them.

Barik, who was on his way to help Herja, spun around just as Corvus' energy hit Vidar, knocking him off his feet. Barik changed course and charged toward Corvus. Corvus flicked his hands, releasing another energy globe that struck Barik in the chest. However, the massive stone-like giant hardly faltered. His club swung around and landed just inches from Corvus's head.

More Lokrum soldiers entered the cavern, rushing toward Draugr, who was now standing. His eyes blazed with hatred, shifting from Elric and then settling on me. He muttered something to his men, who were all now facing me with their weapons swinging excitedly at their sides. Their masks concealed their deadly expressions.

"Healer," Draugr yelled. His eyes narrowed, and without taking his eyes off me, he shouted to his men, "Kill the elf, but do not kill her. She needs to be alive."

I felt the energy flow down my arms and pulse through my fingers. Magic itched to end Draugr once and for all. But when I raised my hands, the golden light pooled around me—flattening against an invisible barrier. I pushed my hands forward again, hoping to break the wall blocking my magic, but nothing happened. Draugr started to laugh—an amulet swayed in his outstretched hand.

"You cannot hurt me, Healer. Surrender, and we will spare most of Wynfalle from certain death."

Stunned, I shook my head slowly.

"How are you . . ." I sputtered, throwing my hands out again with more force. Finally, the golden light swerved around the barrier, knocking the two soldiers flanking his sides into the air, but unfortunately, and by some miracle, leaving Draugr still standing—laughing and now running towards me, sword held high above his head.

Panic momentarily gripped me, but I refused to cower. Fixating on his raised silver blade, I prepared myself for a deadly strike. His declaration of not harming me now was a fleeting thought. A sadistic smile curled on his lips. My eyes closed briefly with a mix of anticipation and regret. My mind drifted to Elric and then to my grandparents—feeling the ache of losing the newfound love of family and friends. But with these last sinking regrets, harsh whispers echoed inside—how could I give up so easily when the very family I was thinking of was in danger?

Fight and defeat them, Anwen.

Before I had a chance to open my eyes and face Draugr with renewed purpose, the clang of two swords resounded.

Crossed swords flashed in front of my eyes.

"You cannot have her, filth," Elric seethed.

With a murderous roar, Elric charged Draugr, metal clashing against metal. Elric threw out his hand, letting his energy escape, but like mine, the force did not hit Draugr.

How could this be?

Why was Draugr immune to our magic?

Elric quickly recovered from Draugr's resistance to his powers. They circled each other, each gripping their blades with both hands, shifting their weight from foot to foot. Unyielding stares challenged one another.

"So, Volun," Draugr fumed. "How can you be kin to our grand Mage? And his son? You must be proud to know you have greatness running through your veins."

Elric met his gaze, refusing to let his remarks distract him.

"What say you, traitor?" Draugr spat, continuing to provoke him.

Losing patience, Elric lunged at Draugr, swinging his sword upward and sideways. Draugr responded, both blades clashing loudly until they faced each other, swords now crossed, arms strained as they fought for the upper hand.

Instantly, Elric's tattoos began to pulse, emitting a strange glow, his tunic coming alive with blinding silver light. He growled, his face red and contorted. His sword also started to pulse with a bright light, pushing Draugr away from him. Elric hunched over, hands resting on his knees—the episode drained what fighting strength he had left.

Taken by surprise, Draugr was thrown at least ten feet away, but he quickly regained his footing and lunged to strike again. Elric twisted out of the way of Draugr's blade. However, his efforts weren't enough as the blade sliced through Elric's sword arm, cutting across the top of his wrist.

Panic and dread returned. My eyes scanned the cavern. The battle blurred into one slow-moving sequence. Another unsettling explosion erupted, this time causing part of the wall to crumble. The force knocked everyone off their feet—stunned by the close-range blast.

A soft mumbling cry drew my attention. Looking quickly around to find the source, my eyes landed on Anu, still tied with Herja's magic, underneath a pile of rubble.

Herja, now crawling on her knees, reached Anu and clawed at the rocks to free her from her prison.

"Hold on, my daughter, hold on," Herja raised her hands, trying to channel her energy. But she was too exhausted.

With a final glance at Elric, I stumbled toward Herja, kneeling to aid her. The entire mountain quaked again, knocking us flat to the ground. A tremor vibrated beneath us. Cracks appeared around us, making it hard to keep our footing.

Anu thrashed against her bonds, eyes wild as she tried to scream out. The black wisps wrapped tighter, making it harder for her to move but also making it more difficult for us to rescue her.

"Anwen, grab those rocks around her head before they fall," Herja whimpered. Her anxiety for Anu's safety overwhelmed her as Anu continued to thrash wildly.

Herja was about to lose consciousness. She clutched at the rocks. Blood was now flowing freely from the wound on her head.

A loud cry echoed from across the cavern. We immediately paused our efforts. My heart skipped a beat when I saw Vidar doubled over, pain coming through with every movement. Corvus stood over him, gripping a strange-looking dagger.

"NO!" I yelled.

Barik roared in distress. He threw his club across the cavern, hitting Corvus in the side and knocking him down.

I quickly rose to help Vidar but stopped when a flash of unnatural light shone from the water's surface. My brief hesitation, however, proved costly. A presence materialized behind me. Turning swiftly, a muscular arm wrapped around my waist, pinning me to the solid figure. Rough fingers grabbed my chin, forcing me to look up into a face I didn't recognize.

"Do I have to do everything for the humans?"

TWENTY-FIVE

The tall, broad-shouldered figure grasped my chin more firmly, bringing his face within inches of mine.

He offered a strange, uneven grin.

"So, this is the savior of the gods?" He asked, more to himself than seeking an answer from me.

"How strange. You are just a helpless girl," he continued as he examined. "But how do you work?"

He lifted my right arm, bent down to my level, and inspected the skin.

"Where are the markings, little one?" he asked, perplexed.

Gathering my nerves, I pulled my arm away from his grasp, glaring at this strange figure.

"Who are you?" I asked angrily.

He quickly straightened his tall frame, peering down at me with skepticism and a touch of boredom. Tossing his long, dark hair aside, he raised his other hand, wielding a small yet deadly-looking gold dagger.

"Corvus," he bellowed suddenly, though his eyes never left mine. "Shall I kill the girl?"

A quick gasp sounded behind me—Herja's face showed a mix of fear and reverence.

Panicking, I kicked the figure, hoping to maim him so I could escape, but my landing was off, and I ended up losing my balance instead. His free hand grabbed my waist and pulled me to him.

"No, Great One, she is the key," Corvus exclaimed across the cavern, too busy holding Barik at bay.

The figure looked up with disdain at the fighting around him. He nonchalantly swept his arm across the cavern. To my surprise and dread, everyone dropped to their knees, including Draugr and Corvus.

Who was this man?

Who could possess such power and act with such arrogance?

The answer to my question surprised me when an angry voice rang out behind us.

"LOKI!"

Freyja stood at the water's edge, her fists clenched at her sides. Her face twisted with rage.

"Let her go, Loki," she said vehemently. "You must stop this irrevocable vengeance upon these people."

I felt his fingers dig deeply into my skin, pulling me closer to him. I was stunned to realize this large figure was Loki, the god responsible for such death and chaos around us—and who aimed to use me to bring about the destruction of our world. A chill ran down my spine.

Loki must have sensed my trembling. He chuckled softly and pulled me even closer to him. But he didn't say anything; he kept staring at Freyja, that uneven grin reappearing.

"My dearest Freyja, have you come to wish love and forgiveness for your traitorous schemes against your Loki?" he declared with a hint of venom edging his last words. "What? Does it not surprise you that I am not marred by the treacherous punishment that the great gods bestowed on me? That the wretched serpent torturing me endlessly and without mercy could be easily defeated?"

Freyja remained unfazed—refusing to give in to Loki's taunts directed at her and the other gods.

"The Mage healed me, giving my face—my body—a new glow." He sneered and then, with barely a murmur audible only to a few, said, "Venom did not stop me from taking my revenge, deceiver. Nor will your elf toy save your precious world from my wrath."

Freyja moved forward, sensing the danger in what Loki was stating.

"You will not harm these beings or destroy this world, nor will you harm the Healer, for she will not give you what you desire, Loki. The gods have succeeded in thwarting your evil plans. Come back with me, talk to the All-Father, and we shall leave this world to heal from your deceiving heart."

Silently, Loki appeared to ponder Freyja's request. A gentle chuckle escaped his lips, gradually turning into a maniacal growl. His hold on me loosened briefly but then tightened into an even firmer grip.

"Your love for these beings makes you weak, my love. Tell me, how does she work? How did the Almighty Odin evoke the spells?" he asked as if having a normal conversation with Freyja—his arrogance beginning to grow bolder with each question.

"Great One, her powers seem to manifest when she gets angry. Even more so when someone she cares about is in danger," Corvus said.

As if reading Loki's mind, Freyja suddenly called out.

"Loki, NO!" she yelled as Loki's eyebrows arched, contemplating his next move. We didn't have to wait long, as he swiped his hand toward Vidar, who was already injured.

Almost as fast as his movement, a soft muffled sound escaped Vidar's lips. A gold dagger pierced his chest.

"NO," I yelled.

Vidar turned his head toward me, pain shadowing his face as the dagger slowly twisted inside him.

"Anwen, don't show him your powers, not now," he whispered, blood trickling from his mouth.

I heard other pleas, but darkness had already clouded my vision—the glow from my hands forming a bright halo around me. It was too late to hold back.

"Yes, little one, yes, show me," Loki peered down into my face, anticipation vibrating through his body.

My hands instinctively rose to his chest, prepared to unleash my power on him, but he grabbed them before I made contact. I pushed against his grip. My golden light flickered around his fingers. His eyes scanned my body, impressed by the sudden appearance of my markings.

"Yes, I see them," Loki exclaimed like a kid on Christmas, opening his first present. His enthusiasm only made me angrier.

"How clever, my dear Freyja," he said, looking up at her with amazement. "Odin surely deserves a lot of praise for this ruse."

With as much grandeur as Loki's entrance, Odin appeared before us. Bright light radiated around him.

"I should not accept your praise, Loki, as you will only use it against me in the future for trickery and maliciousness," Odin barked. "Stop this nonsense . . . now."

You could hear a pin drop inside the cavern. Loki shifted slightly backward. The sight of Odin made his heart race, but he kept holding onto my glowing hands. He looked down at me, expecting to see the marks, but found they had disappeared.

My arms were bare, and my glow was fading. With a faint smile, I looked up at him.

"You lose, Loki. I have control of my body, not you," I murmured to him, hoping my voice didn't tremble like the rest of me.

"Be done with this. Release her along with the others. The gods shall not intervene in their disputes again, Loki. Let them fight their own wars," Odin said, glancing at Freyja. "We have learned our lesson, my brother. Let us leave this world."

For a brief second, Loki paused in thought, but soon, his boyish grin spread across his face. His hand moved up and grabbed the side of my neck, pressing firmly against the skin under my ear. Heat raced down my neck—burning the flesh and making my legs buckle from the intense pain of his touch.

The muffled shouts from Elric and Freyja echoed through my mind. I began to lose focus, and as quickly as it started, the pain subsided. Loki's hands let go of me. My body pitched forward. Laughing victoriously, Loki disappeared. Odin followed in pursuit.

I dropped to my knees, rocks pressing into my skin. But I didn't feel the pain—all I sensed was a strange emptiness. As if a part of my soul had been torn away from me.

Hands wrapped around my waist. Nausea took over me. My body began to shake. A scream, not a whisper, shattered my mind. Chaos and death filled my thoughts. A feeling of loss twisted inside my heart.

What did Loki do to me?

Darkness lurked at the edge of my mind. A painful sob broke free.

"What—what happened to me?" My eyes held Elric in place, a silent plea for the truth. Something was wrong. I felt everyone's trepidation—their eyes refusing to look at me.

Corvus, Draugr, and the Lucian soldiers disappeared with Loki. But Anu stayed behind, now free from the debris and magic. She sat quietly beside an unconscious Herja.

I strained to see beyond Elric, searching for my uncle, but couldn't find him among the gathering group of soldiers.

"Anwen," Freyja called out, her tone gentle and remorseful. Panic flooded through me.

Freyja stood next to Barik, who was kneeling over my

uncle's broken body. I scrambled to his side.

"No," I muttered. "Vidar? Can you hear me?"

With bruised and damaged skin darkening his features, Vidar inclined his head toward the sound of my voice. A broken smile tugged at his lips. Blood stained the corners and dripped down his neck.

"Anwen?" he murmured. "Did he hurt you?"

I fought back the sobs rising in my throat and the tears falling from my eyes. I shook my head and gave him a small smile. "No, uncle, I am fine. Loki is gone . . . everyone is gone now."

Blood-filled eyes struggled to focus on mine. He lifted his arm but winced in pain. The dagger was still lodged in his chest, and another wound was bleeding at his side. He was losing too much blood. I had to heal him.

"You're hurt?" he asked again.

"No, no, I am fine," I answered, not certain why his eyes kept drifting to my neck. "Let me help you."

I placed my hands on his wounds; the golden glow intensified and pulsed, prepared to be released.

"No, Anwen," he demanded, wheezing as blood filled his lungs. "I cannot be healed. Not now. It is my time, dear one."

Tears now streamed down my cheeks. Memories of a different time and place echoed inside me. The same words whispered. The same emotions resurfaced.

I won't fail again—I can't lose him, too.

"No, let me save you, please," I pleaded.

Elric reached out and gently took my glowing hands.

"Anwen."

My name was lost and forgotten when a bright light appeared in front of us. Sparkling with an array of colors, the light pulsed with intense energy. The smell of magic drifted around us.

Squinting against the sun-like glow, I lifted my hands to shield my eyes.

Vidar looked up, eyes filled with wonder.

"Eira?"

The light dimmed, revealing my mother.

"Yes, my brother," she whispered lovingly. "I am here to bring you home."

TWENTY-SIX

Radiant and stunning in her feather-like white and gold armor, my mother smiled down at Vidar. Red hair haloed around her.

"What is going on?" I asked, glancing down at Vidar again, not really understanding why my mother was here.

Vidar's eyes stayed fixed on Eira. The glow surrounding her—or was it emanating from within her—reflected in his eyes. I looked at Elric, who seemed to understand why she was here. He bowed his head, his arm crossing his chest in respect.

"Elric, what's happening? We have to heal Vidar. Please help me," I begged, grabbing his hand. "Please."

"Anwen." Sadness flickered in his eyes. "Your mother is here to take Vidar."

I held my mother's gaze for a moment, desperately hoping that Elric was mistaken. Her angelic appearance scared me.

"No, what do you mean? Take him?" I asked, not immediately understanding his words and their meaning. "Take him where? To Vardia?"

When no one spoke, understanding quietly entered my mind.

Freyja knelt beside me and put her hand on my shoulder.

"No, dear one," she whispered. "Eira will guide him to Valhalla to greet Odin and then to the halls of Sessrúmnir. It is a great honor for a brave warrior of Vardia."

I knew the mythology, but still, what Freyja proclaimed was impossible. Elric placed his hand on mine, his finger slowly tracing a pattern on the back of my hand. I recognized the spell—a prayer for loved ones who had crossed into the afterlife. The pattern changed—offering comfort and serenity to those left behind in their grief. Feeling the magic flowing through my blood brought me comfort, but only for a moment, because denial quickly pushed it away.

Noticing my reluctance to accept my mother's task, Elric pulled me into his arms.

"My love, your mother is a Valkyrie. She is here to escort General Vidar to our ancestors—to the great hall of fallen warriors," he murmured softly into my hair, kissing me gently.

Denial still clung to me. I couldn't stop the tears from streaming down my face. A gentle squeeze of my hand drew my attention back to Vidar. His eyes were now fixed on me. A faint smile touched his lips.

"My dearest Anwen, please, do not despair." His voice was calm, but his breathing was more labored. "I love you, dear one, and I know you will save our people. Be strong and vigilant in your faith, Anwen. Trust your instincts . . . always have hope."

His eyes lingered briefly on my face, but then moved to my

neck. "My heart aches for your new obstacle in these dangerous times."

Eira kneeled beside Vidar, took his hand, and smiled.

"Are you ready, my courageous brother?" she asked before turning to me. "I will always be with you, my dearest daughter."

Her free hand gripped mine, uniting us in the final moments. A gentle burst of light erupted around her, and I closed my eyes against its brightness. When I opened them again, my mother and Vidar had vanished.

My hand dropped to my side. I looked at the empty space. Now, the only sign of my uncle was a shining red stain on the ground. Elric took my hand and kissed it—his emotions passing to me during the brief touch. His magic couldn't stop the emptiness quickly filling my heart.

"Anwen, look at me." The harshness in Freyja's voice startled me out of my numbness. She grasped my face firmly, turning my head to the side. A sharp breath escaped.

"Odin, it is of dire urgency that you come to me now," Freyja exclaimed loudly into the air.

The deep rumble of voices echoed down the tunnel and through the cavern. Another explosion shook beneath us. Even though Corvus and Draugr vanished, the rest of the mountain remained under attack.

Freyja called out again, and within seconds, Odin appeared. She yanked me up and turned my head to the side. I wasn't sure what she was showing him, but his features twisted in fear.

This could not be good.

"Laga, she is in danger," was the only word escaping Odin's

lips before he vanished again.

Another blast sent us reeling, losing our footing and dropping to our knees. Unfazed, Freyja knelt beside me and gripped my shoulders firmly.

"Anwen, you need to save the ancient knowledge; you must be quick," she said, grabbing Elric. "Take Herja to safety. The rock warrior will help you."

"Go, Anwen," Freyja begged. "Before it's too late. Hurry now, because the mountain can't take much more bombardment. I will come to you soon."

In a blinding flash of light and flying debris, she disappeared.

I jumped up just as Elric swung me around to him, ignoring Freyja's urgent command.

"Where are you going?" he demanded.

"You heard Freyja. I have to save the ancient knowledge. In Herja's room, her books, I need to find something that will help us defeat Loki," I explained breathlessly. From the look on Elric's face, he wasn't going to let me go.

I placed my hand on his cheek. "I have to go. I'll be quick about it, I promise. Now, get Herja out of here."

Doubt still clouded his features, but he nodded quickly in agreement.

"Be swift and stay alive," he said, his voice cracking. "I love you."

Before I could respond, he pulled me into his arms, his lips crushing mine in a desperate embrace. Reluctantly, he slowly pulled away, his attention now on an unconscious Herja.

Amid all the chaos surrounding Loki, Anu was overlooked, but now I notice the desperation in how she gripped Herja's hand. Surprisingly, she doesn't resist when Elric lifts Herja into his arms or when Barik wraps a rope around her hands. With a final glance, Elric leads Barik out of the cavern and into the tunnels, leaving me alone.

The only sounds now were the distant commands and clanging metal of the Wynfalle warriors, only interrupted by the occasional tremors of more explosions.

My mind drifted to Vidar.

And my mother—a Valkyrie.

Despair gripped my heart once again. When I last saw my mother, she never told me she was a Valkyrie. How could she keep such an important secret from me?

I shook my head, trying to halt my wandering thoughts and focus on the task—stopping Loki and Corvus from destroying Emberval. Grieving could wait.

Gathering my courage, I sprinted out of the cavern and down the tunnel. I wasn't exactly sure where I was headed, but I soon recognized the strange path leading to Herja's quarters. The debris-filled tunnel made progress difficult—shards of rock quickly pressed into my boots. I stumbled and fell multiple times, blood covering my hands and streaming down my leg. The pain brought fresh tears to my eyes.

How was I supposed to find my way out if I could barely make it through? The tunnels crisscrossed in irregular patterns, confusing my sense of direction. I paused more than once in panic, glancing desperately around me. Closing my eyes, I concentrated—trying to connect my energy with something, anything from Herja's room.

And then I felt him.

The strange owl-like creature was still in his cage.

Frightened and confused, its energy turned into a beacon, so I reached for its light.

Once his energy connected to mine, a shimmering trail lingered in the air. I sprang into action and followed the floating mist, running as fast as I could without tripping. Time was against me—the cracks along the tunnel walls kept spreading deeper. The ground shook beneath me. I braced myself against a large boulder, hoping the mountain wouldn't come crashing down around me.

The section behind me exploded. I dropped to the ground as a stone splintered near my head—knife-sharp shards cutting into my exposed skin.

I grunted in pain, wiping away a drop of blood from the corner of my eye. I stumbled again as another explosion rocked the mountain—my wounded leg now nearly numb. Regaining my balance, I let out a frustrated cry—I had lost the trail of the energy. I leaned against the wall, forcing myself to stay calm. I needed to relax and focus. A familiar voice appeared in my mind, filling me with clarity. I slowly opened my eyes and saw the shimmering mist once more. It was stronger and more vibrant. I knew I was close to her room.

With thick dust filling the tunnels, I relied on the wall to guide me. I pushed forward, gasping in the dusty air. Coughing and disoriented, my hand suddenly reached into empty space.

The glittering trail wavered down the dark hallway of Herja's room. I quickly found the cage. The creature screeched with gratitude when I unlatched the door.

"Go, fly to safety," I said, coaxing it out of its sanctuary.

He let out a panicked squawk and flew out of the cage and down the hall.

The shimmering mist dispersed, leaving an eerie darkness. I quickly lit a ball of golden light. Raising my hand, the glow revealed massive destruction to Herja's sanctuary.

Broken bottles and splintered furniture littered the room. I shone my light toward the bookshelf, which was in shambles—needless to say, the books were in much worse condition, if not beyond saving. Most were buried beneath the rubble. A few peeked out from their rocky grave, but they looked too torn and beyond repair. I fell to my knees anyway, digging through the small piles of surviving books and hoping to find any old ones. I scoffed at that idea—all the books seemed ancient.

Minutes passed, and my search yielded nothing useful. Time was slipping away, but the danger grew—tremors became more frequent and more intense.

"Where are you? What do you look like?" I pleaded into the air.

I glanced around the chaotic room, thinking Herja wouldn't have left special texts in an obvious spot like the open bookshelf, right?

Where, though, would she hide something so valuable and so important?

My gaze settled on the fireplace.

The scykra.

Something special to her. The small trinket might hold the answers.

I ran to the fireplace—the mantel torn from the rock and hanging on its side. I began to sift through the debris, hoping the black soot would reveal the scykra. But my hands came up empty.

Maybe she took it?

Desperation grew inside me.

I couldn't give up. Not yet.

The gods depended on me. Vardia depended on me.

As I continued looking around the room, the aftershocks from the explosions grew stronger.

Knowing time was no longer on my side, an anguished cry burst from my lips—this couldn't be the end. My eyes scanned the books again, calling out to any and all magic within the space.

Please . . . hear me . . . help me.

I fell to my knees and brushed over the pile of books again. A sharp rock cut my finger, drawing dark crimson blood to the surface.

As I reached for a random book, a steady stream of blood dripped onto one of the covers. The blood bubbled and sizzled on contact—and then vanished.

Cautiously, I picked up the fragile book, but it immediately slipped out of my hand. When it hit the floor again, the pages fluttered rapidly as if a gust of wind swept through the room. A burst of darkness erupted from the pages, hovering above my head. Suddenly, the book snapped shut with a loud crack. My eyes kept following the black veil floating above me. A tendril snaked out and floated downward, nearly touching me, but then retracted back into the misty cloud.

Or so I thought.

A gentle caress brushed against my cheek, almost tenderly, while a softness circled around my neck, resting beside my mark. I closed my eyes at the gentle contact as a sigh of contentment escaped my lips, and a sudden awareness of something delicate yet powerful settled deep within me.

That awareness jolted me out of my trance. I stumbled backward and fell on my backside, surprised not only by the ghostly gesture but also by how I reacted to it.

My eyes lifted back to the winding mist. Another finger extended downward, but instead of touching my face, it curled toward my chest and hovered over my brooch. Several misty tendrils sprouted from the finger, brushing against the swirling symbols. A sudden gust of wind burst from the dark cloud, encircling my body and trapping me within a black tornado. Warmth surrounded me.

And then I heard it—the softly swirling whispers invading my thoughts. Slightly spoken but powerful in its tone, the crooning settled deep within my body, warmth gathering in my stomach and then radiating outward, filling every nerve, muscle, and bone. It took hold like a sudden gust. My breath wavered.

Soft words entered my mind—a steady mantra spoken with gentle affection.

Anwen. Anwen. Anwen.

Vér eruey sem einn. We are forever as one.

My hand reached for the book. My finger carefully traced the pattern carved into the cover. The movement triggered an immediate reaction with the brooch clipped to my tunic. An electric charge curled around my hand and connected with the silver, producing sparks of light.

I jerked back in surprise. I remembered this book from earlier. The pattern on the book mirrored the design of the brooch—Elric's gift. The trefoil pattern suddenly shimmered red, and blood seemed to flow along the scrollwork until it disappeared into its black depths. The whispers stopped, leaving an emptiness I couldn't explain.

Another explosion reverberated through the tunnel.

Someone called my name.

My breath faltered, hoping the sound came from the book again, but my name echoed through the tunnel. Not the treasured object in my hands.

"Anwen?"

Elric.

"In here!" I yelled back.

I looked down at the book again with curiosity, and without hesitation, I slid it into my bag—just in time as Elric entered the room, a silver ball floating in his hand.

"Anwen?"

"Yes, I am here," I called out again, running into his arms.

"Thank the gods, you're alive. We need to go now. The mountain is destroyed. There's no more time," he grabbed my hand, pulling me with him toward the door.

He stopped suddenly. "Did you find what you were looking

for?"

I shook my head in defeat.

"No, no, I couldn't find anything resembling Freyja's description." My eyes dropped to the floor, hoping he didn't catch the lie in my words. "I failed her."

"We will make do with what we have, Anwen. There is no failure in times like these. Freyja will understand."

We rushed back through the tunnel, dodging falling debris from the ceiling. Fear shot through me—the tunnel was nearly buried in rubble. I waited too long, and now, I was sure we were doomed.

Wait.

I moved my bag around, searching the bottom until I found what I was looking for.

"What are you doing? We need to keep going," he yelled over the noise of crashing stones falling around us. "By the gods, we are not going to make it!"

I grabbed his hand and pulled him to a stop.

"No, we need a little help . . . a little flying speed," I said to him, brandishing the small figurine in the palm of my hand.

He smiled down at me, and understanding dawned.

My energy engulfed the figurine, transforming it into a familiar creature, its wings outstretched in all their glory. Its head reared back, and with its beak pointed upward, a deafening screech echoed.

"Bane, we need help now," I shouted.

He crouched low enough for Elric and me to jump onto his back. With a powerful push from his hind legs, Bane leapt into the air, twisting and turning through the gaping holes in the rubble stacked inside the tunnels.

With each breath we held, Bane guided us through the thick, suffocating dust that hung like a dense fog. Bane moved swiftly through the tunnel, dodging sharp rocks and fallen debris. Speeding rapidly through the crumbling black stone, we finally burst through the mountain's gates. I risked a glance back to see the mountain's mouth collapse with a thunderous crash. A cloud of dust billowed into the air. I shivered at how close we came to disaster during our escape.

Turning around, the bright blue sky of freedom welcomed us.

TWENTY-SEVEN

Shielding my eyes from the bright sunlight, I tried to scan the ground below, hoping and praying to see people escaping the destruction of the ruined mountain. Anxiety overwhelmed me when no signs of survivors appeared.

Elric leaned in toward my ear.

"Look—over there," he said, pointing to a small clearing between several jagged rocks.

A group of elves appeared from behind them—some blending in with their snow gear, while others wore simple, flimsy tunics and pants. Several small groups huddled along the ridge, trying to share body heat against the cold, icy wind.

To my surprise, several of the rocky pillars began to move, and then, to my delight, the figures of the Rock Giants gathered the elves to their bodies, shielding them even better from the cold wind. Nervously, my eyes searched for one particular rock giant and his companion. I sighed in relief when Barik noticed us, separated from his warrior brethren, and started to run toward us. Soon, the figures of the ambassador and Halvard followed him, waving at us.

Bane, who knew what to do, descended to the ground. But my eyes kept scanning for another figure.

Where was he?

Coldness seized my heart. Then it struck me like nothing I had ever felt before. My hands slackened from Bane's neck. I frantically tried to turn around, but Elric's arms tightened around me, keeping me upright.

"Anwen?" he whispered in my ear. "Are you alright?"

"Where is he?" I asked softly, mostly to myself.

"Who?" he asked, but quickly paused, recognizing the person I mentioned. His arms clenched tighter. A look of concern now appeared on his face.

"Vidar," I hissed back more urgently. "He—he was fighting Corvus . . . and then, I saw him fall---"

A vision of my mother surfaced in my mind—a shining beacon of light clad in white and gold armor.

Elric's silence grew between us. I needed him to say Vidar was fine, that it was all a dream, and that my mother didn't take him away from me. I frantically tried to turn around and confront him.

"Elric?" I asked him again, this time more sharply.

"Anwen, please, let us land first," he whispered in my ear. His warm breath, followed by a brief touch of his lips, made me pause. I closed my eyes as a single tear rolled down.

"No, please, say it was a dream," I murmured, trembling and taking a quick gulp of air.

His arms briefly squeezed my waist, almost desperately. I leaned my head back against his shoulder, closed my eyes, and tried to will away the gnawing grief that spread within my chest. The reality of it all was not just the sadness, the emptiness of losing my uncle, but also the relentless crush of guilt—how many must die because of me?

Elric's lips gently brushed my temple, showing understanding.

"It is not your fault, little one," he said softly as Bane finally landed on the ground, jolting me up and away from Elric.

He jumped to the ground and turned to me with his hands raised. I slid into them, wrapping my arms around his waist—if only until the harsh reality settled in, before his people needed healing, before my people had to face the fact that their brave and kind general was gone.

He pulled back and cupped my face with his hands.

"Let us gather the people, deal with the aftermath of this horrible battle, and then talk, grieve, and prepare for whatever may come to pass with our people. Vidar was a great warrior, Anwen. There will be time for sorrow," he pulled me back into his arms, his hand smoothing the unruly stray hairs away from my face.

Bane screeched a warning when our friends came near us. Elric pulled back a little, though his arm still held my waist.

The ambassador and Halvard were the first to arrive. Halvard greeted Elric by clasping his shoulder, while Ragnhild pulled me into an embrace.

"My dear, how my heart sings to know you are safe," she

peered at Elric, laying her hand on his arm. "That both of you have escaped and are safe."

She tilted her head toward another group approaching us.

"We are uncertain what actions to take. Lieutenant Halvard and I are trying to gather the injured in one spot, but it's quite challenging. Elric, your people need guidance. Sigrún . . . she is overwhelmed by grief, and Herja remains unconscious," her voice faded. "Wynfalle has been so isolated, and the people haven't wandered far from their homeland. By the gods, they seem lost outside their mountain."

Halvard stepped forward, his hand reaching toward me before dropping quickly to his side. With his head bowed, he opened his mouth to speak, but then stopped.

When he finally looked up again, our eyes met, and I understood what he was feeling, what he truly wanted to say, but the words couldn't come out. Because saying them aloud would only confirm the awful truth of Vidar's death.

I grasped his hand with understanding.

"I know, Halvard," I murmured. The words felt thick and harsh, grating against the numbness in my throat.

Barik approached our group with several of his warriors.

"My heart is full of sorrow," he said. "The general was a fine elf, a good talker, and a brave warrior. It will be with a heavy mind and heart that we go back and tell King Grannir of his death."

"Thank you, Barik, my oldest and dearest friend," Elric said. "Thank you for coming to Wynfalle and bringing your brave and honorable warriors to help us in our time of need."

A quiet voice spoke behind us. Sigrún and a few of her warriors showed up.

"Yes, thank you, Barik, great warrior of Wynfalle, for coming to the aid of my people. Your act of heroism shall never be forgotten," she stated. "Please, send word to King Grannir that King Torvald is dead and that I, his faithful daughter, have humbly and respectfully accepted the crown from my people."

She looked at each of us with a cold, piercing stare—challenging us to deny the crown she had rightfully earned. Her gaze stayed on Elric the longest, until she finally turned back to Barik.

"With permission from your king, Wynfalle will need refuge in the valley. I do not know how long we will be at your mercy, but when you return to your kingdom, let him know our condition and our need for his help."

I studied her, aware that it hurt her to say those words—not necessarily out of disrespect for Barik and his people, but because she knew this would be a tough time for her community. Their solitude has left them vulnerable, and Wynfalle might see this as a weakness.

Elric surprisingly shook his head in disagreement with her decision.

"Sig . . . " he paused. "Queen Sigrún, by all accounts, staying here in the valley is dangerous, to say the least."

He glanced toward the ambassador again for confirmation. "With the consent of Ambassador Ragnhild, the people of Wynfalle shall have sanctuary and protection in the Kingdom of Vardia. In this time of need, it is only right that Vardia offers asylum to our mountain kin, especially after the fall of King Torvald—Vardia will provide your people with stability as you plan to rebuild your kingdom."

Sigrún frowned at the offer.

"I cannot ask Vardia to shelter my people forever. And with so many injured, traveling will be too hard," she rejected. "No, Volun Elric, we will endure our current homelessness within Wynfalle—our kingdom, our land—until we rebuild our home."

Elric was about to reply when the ambassador placed a hand on his arm, stopping him.

"Queen Sigrún, with all due respect, your people—alas, your children—need protection, not only from another potential attack but also from the harsh elements that the mountains will surely bring this time of year. The journey to Vardia will be long and arduous, and rebuilding your home could take months, if not years—let Vardia give you sanctuary until you can reclaim your kingdom." The ambassador paused, allowing her words to fully resonate. "Commander Elric is correct in his assessment and offer. King Ansgar and Queen Eydis would welcome you with open arms—especially in a time of great sorrow. Once they learn that their son, our General Vidar, sacrificed his life for your people."

I cringed at the mention of Vidar in such a way to invoke support for her proposition, but I understood it. She was right. No matter what disagreement I had with Sigrún, she was Wynfalle's queen now, and her people—Elric's people—needed our help.

Everyone waited as Sigrún contemplated the invitation. I

expected her to argue again, but when she finally spoke, her eyes met mine, and to my surprise, she smiled faintly.

She nodded her head and agreed.

"Wynfalle is proud to renew our connection with our Vardian brothers and sisters," she paused. "I would be forever grateful for the offer of sanctuary, and I accept on behalf of my people. We are unquestionably in your debt."

She turned to Barik and his warriors.

"Once our kingdom is re-established, Barik, I will inform King Grannir. Until then, let him know we value his help during this difficult time and look forward to further talks about the fall of Lord Kenrick and the Lokrum."

She quickly turned to us, her woeful eyes saying everything as she gestured to the injured and dying.

"Please, Elric . . . Healer Anwen, my people need help," her gaze slowly swept over the groups of elves lying in the valley. "Many are dying or in need of healing. Especially the children. Many were struck down while attending their studies. Please, go to them first."

Her voice faltered when her eyes drifted to a certain part of the group. My eyes followed her gaze. I grabbed Elric's arm in alarm. The air left my lungs quickly when I saw the small bodies on the ground.

By the gods, there were so many.

My feet moved forward automatically—an irresistible pull drew me closer. Even though I was terrified to see what atrocities the Lokrum committed against the children of Wynfalle, all I could think of was Jack. And the complete disregard for any life at the hands of Kenrick and Corvus, all for the pursuit of absolute power.

And Loki.

How could a god hate the very beings created to worship him and help him in times of need? Using innocent people for his own selfish revenge against his own kind?

I stopped at the first child, and even though I felt Sigrún and Elric beside me, my focus was on the injured group ahead.

The number of children gave me pause. Vardia had children, but not as many as Wynfalle. Hundreds of children, if not more, appeared to be no older than five years by human standards. Most lay on blankets or clothing, grabbed at the last minute during the evacuation. Even as I looked out across the valley, parents or relatives surrounded them, taking clothing from their own backs to give to the little ones. Half, if not more, sat alone, leaning against an adult or another child—injuries that seemed minor covered their bodies. But the others, those lying on the ground with their soft pleas slipping from bloodied lips or with hardened stares searching for relief in the sky, bore far more devastating wounds.

"No matter where I go or what world I am in, children always seem to pay the price for their elders' negligence," I murmured in anger, choking back tears.

Elric placed his hand on my shoulder. I turned and noticed the same emotions flickering across his face.

"Come, let us start here, Elric." I knelt beside the first child.

Pain-filled eyes looked at me. I placed my hand on her cheek. Tears traced down her face, covered in black soot. Her long, black hair spread around her head, forming a halo against the white snow beneath her. A small wound seeped red across her white tunic.

Her eyes widened when she saw who I was, and she pulled away from me. I wasn't sure if I should continue because of her distress, not wanting to make things worse for her. But Sigrún knelt beside the girl and leaned in close to her ear.

"Fanndís, you are safe now, my dear. Healer Anwen will help you," she whispered. "Please, let her lay her healing hands upon you."

Fanndís looked up at me. Fresh tears shimmered in her dark eyes. She nodded, granting me permission to help ease her pain.

I smiled at her and touched her cheek.

"Close your eyes, little one. This will not hurt," I reassured her.

She immediately shut her eyes. Briefly, I glanced up at Elric, who was kneeling beside me. He offered a faint smile and squeezed my arm.

"I will go help the others," he murmured. "You know what to do, Anwen. Have faith, my love."

From the corner of my eye, I saw Sigrún bristle at Elric's affirmation but quickly regain her composure and place her hand on Fanndís' arm. She murmured a few words in the Wynfalle language.

I closed my eyes and placed my hands over her chest, then slowly moved them down to her wound. Pale gold light pulsed and flickered until a steady stream of energy hovered around the injury. As the heat intensified, Fanndís clenched her fists. Her lips pulled back into a grimace, revealing a small red line across her face. Her body trembled as the magic began to heal her wound.

When I felt my energy fading, I opened my eyes. The dark gold light filtered through my fingers until only a small halo of light remained. The wound was now just a tiny white line, barely visible on her already pale skin. A group of children and adults gathered around us—their expressions showed deep reverence.

A hand pressed down on mine. Ffanndís' stunned but smiling face looked up at me.

"Thank you," she said.

I leaned in so I could see her face more clearly.

"You are so very welcome, little one," I whispered with a smile. "Now, rest, and I will have someone come and wash you up."

I looked at Sigrún, who still held Fanndís' hand. She gave me a smile—one of hope and gratitude. But it also signified a truce. An understanding formed between us, something we both could see—our people, both Vardia and Wynfalle, were united once more.

United after thousands of years.

And now, our only goal was to take down Lucia and Loki once and for all.

TWENTY-EIGHT

Elric and I worked tirelessly throughout the day and into the early evening. Many of the injuries his people sustained were quickly attended to and healed as best as we could. Now, sitting alone by a rocky ridge, I gazed out across the valley, the quiet, moonless night stretching over the small fires and makeshift tents of the homeless Mountain Elves.

My thoughts raced as I tried to make sense of everything since we arrived at Wynfalle. I rubbed the back of my head, hoping to relieve the tension in my muscles, but instead, a sharp pain shot up my arm and then painfully snaked down the left side of my face.

I grimaced at what remained of the gash below my elbow. Earlier, Elric had to make me sit down long enough to heal me—in the middle of my healing sessions, I didn't realize I was bleeding out until one of the wounded stopped me. There was so much blood that I couldn't tell the difference between my blood and the blood of the healed.

I wiggled my fingers through the thick strands of my hair, then found skin to knead the stress of the day away. Although my body had cuts and scrapes from the fight—wounds on the outside—it was the injuries inside that hurt me more. Wounds that couldn't be healed with a single touch of magic.

No. Magic was the injury this time, the cause of heavy emotions swirling inside me.

My markings. My body.

What was once considered a blessing for many gods has now become a curse—marks meant to protect the gods could now lead to their downfall. My downfall, if Kenrick, Corvus, and Loki got their way. Loki has the power to locate the gods with just a single touch—but what does he do with that knowledge?

I turned my attention to the small fire dancing erratically in front of me. The spiky flames wobbled back and forth, as if uncertain where to point their fiery blaze next. Its hesitancy reflected my own feelings about my current predicament. Where do I go from here with the knowledge that I hold the fate of the gods within me?

My eyes drifted across the clearing to the small group gathered around a large fire. Ragnhild and Halvard were deeply engaged in conversation with Tyr and a female elf I didn't recognize—their hands waving occasionally as if making a crucial point. Barik and another giant warrior sat on the other side, away from them, but looked up now and then to share their opinions in the discussion.

My eyes drifted slightly to the far corner where two figures sat—close enough to the fire to stay warm but far enough to keep their privacy. Heads close together in thought, with words spoken so softly that their lips barely moved.

Sigrún and Elric.

I slightly bristled when Elric leaned toward her, focusing on her mouth as she whispered something to him. A faint laugh escaped her lips while he shook his head at her words, replying to her witty banter, which prompted a slight smile from him.

I quickly turned my head away. I shouldn't be upset at them because I was the one who wanted to be alone. I needed time to think. Time to mourn what was lost today in the mountain. But the reason for my restless thoughts and emotions made me angry—who was I mourning for right now?

Vidar, obviously.

Or maybe, strangely enough, me.

My hand instinctively touched my face again. Just a few hours earlier, after Elric and I finished healing the injured, he took me aside and finally mentioned my new markings—the spells that protected Laga. I had totally forgotten about them, no longer feeling the pain because of the other duties I had to handle. But as soon as he pointed my attention back to my own injuries, everything flooded back to me.

The spring. Odin and Freyja. Loki. And Vidar.

I turned away from him and told him to leave me alone for a while. Of course, he wouldn't hear of it, but I insisted—well, that's putting it mildly. I totally lost it, yelling and pointing at everyone like a madwoman.

Okay, so I went a little crazy. But no one said anything—actually, no one even flinched at my wild behavior. All said and done, I was ashamed that I was that out of control—that angry.

And Elric. He took it in stride and let me vent, let me accuse everyone around me of conspiracy. Even accusing him, which surprised him, and of course, surprised me.

How could I be so in control one moment, helping save the Urora and healing the Mountain Elves, and then suddenly be so angry at everyone? My friends, my family.

My feelings rushed back inside me again. My thoughts spun chaotically.

I was angry—because I felt different. I tried to tell Elric how I was feeling, but he refused to listen, insisting that I was the same person. However, he didn't understand—no one did.

I was different, not just physically but emotionally and mentally, call it whatever you want. Something changed in a way I couldn't quite define. It was like I was shedding my old skin for a newer, better, more resilient one. A new sense of myself—and it should have frightened me, but it didn't. I felt stronger and more alive—more like myself. It was a different feeling than when Hrafn's magic entered my body.

Loki did something to me when he revealed that spell—the words came alive within me. The strange feeling thrummed through me when all of the markings appeared on my body briefly as I used my powers. Then they vanished, and the words lost their strength. But now, with just one spell exposed, I can feel the words inside me—resonating through my bones, veins, and blood.

I couldn't explain it to Elric or the ambassador. My explanation even sounded crazy to me.

So, secluding myself from everyone became my solution. I built a small fire and sat far away from the group—or as far as Elric thought was reasonable. It was my time alone to think about the next steps, because I knew, without question, that only I could do what needed to be done. No one else. I was the key to something bigger than anything ever seen in this world. The pressure to succeed felt overwhelming.

An abrupt whistle followed by a quick squawk interrupted my thoughts. I glanced sideways at the lounging creature next to me.

"Can you feel it too, Bane?" I murmured as I stroked my hand down his warm, feathered neck. "Can you sense the change in the air as well? The change in me?"

Sighing, I leaned my head on his shoulder. "I wish Hrafn were here. He would know what to do. What to say."

And as if on cue, the faint cries of the Okri began to echo in my mind. Throughout the day, the Okri remained silent—almost as if they knew I had enough to worry about without alerting me to their situation. I closed my eyes and tried to calm my breathing.

Screeching again, Bane lifted his wings to shield me, repositioning himself so I could lie down beside him. I smiled once more, curling up against his warm, feathered silk. As I closed my eyes, Elric lifted his head from his deep conversation with the queen and glanced in my direction.

But I didn't acknowledge him—I knew he felt the Okri cries within me. Emotions flooded through him, but I didn't respond to his curious thoughts. I needed this time for myself. Away from everyone—away from him. Especially now. The ancestors cried out one last time before my eyes shut, and darkness embraced me.

***

"Anwen? Sleepy, sleepy one. Wake, my dear one," a soft voice called out.

I opened my eyes slightly and was greeted by a rippling, velvety golden light. Freyja sat in front of me, legs crossed at the ankles, her chin resting casually on her palm as she looked down at me.

Slowly, I pushed my body up into a sitting position while rubbing my eyes, hoping to clear the strange fuzziness from them. But when I opened them again, the weird, hazy glow continued to emit from my surroundings.

"Why does everything look so strange?" I asked Freyja.

She swished her hand to the side and smiled softly. "Because I am in your dream, Anwen, only within your thoughts. I did not want to risk visiting you in the open with the others so close."

Now sitting upright, I hugged my legs to my chest and sighed.

"I'm pretty sure no one would have noticed you here anyway. They're all busy with their own plans and not paying any attention to me right now."

Freyja smiled and shook her head. "My dear Anwen, you are the one who isolated yourself. And don't believe that your young Volun and your new friends haven't been keeping an eye out for you. They care for you deeply, young one, and when you are hurting, they also hurt. They are not indifferent to your situation, especially now that you feel the effects of our goddess Laga's spell."

I shook my head. "I don't understand. Who is Laga?"

"Laga was the guardian of all the water sources that contained many of the spirits of the ancestors." Freyja turned away. "She was well loved by everyone, especially our All-Father."

"Was?" I asked. "What happened to her?"

Freyja looked away and blinked several times, trying to hold back the tears. Suddenly, she spun around.

"With the knowledge of Laga's spell revealed to Loki," Freyja's hand reached for my face and touched the markings. "He killed her."

Freyja's hand fell to her lap as sorrow spilled from her next words.

"What have we done, Anwen?"

She looked back at me. "We turned our backs on Loki, and brought a heinous punishment upon him and his loved ones, but we never thought it would come to this . . . that our own insolence with each other would hurt everyone around us. All beings, all worlds, that Loki would retaliate this way. The hatred is so deep."

"He killed her? A god?" I asked again. The heat of Laga's spell coursed through my blood. "Why does he hate you so much?"

"Your mark . . . Laga's spell . . . when it was revealed to

Loki, he took that knowledge and destroyed her," Freyja whispered as her eyes moved to the side of my face. "I am not sure how he made the spell reappear without your power, but we are now, more than ever, afraid that Loki will succeed in destroying us and destroying this world and everything within it. As for his hatred, Loki defied the gods and so the All-Father—no, not just Odin—but all the gods punished him by condemning him to eternal pain, enduring the poison of a serpent while his lover watched him in agony."

I looked away, not fully grasping the reason behind the terrible punishment. All I knew was the present moment and that Loki could kill a god so easily. In this world, Loki fought in the name of Kenrick, and he had to be stopped. Something surged inside me—a new understanding of my powers.

"But Loki has allied with Kenrick and Corvus."

"No," Freyja interrupted. "Do not think that Loki pledged allegiance to anyone, Anwen. Whatever he has told Kenrick and his Mage is a lie. Loki is out for revenge against the gods, and he will take everyone down. There is no loyalty. Creating chaos is his only goal."

Freyja pulled out a small bag from her side, her hands briefly caressing the latch before she opened it and revealed the contents.

"And this is why I'm here, dear one. To give you this," she said as she pulled out Loki's gold dagger—the one that killed Vidar.

"No . . . no," I shook my head vehemently and started to move away from her. "I don't want that awful thing. Get it away from me."

Freyja grabbed my arm, stopping me from stepping back any further. "Anwen, take it. It was once mine and was given as a token of love to Loki. I know it has taken someone you loved dearly, but it is powerful and highly loyal to its owner. I have reclaimed it and now I am giving it to you as a symbol of my love and trust."

She gently pressed the dagger into my outstretched hands and then folded my fingers over the smooth hilt. I closed my eyes with sadness and guilt. Instantly, anger welled up inside me, hating Freyja for giving me the dagger.

"I understand your feelings, my dear one, as I wish your Vidar had not perished. But know this, he lives within my halls as a noble and courageous warrior, and he dines with his beautiful and brave sister," Freyja placed her hand on my cheek.

I felt her pull away, so I quickly opened my eyes and scrambled to my feet.

"Please don't go," I yelled out frantically. Anger now faded away along with the need for more answers. "I have so many questions. Why do I feel so different? Why do I feel so . . . so . . ."

"Angry, sad, guilty—powerful," Freyja finished, perfectly capturing how I felt. She smiled faintly, a hint of sadness in her expression. "Because you *are* different, and those feelings are fueling your magic now. You have Laga within you, Anwen. Her knowledge and energy flow through your veins. With her death, she has given you a part of herself, and that is what makes you different. Feed off those feelings, Anwen. Learn from her power, but don't let it overpower you."

Freyja looked over at my bag sitting next to Bane.

"Be careful, my little one. The new powers developing inside you are wondrous, but when mixed with the Shadow—without control or proper training—it can be dangerous at best. Although I am the one who told you to seek that knowledge, it seems that the Shadow calls to you for other purposes."

My eyes moved back to my bag, where the black book was hidden among the dark folds.

The Shadow.

Was it the Shadow whispering to me in Herja's room?

I felt the finger of overwhelming power beckoning me, even though it was hidden by my bag. Still, I was sure I could handle the contents. It was only a book.

As if she could read my mind, Freyja frowned but didn't give me any more words of wisdom, just a warning.

"Heed my words, Anwen," she whispered and turned around with a surge of brightness, disappearing into the night.

***

I lurched forward. A muffled scream escaped my lips. My eyes quickly swept my surroundings in fear, only to realize that the terror of my nightmare was nowhere to be seen. The warmth around my hands was not blood from my dream, but rather the handful of skin and feathers from Bane's neck. He screeched as I loosened my grip. I muttered an apology.

The night still covered the valley. The voices across the clearing grew quieter as more people went to sleep. I looked at

Elric's group and saw that most were asleep, except for Barik, who stood guard as still as a stone. His watchful gaze cut through the darkness.

I rubbed my hand across my eyes, trying to remember the dream, but it slipped away. I grabbed a small canteen at my feet and took a quick sip, enjoying the ice-cold liquid flowing down my dry throat. When I put it back down, my eyes landed on my bag—a glint of gold peeked out of the opening.

Loki's dagger.

Cautiously, I reached down to slowly open the bag even more. And there it was—the dagger that killed Vidar. My dream rushed to the front of my mind. My hand hovered above the bag's contents. My finger gently caressed the top of the hilt, circling the large amber stone shining brightly in the firelight. As I slid my finger down further into the bag along the blade, my hand landed on the book. Blurred, almost wild images pierced my thoughts—strange figures swimming in and out of turbulent water, yelling at a dark figure standing on a cliff. A tall obelisk loomed in the background—black and gleaming red.

A coldness settled over me. A sudden jolt shocked my mind. My vision blurred as another attack tore through my thoughts. I pulled my hand out of the bag and immediately looked around at the other fires burning in the night, hoping to spot the culprit. But then it hit me—the only person brave enough to try invading my thoughts.

Herja.

She must be awake.

I hurried through the darkness. Her camp was separate

from the others, just like mine. But unlike me, she wasn't alone. Anu sat with her back against a withering pine tree, in her true form, with her hands unbound.

"Well, good evening, or should I say good morrow, to you, Healer," Herja murmured into the darkness. Her eyes searched the blackness. "Do not hide from me. You are welcome here, as always. I sense your hesitation, young one. My daughter will not be treated like a prisoner when she is with me. Rest assured, no harm will come to you."

I walked into the circle of light.

"You seem surprised that I have come to you, Herja, when only a few minutes ago, you were trying to see into my mind," I said, sitting diagonally from her, a good position to have both Herja and Anu in my line of sight.

Herja laughed at my boldness.

"Yes, yes, my dear Anwen. I do not deny that I am still trying to understand that strangely sealed and seemingly impenetrable mind of yours," she said, but then immediately sobered and frowned with concern. "How are you, my dear?"

Her eyes trailed to the spell inked along my neck.

"As well as to be expected, I guess," I shrugged. "I am fine, Herja. Nothing has changed."

So, I lied. But I wasn't going to tell her the truth, not yet. Not with Anu very much awake and staring hatefully at me. She was the enemy, no matter who she was to Herja.

With my eyes never leaving Anu, I couldn't help but feel the irritation gradually taking hold in my mind.

"And you, Anu?" Her name came out as a slow, spiteful

drawl. "How does it feel now that you were left behind by *your* trusted Master?"

Herja clicked her tongue in irritation. I shot her a piercing stare.

"No, no way, Herja. You cannot sit there and expect me to be all warm and fuzzy with her, not now, not ever," I seethed. "Not with what she did to my people, to the Okri . . . and to Jack."

Anu tried to speak, but the words wouldn't come out. Instead, she turned her head away from me, finally breaking her dark stare, but not before I saw a flicker of guilt and shame cross her face.

I began to laugh, loud and cruel. Herja's head snapped around, the harshness catching her off guard. Her brow furrowed with caution.

"NO! You have no right to feel anything towards Jack. You may not have directly caused his illness, but you knew what they were doing to him. You are despicable."

Anu's head snapped back toward me. Sparks flashed in her coppery-black eyes.

"You have no right to judge me," she muttered sharply.

But all I could see was red at those ridiculous words.

"I. HAVE. NO. RIGHT?!" I erupted, quickly scrambling to my feet. "How dare you sit there and say that to me!"

"Anwen!" Herja jumped in front of me, her face twisting with shock at my outburst.

My eyes lingered a few seconds longer on Anu before slowly turning to Herja's unwavering glare. The heat of my energy pulsed through my hands and into my eyes. A gentle glow shaded Herja's face, but her eyes never left mine; they only narrowed slightly, silently warning me—she wouldn't let me harm her daughter.

My hands clenched into fists, itching to lash out. Everything around me looked golden—except for a dark halo surrounding Herja. The black, wisp-like fingers flickered like grass in a breeze—almost as if they were protecting her.

I closed my eyes, trying to push aside the vengeful thoughts. The pressure kept building behind my eyes.

"Calm yourself, Healer," she whispered fiercely. "Or I will demonstrate my powers for you. I will not show mercy."

Trying to calm my breathing and realizing the threat that Herja just sent my way, I sat back down. My eyes fixed on the flickering flames of the fire, and I silently seethed inside.

"Now, let us keep our voices low and our minds clear," she declared, sitting across from me. But she remained rigid and cautious—maybe Herja felt the new power surging inside me now. Still, curiosity gradually took over her. Her eyes scanned my body for any signs that I was different. She almost gave up her search until she narrowed her eyes, catching a glimpse of silver beneath my cloak. A slow smile spread across her lips. Her eyes met mine.

"You *are* full of surprises, Healer."

I let her speculate, choosing not to pander to the questions forming on her tongue. Instead, I stayed silent while continuing to stare into the fire. When I finally looked up, I saw Anu watching me. Our eyes connected, and suddenly, I sensed her pain, her remorse, and her anger. But this time, the anger wasn't directed at me. No, it was aimed at someone else now. And she was fading quickly, as if her exhaustion from hating the world was finally catching up with her.

Sucking in a shaky yet calming breath, I realized how similar our struggles were. How we both were thrust into lives we were never meant to live—willing or not, we were pawns in a game we didn't know how to win. Life or death was a simple choice—but it really wasn't ours to make anymore.

I started to laugh softly, sighing and shaking my head at our predicament. Both Anu and Herja looked at me with fear. I was sure they were both thinking that I was finally losing it. I could sense their confusion.

But then I stopped, realizing tears were streaming down my face.

"I am sorry, Anu," I carefully formed my words, testing the sound and sincerity on my tongue. I looked up and met her gaze.

She didn't say anything, just nonchalantly raised her brow—certainly questioning my sudden change of heart.

That made two of us.

Now, as my fingers absentmindedly toyed with a lone, ragged thread hanging from my jacket, I sensed a slight vibration just inside my tunic. Lifting my hand and feeling the familiar shape—my beloved brooch.

Elric.

I quickly looked toward his camp, but he was too far away to see.

But I sensed his presence. He knew I was here—and he was

thinking about me.

Sending me courage and guiding my faith.

Why was I really here?

My eyes moved over the fire and landed on Anu, still waiting for my next words.

And then it hit me.

Freyja.

My breath quickly faltered. Understanding dawned.

"You!" I exclaimed. "It was you all along!"

Herja reacted quickly to my outburst, standing up and positioning herself in front of Anu, prepared to fight if I lunged at her daughter.

But I didn't move. Suddenly aware that the loathsome person sitting in front of me—throwing phantom daggers with her dark glare—might hold the answers to saving Emberval.

It was as if Freyja descended and held up a giant blinking arrow, pointing directly at Anu, revealing the answer I should have figured out hours earlier. Freyja's words about finding the ancient knowledge, traditional magic, and understanding the past—the answer was so clear now.

I shook my head in disbelief, completely surprised and struck by the irony of it all.

I stood and walked towards Anu, but Herja's expression told me she still didn't trust my sudden movements.

My hands rose to show her that I wasn't a threat, that they appeared normal and had no glow.

"Don't you see, Herja?" I asked, as if pointing out what was obvious. "Freyja told me to learn from you—the traditional magic, the ancient knowledge, and your past—learn the Shadow. The answer to defeating Loki. But I thought it was scrolls, texts, spells, found in your books, your library. No, it was right here all along."

I waved my arm at Anu.

Herja furrowed her brow in confusion and followed the sweep of my arm. Suddenly, clarity lit up in her eyes.

"Anu?" she asked. "My Anu?"

TWENTY-NINE

"Yes, yes, of course," Herja's voice hurried out. "How could I have missed this revelation?"

Anu, now glancing between us, shook her head in confusion.

"What are you crazy fools talking about?" she asked, her anger rising. "What revelation, Seer?"

I rushed forward, kneeling a few feet in front of her. She glared at me for a few seconds but then turned her head away.

"Go away," she muttered in disgust. "I am finished talking to you."

"Anu, look at me," I begged. "Please."

I saw her dark eyes dart to the side quickly, but just enough that I caught the surprise in her expression at the kind word.

"I believe," I said slowly and thoughtfully, "that you might be what I was supposed to find—what our goddess, Freyja, wanted me to locate so I could find a way to defeat Loki."

Now Anu stared directly at me, her eyes just slivers as she

gasped in disgust.

"You are mad, elf," she muttered. "What do I know that could defeat the great Loki? Nothing—that is what I know. Anyway, Loki would have known my importance to his agenda. He would have worshipped me, not treated me with disdain. And . . . and even if I did have this knowledge, why would I help you?"

She started to walk away from me, but I kept following her, my hand resting on her arm.

"Hear me out, Anu. I know you are scared," I stated.

Her head immediately spun around.

"You are wrong," she started, but I held up my hand to stop her.

"I'm scared too, but I know we can defeat Loki. And I have no idea why Loki let you go if you have what I think you do inside you, but I truly believe you have some kind of knowledge—somewhere hidden, maybe—that can defeat them. I don't know, but if I am right, we can stop Kenrick and Corvus from destroying our world if we work together," I said earnestly. "I know this because we are both different now—we both have something to live for, people to fight for, loved ones to save. And if we work together, we can succeed."

Anu stood silently, staring at me. But I sensed her mind working through my words, grappling with the truth of belonging and the fight to save someone else's life.

"Aren't you tired of running? Of hating everyone around you?" I asked. "Are you tired of others telling you what to do?"

I moved closer to her. "Then do something about it. Help

us. Help Vardia. Save Wynfalle. Your people, Anu. No matter what you say, you belong here with your people. With your mother."

I took Herja's hand and pulled her toward us.

"Kenrick and Corvus have turned you against everyone who loves you. Why would they do that? Surely not because they want to protect you, because they care for you? Otherwise, why would they have left you here? In their eyes, you failed in capturing the Urora. What use are you to them?"

Anu turned away from us and stepped outside the circle of firelight—her dark figure blending into the shadows. For a moment, I thought she was going to run away. My eyes searched desperately to spot her.

But she walked back to the edge of the glowing circle, her eyes shimmering in the night as they absorbed the flames' flickering radiance.

"Do not think for a second that I did not know what role I played in their grand plan. I am not foolish or unaware of how they viewed me—they treated me with little respect and even less affection. But at least I understood their intentions. They never lied to me. Unlike others throughout my life," she whispered with a surge of emotion. "I rely on my own intuition, for that is how I have survived for thousands of years; nonetheless, what you say is logical; I cannot deny."

She stepped back into the light, her expression stern and her voice cold. "I shall think on your proposal, but with a few conditions."

"Go on," I replied hesitantly.

"I will give you my answer within a sennight, but I will not be bound like a prisoner, and I shall be treated as an equal among the people of Wynfalle and Vardia." Her head tilted stubbornly.

She was asking me to trust her and forgive her past actions against everyone I loved. But didn't my little speech already show that I was willing to give her that? For now, I knew I had to eat my words and simply accept her terms.

Anu misunderstood my hesitation as a rejection of her request. She began to turn away again.

"Wait!" I exclaimed. "Okay, I mean, yes, I accept your conditions, but I expect an answer before we get to Vardia, not later."

Herja squeezed my hand in approval, smiling as she sat back down by the fire. Anu nodded and did the same, tilting her head back against a tree and closing her eyes, dismissing me.

Without another word, I began to walk back to my fire and the comfort of Bane's warm feathers, hoping sleep would take me. But as I sat down again, nestling my body closer to Bane's side, I thought about what I just agreed to with Anu.

I made a deal with the enemy. The same person who not only stole Vardia's sacred Okri and handed them to Kenrick, but also tried to do the same with the sacred Urora.

And I made this decision without the advice of both Vardia and Wynfalle.

Oh boy. Elric was going to kill me.

***

"You did what?" Elric snapped, grabbing my arm and pulling me away from the ambassador and Halvard.

"I told you, I made a deal with Anu last night," I said calmly. "And before you scold me about making the decision on my own, it really wasn't. It was Freyja—she was the one who helped me."

Elric stopped suddenly once we were in a secluded enough spot away from the others.

"What do you mean? Did she visit you last night?" he asked.

"No, no, it just came to me last night, her words at the lake and then at the Sacred Spring," I said quickly, hoping my lie didn't show through how fast I responded.

I told him about the latest revelation while I was talking with Herja.

Elric paced back and forth, courteously listening to my new discovery.

He stopped in front of me, rubbing his temples as if summoning long-hidden answers to my surprise. I couldn't help but smile at his new habit.

"So, the answer to defeating Loki is somewhere in Anu, though she denies knowing anything about this hidden ancient knowledge?" he asked. "How do we obtain it?"

I shrugged my shoulders. "I have no clue, but I am hoping Herja may know how to access this information? She is the only one who knew the Lirreans. Somewhere within Anu, there has to be some clue."

Elric watched me closely for a long moment, his eyes now fixed on my new markings.

He seemed unsure about something—his expression

guarded. He began to raise his hand toward my face, but immediately decided against it and let it fall to his side.

"Are you well, Anwen?" he asked quietly. "Yesterday, I knew it was hard. It was a difficult day for all of us. I felt your high emotions; your pain was so severe last night, but I couldn't see through the cloudiness of your thoughts. Do your marks pain you now?"

I really didn't know what to say.

Did I feel pain?

No.

But how could I explain what was coursing through my body right now, a budding power that even I couldn't understand.

He raised his hand and gently caressed the Odin mark, then trailed his fingers down my neck, where they lingered lightly, tracing the dark runes.

I closed my eyes. His touch relaxed me. When I opened them, his eyes were wide with wonder.

"I feel the power, Anwen," he murmured. "Is this what you are feeling now?"

I nodded my head. The words got caught in my throat. His gaze was warm and intense.

"If I could take away the past hours, take away your heartache, I would," he whispered as he leaned his forehead against mine.

"And I would also take yours away," I replied.

Although Elric hadn't mentioned the revelation about his father, I knew it weighed heavily on his mind.

Elric stepped back, pulling away a few paces from me. His face was now clouded with a mix of emotions—unease, anger, doubt.

"Do you know why Herja kept his deception a secret?" I asked softly.

Elric turned away from me and started to walk off.

"I would rather not discuss this right now, Anwen," he said over his shoulder. Anger clearly marked his words.

I ran up and grabbed his arm, pulling him around to face me.

"I understand, Elric, believe me. But we need to talk about him sooner rather than later," I said. "He is dangerous, and now, with his identity exposed, I worry about you and where your head is."

Hurt flashed across his face at my words and the implications—how cold and unfeeling they sounded to my ears. I quickly wished I hadn't brought the subject up.

"I'm sorry, Elric, really," I stammered. "That sounded so terrible. I trust you completely—I didn't mean anything against your loyalty to Vardia. I know you haven't had much time to think about your father right now, but we need to go over our next steps against Kenrick."

Elric looked down at my fingers, white from grasping his arm in desperation. I loosened my grip, but he gently placed his hand on mine.

"But, alas, my mind has found no refuge from that very thought, Anwen," he said sadly. "I must talk to Herja first before a strategy is devised. I can only believe there are more secrets to be revealed, and truth be told."

"The truth about what?" a voice asked from the side.

We both turned around in surprise to see Sigrún standing just a few feet away from us. Elric quickly pulled himself away from my hold.

"My queen, it is nothing of concern right now," he said as he bowed his head. "We only hope to discover the truth about Loki and Kenrick's devious plan for our people."

Sigrún narrowed her eyes, trying to figure out if we were hiding something from her. But she nodded and extended her hand to Elric. After a brief hesitation, he took it—much to my dismay.

"Yes, we shall discuss this right now, for a small council has gathered by our fire," she said as she placed his hand into the crook of her arm. And while walking away from me, she called over her shoulder, "Anwen, please, you are invited as well."

Well, wasn't that just so kind of her to invite me to her precious council.

I snorted softly in disdain, mostly to myself but loud enough to make Elric turn his head slightly, a smile curling one corner of his mouth.

***

A large group sat around the bonfire. Elric and I sat together while Ambassador Ragnhild and Halvard sat near the queen. Other council members spread out around the circle, mingling with their people, arms crossed over their chests with worry.

But determination clearly prevailed with the number of elves and giants gathered for the meeting.

I recognized most of the council members except for two from the royal court—the two who survived unharmed from the attack—Flóki, an older male elf with short, white hair clipped close to his scalp, and Elley, a younger female elf with similarly cut, jet-black hair.

Herja joined the group, arriving without Anu, and sat across from us while Barik and one of his warriors, Thrym, stood behind us, away from the fire, preferring a wider view of the council. Tyr stood with the same unidentified female elf. This elf, in particular, held Elric's attention. She was quite beautiful, with long black hair pulled up into a loose knot on top of her head. She held her dark blue robe close to her body—her back stiff and her face expressionless.

Sigrún sat on a makeshift chair made from a fallen tree, looking a little bewildered in her new role as leader. Flóki and Elley sat close to her on either side, continuously whispering in her ear, but her attention was fixed across the valley toward her mountain. In my own grief for Vidar, I had forgotten that not only had Sigrún lost her king, but she also lost a father.

I glanced down at my hands, clenched in my lap. I knew she, like me, was also saving her grief for another time. When the chaos had been dealt with and the crowds were safe, the mourning would take place in peace.

Queen Sigrún cleared her throat, and the murmur of private conversations faded away. Her eyes slowly scanned our group, branding each face in her memory. Her once reserved demeanor had become friendlier toward those around her, an appreciative smile briefly shadowing her face.

"I am humbled and honored to stand among you today. In Wynfalle's time of need, those of you who were once considered our enemies have become our brethren."

Sigrún's eyes briefly met mine, then she looked out over her people gathered in the valley.

"Wynfalle, my people, need a home. In the meantime, we will travel to Vardia tomorrow, and once we recover from this terrible attack, I will appoint a special council to find us a new mountain," she stated. "But don't think that the destruction of our home will stop our preparations for retaliation against Kenrick. An alliance has been renewed with the Vardians and with King Grannir of the Rock Giants as well."

Ambassador Ragnhild nodded her head in agreement; Barik and Thrym bowed their heads and crossed their mammoth arms on their chests.

"Earlier this morning, I sent my best warriors to scout for the Lokrum. They will report back to Vardia only when they have vital information," she bowed her head. "May their journey be safe and successful in their endeavor."

"As we move forward, I will ask Seer Herja, the Volun Elric, and Healer Anwen to recount the events that took place in the Sacred Spring. She looked in our direction, patiently waiting with her hands folded in front of her."

All eyes turned to us. Herja started her story at the moment she appeared in my bedroom, voicing the mutinous Geir's intentions, and then recounted the attempt to summon the gods to answer our questions.

When she described the appearance of both Freyja and

Odin, everyone around the fire gasped—moving closer with eyes wide in anticipation and reverence. I risked a glance at Sigrún. Her body leaned forward in her seat; her eyes full of admiration.

But soon Herja stepped back and signaled to me. Hesitantly, I knelt beside her. She gently brushed my hair away from my face.

"Odin, our great All-Father, laid his hand upon Healer Anwen and blessed her, giving her his mark," she said, and then drew everyone's eyes to my neck. "And the great god Loki brought forth the mark of our goddess, Laga."

I looked at all the faces, now showing a mix of admiration, skepticism, and fear in their eyes. Questions quickly formed on their lips; murmurs of disbelief echoed around the fire.

"Silence," Sigrún hissed. "Please, continue, Seer."

But doubt also crossed Sigrún's face.

Herja continued our story in the Sacred Spring, quickly skipping over the account of our capture and the king's murder.

When Herja approached Corvus, she hesitated, uncertain if it was the right moment to reveal the truth about their once-loved Volun. But Elric nodded, giving her permission to expose the true identity of the Mage—his father.

And with this new revelation, alarm and anger erupted throughout the group. Everyone except Sigrún and the woman standing next to Tyr displayed their surprise.

Tyr noticed his companion's passive stance.

"Mother?" he questioned, doubt flickering in his eyes. "Why are you not startled by this news?"

When she didn't respond but only bowed her head in regret, he grew more aggressive.

"Did you know about this? That Brynjar was a traitor to our people?" His low voice echoed around the fire, silencing the murmurs.

He looked at Elric and then back to his mother, understanding now flickered across his face. "Was that the reason why Elric was banished? For the misdeeds of his father?"

He swiftly looked away from her in disgust.

"Tyr, it wasn't Inka's fault or her decision," Sigrún said regretfully. "The king ordered her to remain silent—never to mention Volun Brynjar's betrayal. Only a few of us knew about it."

The hurt expression on Elric's face tore at my heart—knowing his family understood the reason for his banishment, and that they agreed with it, cut even deeper. The murmurs among the council grew louder. Elric raised his hands, silencing the disdain and threats from spreading any further.

"Please, Tyr, council members, let us not dwell on the reasons and accusations, for I was, no, I am still reeling from the fact that my father is still alive and a traitor to his people, to our world. But it does not change what we must accomplish to defeat him," he asserted as he finally turned back to the queen. "There is more at play here than just the past transgressions of Brynjar—my father. Kenrick and Loki need Anwen for their own purposes, and I plan to stop them at all costs."

Sigrún turned to Herja.

"Seer Herja, for what purpose does Anwen play in

Kenrick's and his Mage's plan? Why did Loki give Anwen the goddess Laga's mark?" Sigrún asked.

Elric rose and extended his hand to me, grasping it and pulling me closer to his side. All eyes fixated on me—searching and judging. I winced under the attention, but Elric pulled me in even tighter.

"Because Loki is waging war against the gods, heralding the destruction of their realm and the fall of our world. He is aiding Kenrick and Corvus, his mage—my father—in this. Their reward is unknown, but it cannot be for the good of Emberval. The solution can only be evil and chaotic." His eyes met mine. "Healer Anwen is the key to stopping their loathsome plot. And we must help her fight for the survival of our world."

All eyes were on me. I knew my past, my history, needed to be revealed now. Drawing strength from Elric's presence and the newfound power of the gods flowing within me, I started my story—beginning with my family in Lucia.

THIRTY

Lifting my hand, I stroked the warm, downy feathers, enjoying the thunderous purr-like sounds beneath my cold fingers. Ambassador Ragnhild, along with Queen Sigrún, thought it best to send Bane back home ahead of us, giving King Ansgar and Queen Eydis time to prepare accommodations for the thousands of Wynfalle refugees traveling to their kingdom.

"I know, my friend, I hate for you to leave, but the ambassador needs you to deliver the message to Ansgar and Eydis," I whispered, leaning my head against his neck.

Closing my eyes and listening to his soft screeches of disapproval, I couldn't help but smile at his protectiveness.

My thoughts drifted back to no more than an hour ago, when I finally opened up to everyone about my past and my family, about Jack, and what happened when my energy ignited something within me, when the markings appeared, and what that meant for the fate of this world. I felt a heavy weight had been lifted from my shoulders.

That part of my life was exposed—the part that Elric knew about—but I didn't reveal the latest revelations. Laga's power, Loki's dagger, the book of Shadow—all needed to stay hidden for now. Until I can understand it and figure out how they all connect to defeat Loki. A puzzle with no clear borders and pictures to unlock the answers.

When the plan involving Anu was revealed, it was met with little enthusiasm. The reaction was expected, especially from Ragnhild and Halvard. However, the key fact remained that Anu could help us find the Okri and, in an undiscovered way, might also help us defeat Loki and, eventually, Kenrick.

Another presence was felt beside me. The energy was turbulent but still reassuring. I opened my eyes to see Elric staring down at me.

"Anwen, we need to send Bane on his way now. The sun is about to set," he warned me, but gave me a faint smile. "I know your concern, little one, but it is necessary for him to return with the ambassador's report. He will have a safe journey. He has relayed many messages for Hrafn in the past. He knows what to do, and he knows the way home."

Frowning at his brief peek into my thoughts, I looked back at Bane. His beak pressed into my shoulder. I turned my head, ready to rest it against his velvety neck, when Elric gently pulled me away and drew me to his side.

"Did you attach the scykra?" he asked, holding me to his chest.

I rested my head against Elric's soft fur coat and nodded as I patted the small leather pouch buckled around Bane's neck.

Soon after the meeting was adjourned, Ambassador Ragnhild recorded a message on my scykra, informing my grandparents of the recent events at Wynfalle and the return to Vardia with our mountain kin—everything was shared except for Vidar's death.

When she finished her report, Halvard, Elric, and I remained silent—each grateful for saving the bad news for when we were alone with them in Vardia. However, in my heart, I was sure that Vidar's absence would weigh heavily on their minds when they received the message.

Elric pulled away from my arms and looked into Bane's eyes.

"Fly fast, my friend, stop only when necessary, and only then, take care in choosing your shelter," he whispered. "I feel darkness quickly shadowing the valley, and I am afraid it shall follow us to Vardia."

Bane pranced on all four strong legs, anticipation for his mission felt with each step.

I leaned forward, placing my hand on the pouch, then looked up into his deep brown eyes.

"Be careful, dear one, and we will see you soon," my voice cracking with emotion.

It was difficult to let him go, especially now when the absence of Hrafn also weighed heavily on my mind.

Instantly, Bane reared back, wings spread wide and flapping in all their glory. He crouched on all fours and then pushed off, creating a tornado of snow swirling around us. I pressed my hand against my forehead, shading my eyes from the setting sun, and followed Bane's fading figure as he headed back to our home.

Sighing, I turned to Elric and sank back into his waiting arms. After standing there for a few moments, I pulled away.

"Did you have a chance to talk with Tyr and his mother?"

Feeling his sigh, I lay my head back down and ran my finger across the fur of his coat.

"How do you think the rest of your people will react once they find out your father is still alive?" I asked, hoping he would open up to me. But his silence persisted.

I turned in his arms.

"Talk to me, please. Don't shut me out now," I pleaded with him. He began to pull away from my touch, eyes looking past me as he avoided my question.

"Why do you do this?" I asked, anger beginning to flare. "After everything we've been through, you still can't open up to me? I know you're upset about your father---"

"Upset?" He snapped at me, his fists clenched at his sides, as if fighting against his own energy.

I had never seen him act like this, especially toward me. I moved away from him, not wanting to be close in case he couldn't control his energy.

But my sudden movement stopped him. His expression shifted from surprise to agony.

"Do you think that I would hurt you, Anwen?" he asked softly. Hurt and dejection flickered across his already pained expression. "I would never . . . because I am not him."

He stopped and dropped to his knees, clutching his head

with his hands. I knelt next to him and held his face, forcing him to look at me.

"No, of course not," I reassured him. "I know you would never hurt me, Elric."

He shook his head, his eyes filling with unshed tears.

"How can you stand to touch me?" he whispered.

"What?" I asked, not sure what he meant.

"My father killed your family . . . his blood runs within me," he replied faintly. "How can you look upon me and not feel hatred and vengeance?"

He tried to pull away from my hands, but surprisingly, my grip remained firm as I continued to stare into his eyes.

"Can you say the same for me?" I demanded. "Does my blood also share that of Kenrick's? Do you hate me now?"

His eyes blinked several times, realizing the truth of my words. About my family. That we shared a connection now; that somehow fate had brought us together for a reason. Maybe balancing the sins of our ancestors with the goodness of our own lives.

I smiled at his distressed face, tears threatening to fall from my own eyes.

"What our relatives did defined them, and only them. People have choices—they choose to live in hate and despair or with love and hope. You are not your father, just as I am not my uncle," giving him a hard stare. "I love you, and there is nothing in this world, no startling revelation from your past, that will stop the way I feel about you. Do I make myself clear?"

Elric, still speechless, smiled as he raised his hand to gently sweep a wispy strand of hair from my eyes. He softly pressed his lips to my forehead. "You mean everything to me, Anwen. With every touch, every breath, every glance, I feel your love deep inside me. I couldn't ask for anything more in this world, and I will protect and fight for you with every breath I have. My heart will never doubt your love and faith again."

Returning his smile, I gently guided his mouth to mine, ensuring my actions spoke louder than words.

***

The morning sun quickly spread its light across the valley, prompting everyone to start preparing for the long journey to Vardia. Some of the injured still couldn't walk on their own, so travois were built using the sparse wood found around the barren land.

Standing above the large group of elves packing their meager belongings, I couldn't help but feel apprehensive about our journey. The cold wind bit at my exposed face, but instead of covering it, I tilted my head into it, letting the crisp mountain air wash over me and bring the calmness I desperately needed.

Crunching snow broke my meditation. I slowly opened my eyes to see Ragnhild standing beside me. She stayed silent, tilting her head up towards the sky. She closed her eyes and took a deep breath.

"You have brought great honor to Vardia, Healer Anwen," she said without looking at me. "General Vidar and Healer Eira would be proud of you. Hrafn would be proud of you . . . and I am proud of you."

She turned to me and placed her hand on my arm, her face unreadable, but her eyes revealed the depth of her emotions. "Now, let us begin the journey back to our kingdom."

Speechless at her declaration, I watched her turn and walk away, heading toward the group waiting for me to join them.

Taking one last look at the great Wynfalle Mountains, I knew this wouldn't be the last time I traveled to this majestic kingdom. I had faith that I would return again.

THIRTY-ONE

The first day of travel was tough—the bitter cold and deep snow stretched farther than when we traveled to Wynfalle. The people were cold, and some were still too injured for a long trip, and they were held back by their fear of another attack. Despair dominated the people.

And no matter the reassurances of safety, fear of the unknown overwhelmed them—will Vardia truly accept them after their chaotic history? I couldn't blame them for their thoughts. Sometimes, I felt the same emotions twist inside me—fear, vengeance, acceptance. But instead of feeding that despair, I helped the elves appreciate the small gifts offered by the land—the gurgling creek, the scurrying creatures, the new buds of grass pushing through the snow. Strange and unfamiliar terrain became a wonderland. Any distraction eased the worries of the younger children and their injured parents—these discoveries only deepened the allure of a new life waiting ahead.

Most of the elves smiled and appreciated my efforts, but

others still clung to the idea that the queen would change her mind and stay with the Rock Giants until a new home in Wynfalle was found. Both Elric and I tried to reassure them of our new alliance, but the doubt in their eyes remained.

Clutching one of the injured children in my arms and trying to guide Glaesir through the snowdrifts, my eyes drifted to the figures leading our group. More often than not, Sigrún would lift her hand to Elric and gently touch his arm. Her laughter tinkled through the air. My brow creased.

Surprisingly, jealousy didn't grab me with its sharp claws. Elric's declaration of love still resonated in my heart. That wasn't the issue—Sigrún wasn't a concern. My worry was about a much bigger problem. Elric's people, his family, and their influence weighed heavily on my mind. His loyalty to Wynfalle was stronger than ever, and now that the truth about his father was out, he might feel driven, or obligated, to help Wynfalle find a new home, leaving Vardia—and me—behind.

Guilt surged inside me—selfish thoughts tore through me. I closed my eyes, trying to push my worries to the back of my mind. There were more urgent matters to focus on. It wasn't about me.

Laughter echoed through the trees. I shifted slightly in my saddle and watched Ragnhild and Halvard walk beside their horses. Several children sat on each of their saddles, laughing and shouting with joy.

A smile touched my lips—her animated laughter reminded me of Jack. Hope settled within me. Herja promised to take care of Jack—not necessarily promising to cure him, but to try to find the cause of his current condition. And that was enough for me.

Anu pledged her allegiance to Vardia—to find a way to defeat Kenrick and Loki. In exchange for her help, she would be granted asylum with no declaration of retribution from either Wynfalle or Vardia. Of course, it wasn't my place to guarantee any of her requests, and I told her that, but I would put in a good word for her. That was the least I could do for Herja.

Elric raised his hand, stopping our procession. He turned Lyfir around and cantered down the line, telling everyone that we were calling it a night.

As he passed me, he nodded in acknowledgment but kept going until he reached the guards at the back of our formation. I noticed more of his people, especially the soldiers, responded and followed his commands. The past seemed unimportant. All they knew was that their Volun was back, helping the people survive.

My heart faltered—more proof I was losing him.

I turned to the child in my arms and motioned for his father. I carefully handed him down, being careful not to wake him. Jumping down from Glaesir, I led him toward the line of trees where the horses would be stabled for the night.

I gathered my sleeping gear and walked to the clearing where fires were already burning bright. I scanned for the ambassador and finally found her making camp near a strange-looking stone. As I approached the odd obelisk, I noticed several symbols etched along the front, which piqued my curiosity.

Ragnhild noticed my observations. "It is an ancient prayer pillar, but the meaning of the symbols is almost forgotten."

She turned back around to help Herja and Anu with their bags. I kept staring at the runes. My brow furrowed at how familiar the pillar seemed. My hand reached out and began to trace the worn, curved lines of the symbols. A disembodied voice whispered inside me, caressing my deepest thoughts. A thick, unnatural fog slithered along the ground, around the pillar, and curled around my feet. A hand emerged from the stone, urging me to step into the growing light emanating from within. A shiver ran through me—and my eyes opened to a quiet, peaceful forest. Whispers, lights, fog, and ghostly hands vanished. My hand, still hovering over the runes, fell to my side. The silence made me pause. I quickly turned around and saw everyone watching me.

"What?" I asked. "What are you staring at?"

My brow furrowed at their strange behavior. "What is wrong?"

Ragnhild moved forward carefully. "Anwen?"

"Yes?" My patience snapped. My hands rested on my hips in frustration. "In the name of Freyja, what's happening?"

Herja approached me, glaring intently. "Do you not know, child?"

"Know what?" I asked, now getting annoyed by everyone's odd behavior. Even Anu looked surprised by something.

"If someone would stop staring and just tell me," I said angrily.

"Anwen, you just spoke to us in another language. When you touched the runes," Ragnhild said. She stood directly in front of me, mirroring Herja's actions. "How is that possible?

This language is long forgotten, not even . . . " she looked over at Herja.

"Yes, ambassador, not even I know what she said," Herja whispered.

"Well, I have no idea what you are talking about. I don't remember," I said while unfolding my bedding and ignoring them.

Herja looked at Ragnhild and Anu, the only ones who witnessed my brief lapse of whatever they thought happened to me.

"Let us not speak of this to anyone quite yet," she said in a hushed tone, scanning our surroundings for eavesdroppers. "We just witnessed something important, but I will need time to think and discuss with the bones."

Ragnhild and Anu nodded, turning their eyes back to me, stunned.

Sighing, I brushed the hair out of my eyes. "Well, I am going to gather some snow and then melt it for us to clean our faces."

I grabbed the small wooden bowl that Elric made for me and stomped away from their probing eyes. I probably should be more upset about what supposedly happened to me and the strange connection I felt with the stone. But on my long list of concerns right now, that was the least of my worries.

I returned to the camp and saw that everyone was gone except for Elric. His bedding was beside mine.

"Where is everyone?" I asked, as my eyes wandered around the other groups.

"Just across the way. Sigrún ordered a large bonfire to be

built," he said excitedly. "It is an old custom to tell stories around the fire during the first night of a long journey. Platters of food and carafes of wine are enjoyed throughout the night." He shrugged with a smile. "We might not have the food and wine, but we have the stories."

He extended his hand to me and offered a heart-stopping smile. The long-dormant dimple finally appeared. My heart fluttered and raced.

"Come, Anwen, let us sit and enjoy this night."

Together, still holding hands, Elric and I sat around the great fire, flames soaring into the moonless sky and lighting up hundreds of faces before us. Each one captivated as they watched Herja retell the fearless battle of the Sacred Spring—how the alliance between the Volun and the Healer saved Wynfalle.

I couldn't help but feel that these stories would eventually heal the rift between our kin and bring us together forever.

***

The next day of travel passed quickly, even though it was difficult; by the tenth day of our journey, those heavy thoughts and hearts transformed into positive feelings and excited anticipation—hope was a word we could actually feel for the first time since leaving Wynfalle. Especially when the days grew warmer, and the snow disappeared.

Fur coats, gloves, and scarves were thrown away without hesitation or thought. Maybe it was a somber reminder of what the elves endured in their homeland—and a clear sign that it could be a while before they could return to living in the mountains.

But I was hesitant to give up my coat for some reason, so I just folded it as small as it could go and tied it to Glaesir's saddle. I needed the reminder, and it gave me hope that sooner rather than later, Elric's people would have a new home to start over.

And when Elric raised his hand and stopped our group, I urged Glaesir to run faster, pulling alongside him and looking across the river.

The overwhelming feeling of excitement and anticipation burst inside me as I looked across the forest fortress of Vardia, where hundreds of our people stood, waiting for us. In the center, Ansgar and Eydis waved their hands in the air, greeting us and welcoming us home.

THIRTY-TWO

Glaesir dashed off, splashing through the shallow river, not pausing until we nearly reached Eydis and Ansgar. Only then did I slow enough to hop off and jump into Eydis's open arms.

"Oh, Anwen, my darling," she whispered in my ear, hugging me tight. "How we prayed for your safe return."

She reluctantly pulled away, her hands gently cradling my face and wiping the tears from my cheeks. "We worried about you, and then Bane appeared with your message . . . we have been waiting anxiously for your journey to end and finally come home."

I turned just as Elric reached us, bowing and kneeling. Sigrún stood beside him, briefly bowing her head to Ansgar.

Eydis turned to them but was hesitant to let me go, wrapping her arm around my waist.

"Commander Elric, the queen and I are glad for your safe return, and of course, for keeping the Healer safe," Ansgar replied, though his eyes briefly scanned the clearing for Vidar.

Elric, now standing, offered his hand to Sigrún.

"My king and queen, please welcome the newly-crowned Queen Sigrún, daughter of the great King Torvald and his wife, Queen Embla," he said with pride.

Sigrún slowly stepped forward, bowed her head again at Ansgar, then turned to Eydis.

"It is a great honor to meet the mighty warriors of the woodland kingdom, King Ansgar and Queen Eydis," she stated in a firm yet respectful voice. "It is with sorrow and a heavy heart that I must report my father was killed in the battle at Wynfalle, so I am here, a humble servant before you, grateful for the asylum you are providing for my people in our time of great need."

And surprising us all, Sigrún fell to her knees, bowing her head again before Ansgar and Eydis. From what I knew of her, this must have been difficult, especially in front of her people, who all remained silent during her act of humility.

Eydis let me go and quietly knelt beside her. She lifted Sigrún's chin and smiled.

"No, Queen Sigrún, it is with respect and admiration for your people, our kin, that humbles Vardia with your presence," she said, grasping Sigrún's arm and helping her to her feet. "What Wynfalle has gone through is beyond our comprehension, and we pledge our alliance and loyalty to bring justice to your people, to King Torvald."

With trembling lips, Sigrún slowly shook her head in complete disbelief at Eydis's heartfelt declaration. King Ansgar stepped forward, placing his hand on Sigrún's arm.

"My queen has spoken eloquently and with sincerity, Queen Sigrún, for our kingdom is now your home. We have set up tents and other necessary accommodations for your people in a large clearing on the west side of our city," he looked out across the wary faces of the Mountain Elves.

He bowed his head toward Sigrún, speaking in a quiet voice that only our group could hear.

"Do not be offended that your shelter is far from our people. We assumed that recent events would cause hesitation in our alliance. Time will heal our past grievances, and hope and faith will prevail."

Sigrún returned his smile.

"We are very thankful for your kindness and understanding. You are right in your assumptions, King Ansgar, because some still hold resentment toward Vardia, and I believe, in your unspoken words, that the same might be true of your people. However, with time, that will also heal."

Elric's hand brushed against mine—his fingers almost clasping mine, but he stopped before my grandparents noticed. Yet, I knew from his tremors that he was excited about what was happening. A smile played on both our lips—we understood the importance of these first steps toward friendship and solidarity again.

But the joyful moment quickly ended. Eydis stepped away from our group and turned toward the gathering of elves. Her eyes searched for a specific face among them.

"Anwen," she murmured. "Where is Vidar? He should be here with us by now."

I didn't know what to say—words refused to come out. My eyes filled with tears. Elric, sensing my overwhelming emotions and my sudden silence, gently squeezed my hand, assuring me he would be the one to break the news to the king and queen.

"Your Majesties, shall we take a walk by the river?" he suggested, nodding toward the sandy bank.

The king and queen hesitated—a brief moment of fear, dread, and then understanding passed between them.

Quietly, Elric and I led them to the river. And as we told them about the death of their son, not a scream or cry escaped their lips—only the sound of a soft, sorrowful gasp and the gentle ruffling of silk as Eydis and Ansgar fell to their knees, weaving their arms together in shared grief.

Eydis reached for me, clutching my hand to her chest. Comfort was given silently and with tears.

***

He looked so pale. Fine beads of sweat lined his forehead, but he didn't have a high fever. Aside from his sickly appearance, Jack looked like he could jump off the bed at any moment, ready to challenge you with the swiftness of his bow and arrow. I could just hear his contagious laughter. A smile briefly touched my lips, but soon faded. Wishful thoughts ignored the reality of Jack's condition.

I looked across the bed at Herja. She was deathly still except for the gentle motion of her finger touching Jack's palm and the rapid movement behind her closed eyes. Her lips moved slightly, but no sound escaped except for a quick breath every now and then.

I looked down at his other hand splayed across the blanket. I itched to reach over and hold it in my own. But Herja told me not to touch him, not yet, not while she was using the Shadow to find him—to understand his condition.

My hands clenched together, anxious for her to finish whatever she was working on.

Anu stood near the fireplace, her expression cool yet curious. She kept denying any knowledge about Jack's condition—but I didn't trust her. She might have the information to take down our shared enemy, and for that, I was willing to work with her, but as far as Jack was concerned, she would never be alone with him again.

Elric quietly moved behind me, placing his hands gently on my shoulders. His energy flowed through me, calming me, but his touch conveyed other emotions—anxiety, sadness, and protectiveness. He hadn't left my side since we broke the news of Vidar's death to my grandparents. His love and concern touched me, but I also knew he had reasons for staying close—rumors that he would lead a scouting mission back to Wynfalle to search for a new home for his people.

Another gasp escaped. I opened my eyes to see Herja slowly letting go of Jack's hand. A crease furrowed her brow.

I rose with eagerness, leaning over Jack and searching his face for any signs of movement.

"Can you tell what is wrong with him?" I whispered.

She quickly stood up and moved away from the bed, shaking her head in disbelief. She looked at Anu, then back at me, shock in her eyes.

"By the gods," she whispered.

"What!?" I said loudly. "What is wrong with him, Herja?"

Out of nowhere, a small voice appeared.

"Jo?"

My hand shot up to my mouth. Bright blue eyes looked at me—then they suddenly shifted. Black, gold, and blue. All the colors blended together. The air around Jack changed and shimmered. His exposed skin rippled with a strange darkness, as if a vaporous veil had fallen over him.

Elric drew his sword quickly and stepped between Jack and me.

"Jo?" Jack cried out in alarm. "Elric?"

I looked around Elric's shoulder, still shocked, but when I glanced down at Jack, frightened blue eyes looked back at me.

Without caution, I moved past Elric and knelt by the bed, grabbing Jack's hand in mine—unconcerned about the mysterious change I had just seen.

"I am here, Jack," I cried, burying my head next to his and kissing his cheek. "I will always be here."

When I finally quieted him down enough to rest again, I looked up at Herja. Her eyes never left Jack for a second—studying him and listening to him, with no questions asked, even when he stated that he couldn't remember anything after the kidnapping.

"Herja?" I asked. "What's wrong with him?"

"It's as if---" Elric shook his head in disbelief.

Herja, her musings now coming to an end, nodded in

agreement to Elric's unspoken declaration.

"Yes, Volun Elric, I believe you are correct in your supposition," she said, her voice confident and unwavering.

"Would someone please tell me what is wrong with Jack?" I asked again impatiently.

Herja turned to me, sat on the edge of the bed, and took Jack's hand in her own. She closed her eyes again, but this time she smiled faintly.

"Yes, I am quite certain now," she said with finality, opening her eyes and staring at us with a bright smile.

"It seems that your Jack has been hiding a secret from you," she paused, "or I dare say he might not have discovered it yet."

"What do you mean? Didn't know what?" I asked. My eyes examined my peacefully sleeping brother.

Crossing the room cautiously, Anu leaned from behind Herja, hands on her shoulders, and looked down at Jack, pulling back in shock.

This was ridiculous.

Before I could voice my frustration with everyone, Herja turned to me. Her silver eyes sparkled with excitement.

"Healer Anwen, we are blessed twofold—our world will rejoice, for it seems we have another Lirrean among us."

To be continued...

PRONUNCIATION GUIDE

Character Names

Ansgar – ANHS-gahr

Anu – AH-noo

Anwen – ANN-wen

Arnbjorg – ARN-yorg

Áslaug – AHS-lowg

Asmund – AHS-moont

Barik – BAR-ick

Brynjar – BRIN-yar

Corvus – CORE-vus

Draugr – DROW-ger

Einar – IE-nahr

Eir – Air

Eira – AY-rah

Elley – EH-lay

Elric – EL-ric

Elwyna – EL-win-ah

Embla – EM-blah

Eydis – EY-dees

Fanndís – Fan-dis

Flóki – Flo-kee

Frey – FRAY

Freyja – FRAY-ah

Garrick – GAR-ric

Geir – GAYR

Glaesir – Glay-seer

Grannir – Gran-near

Hagen – HAH-gen
Halvard – HAHL-vart
Herja – Her-ya
Hjalmar – HYAL-mahr
Hrafn – RAH-ven
Inka – EENG-kah
Ivar – EE-vahr
Jerrick – YEH-rik
Katherina – kah-te-REE-nah
Kenrick – KEN-ric
Laga – La-GA
Leofric – LEO-fric
Loki – LOW-kee
Lorrin – LAWR-ən
Lyfir – Lie-fur
Menglad – Men-glod
Odin – OH-din
Oswin – AHZ-win
Ragnhild – Ragn-hild
Sigrún – SIG-run
Sigurd – SIG-urd
Sindri – Sihn-dree
Sulwen – SIL-wen
Thrym – Thrimm
Thyra – TEE-rah
Torvald – TAWR-vald
Tyr –Tire
Vidar – VEE-dar

Important Names

Auros – AH-rose

Fólkvangr – FOKE-VAHN-gerr

Jilneim – YIL-neim

Lirrean – LEAR-e-ann

Lohrhann – LOR-han

Lokrum – Low-crumb

Lucia – LOO-sha

Máni – MAH-nee

Okri – OH-cry

Rydlyn – RID-lyn

Saerún – Sah-run

Scykra – Sky-craw

Sessrúmnir – Sess-room-near

Skovmal – Skow-maul

Sól – Soul

Soraynn – SORE-ann

Urora – YOU-oar-ah

Valhalla – Varl-hah-lah

Valkryie – Val-KEE-ree

Vardia – VAR-dia

Wynfalle – WIN-fall

ACKNOWLEDGEMENTS

Everyone said writing one book was hard, but writing two—especially a continuing saga? Nothing could have prepared me for the journey. But I truly love this series and am so proud of the accomplishment. Writing continues to be an addictive ride. But I did not take this trip alone. I have so many people to thank for helping me along the way—some of them directly involved and others guiding me in spirit.

Thank you to my brilliant husband, Joey, and my two boys, Connor and Reece. All my love for putting up with my notebooks, edited papers, and research books strewn around the house and my late-night writing sessions. Your patience and support mean the world to me. Someday, let's leave this cold weather and buy oceanfront property...we deserve it! Love you most.

Mom and Dad, thank you for your encouragement to pursue this dream. I appreciate everything you do and more! So... should I thank you now for promoting and selling copies of my book to family, friends, and strangers roaming the town square? How many books do you need? (Insert devious smile here.) Love you both.

Thank you to Jennifer Noffze, a.k.a. JNo—my editor extraordinaire. Your opinions and support are truly appreciated.

Hopefully, one day we can finally get together and have a proper celebration! I truly miss your impromptu rapping of the Nineties hits after first call... (Insert another devious smile here...)

Thank you to Beth and Dolly. The best fans ever. Dolly, I wish you could have read the second book—you were truly the best advocate for *The Power of Gold*. I know without a doubt you would have loved Anwen and Elric's continuing adventures. I miss you.

Thank you to the ladies of the library for your encouragement, support, kudos, and high fives! Shari and Kiersten—my kindred reading buddies—thank you for making me laugh and for fully realizing that I am not the only one with the compulsion to have at least ten library books checked out, stacked in a designated pile, and ready to read at a moment's notice. Our discussions always make my day!

Thank you to Gabriella Regina from GR Book Covers. I appreciated your patience and wonderful designs that captured the true essence of the story. All the covers are fabulous!

And thank you to all my dear readers—for the support, the reviews, the encouragement. Thank you for following my beautiful and brave Anwen—her journey to find strength, love, happiness, belonging, hope, and family. Thank you, thank you. You make me strive to become a better writer—a better storyteller.

Until next time, and with the continuing story of Anwen and Elric in *The Twilight of Chaos*. Cheers!

www.ingramcontent.com/pod-product-compliance
Lightning Source LLC
Chambersburg PA
CBHW030517310726
48979CB00010B/1710/J

* 9 7 8 1 7 3 6 0 1 4 4 3 1 *